# MISS ASHBURY AND THE ANATOMY OF MENDING A HEART

LOVE FROM LONDON
BOOK FOUR

JILL M BEENE

Copyright © 2025 by Jill Beene

Cover Design by Kari Joy Hodgen

Edited by Jana Miller

All rights reserved.

No part of this book may be reproduced in any form or by any electronic or mechanical means, including information storage and retrieval systems, without written permission from the author, except for the use of brief quotations in a book review.

*For Mary.*
*Thank you for sharing your vast knowledge and for all of your encouragement!*

# CHAPTER 1- VERA

Letters were such funny things, Vera thought. A bit of pulp, a splash of ink—the whole thing weighed hardly anything. And yet, the contents could change a life forever.

She hiccuped a desperate laugh and read the words again.

*Miss Vera Ashbury,*

*Since you have abandoned all daughterly duties, I must assume that you are comfortable abandoning the title itself. And if one is no longer a daughter, one can no longer claim any relation or privileges that would be assigned to a daughter. I wish you the best in your future endeavors.*

*No further contact will be necessary between us.*

. . .

*Sincerely,*
   *Lady Callista Ashbury*

Disowned! She'd been disowned with the stroke of a silver pen. It hadn't even been a new sheet of paper—the bottom half of the parchment contained a scratched-off shopping list. Her mother was in need of lavender soap, gloves, and a new hat. Or, she had been.

Vera wondered—was her father aware? There was no way to ask him. Her mother opened all household correspondence, no matter if it was addressed to her or not.

Vera had known there would be some sort of penalty to pay when she'd left to the countryside with Candace. She hadn't asked her parents' permission to go, after all. She hadn't dared—not when she already knew what her mother's answer would be.

Instead, Vera had stuffed a carpet bag full of her least offensive dresses, tossed it and her shoes from her second-story window into the back garden, and climbed down the elm tree barefoot.

She'd done it a hundred times as a child, but never in stays and a thick dress. She nearly tumbled from the branches several times and had scratched her feet terribly. But she'd made it down without braining herself, slipped on her shoes, and trotted out the rear gate. Once she made it down the street, she walked briskly, head high, as if she had every right to be headed in that particular direction without the chaperone of mother or maid.

Perhaps it had been cowardly to do as she did—to wait

until just before Candace planned to leave London to join her. The idea was that even if Vera's parents found the note she'd left and sent someone after her, they'd be too late to stop the Salisbury carriage.

Vera had soothed herself with the knowledge that at least she'd left a note, vague as it was. She'd tucked it beneath a vase full of flowers on her mantel. Even if no one saw it when they first searched for her, the flowers were days old and would need to be changed soon.

FATHER AND MOTHER,

BY THE TIME *you get this note, I will already be gone. I've decided to accompany Lady Candace Waldrey to the countryside for an indefinite amount of time.*

*Please do not worry—I'm completely safe and well-chaperoned. I won't behave in any untoward way while I'm gone, and I do plan on returning eventually. In short, there won't be a scandal unless you make one of my absence, and I'm certain none of us want that.*

*The only reason I didn't ask permission to go in the first place is because I believe you would have said no, even though it was a perfectly reasonable request. You may send post to the Marquess of Salisbury's London townhome; it will be forwarded to our destination from there.*

LOVE TO YOU BOTH,

*Vera*

VERA THOUGHT that it had been a logical, straightforward letter. She'd assured them of her safety, let them know she wasn't absconding to Gretna Green in some foolhardy match, and assured them of her propriety.

Her mother would doubtlessly find it shocking—her mother was *always* shocked when someone didn't do exactly as she wanted them to.

But Vera had never expected *this* response.

She'd been disowned.

What was she to do?

Travelling back to London was out of the question. Her mother was stubborn enough that Vera would be turned away at the door—of that she had no doubt. Even if Vera could get word to her father, he'd never been good at standing up to his wife. Besides, he might have approved the awful letter before her mother sent it—Vera had no way of knowing.

Perhaps she could appeal to one of her brothers. She chewed her lip, considering. Would she rather act as governess to Bertrand's children—who'd chased away a string of governesses by putting honey into their hair while they were sleeping, among other things—or would she rather act as nursery maid to her brother Campton's squalling twins?

Honey in her hair or several years of changing nappies—Vera couldn't decide which was less offensive at the moment.

Knowing her mother, neither was an option. Not really. Lady Callista Ashbury was remarkably talented at closing the ranks. That was probably why this letter hadn't been delivered until now—her mother had been crafting a narrative to shut down any support Vera's brothers might have given her.

Vera wondered what lie they'd been told, even as she shoved the letter to the bottom of her basket and walked briskly from the village in the direction of Jacqueline's house.

Vera desperately needed advice, and the Baroness Winthrop was just the person to give it.

THE DEVON COUNTRYSIDE was at the peak of late-summer beauty, green growth juxtaposed by interesting rock formations that jutted at random from the landscape. On any other day, Vera would have enjoyed the familiar route that separated the village from the baroness's estate.

As she walked past verdant fields, Vera worried her lip with her teeth. She had never been without a home before. It was a strange sensation—as if she'd been a boat tied safely to a dock, and someone had come along with an axe and chopped through the mooring rope with one strong swing.

Not that she was without a roof—Vera currently resided at the home of Percival Waldrey, the Marquess of

Salisbury, though only because she'd been invited there by his sister. Candace was the newly minted Duchess of Canterbury, and had quite rightly moved in with her husband, the duke.

Now, Vera was in this strange in-between—a bog of uncertainty that grew deeper and muckier by the day. For though she was staying with Percy and his wife, Adelaide, Vera hadn't been invited by them; she simply hadn't *left*. Candace was too distracted by her new marriage—and rightly so—that she hadn't invited Vera into her new household as a guest.

Vera would have headed home to London—she certainly had been *planning* on it, eventually—but she'd put it off in order to delay the inevitable unpleasantness. Call it what she may, Vera had absconded from home, run away like a spoiled child of twelve instead of a young lady of twenty-four.

Now she had no home to return to. Her fingers clenched around the handle of her basket.

Lost as she was in her befuddled thoughts, the baroness's estate appeared quickly, and before Vera knew it, she'd arrived upon the stone steps of Bertforth House. It was a large, stately country home—white painted brick, with large arched windows that gazed owlishly at the circular front drive. Trim decorated the space where the brick and the roofline kissed—a small swath of lace upon the throat of a grand lady.

Vera rapped the brass door knocker that was shaped like a fox and wondered—not for the first time—where the baroness had found such an item. Knowing the lady's devotion to woodland creatures, Jacqueline had probably commissioned it.

The butler opened the door, his salt-and-pepper eyebrows lifting with his polite smile. "Miss Ashbury, how lovely to see you. Please, come in. The baroness is in her parlor."

Vera thanked him, relinquishing her basket, gloves, and cloak to his efficient care. She'd been a regular visitor here as of late—a natural consequence of sharing a house with newlyweds who were expecting their first child.

Vera strode past the round table that held a collection of blue-and-white pottery, each vessel planted with different forced bulbs. Some were well past their peak, but the baroness found beauty in the entire cycle of plant life, not just the part where the plants were green and blooming. At the moment, Vera felt a special affinity with the papery brown stalks listing to the side.

The parlor wasn't a parlor at all—at least, not anymore. Vera rapped her knuckles against the polished black door, and Jacqueline's muffled voice called out, "Hold a moment! Sheldon is behind the door."

Vera smiled as a gentle scuffling erupted within the room, complete with murmured chidings meant for Sheldon alone. Finally, the door opened slightly to reveal the baroness in her customary ensemble of slim trousers and a nipped-at-the-waist tunic. Her dark hair was shot through with silver at the temples and braided back simply from her face. She clasped a chubby hedgehog to her shoulder.

"Vera!" Jacqueline said, her eyes alight. "I was hoping you'd be by today. Come in!"

Vera returned the greeting, chagrined that the woman always greeted her in such a fashion. Surely Vera would wear out her welcome eventually? But that day had not yet come, and the baroness ushered her in, carefully closing the door behind her and setting Sheldon upon the flagstones.

The baroness fondly called this room her parlor. Perhaps it had once been one in the traditional sense. Now, the room was sparsely furnished, stripped down in service of its true purpose. A set of sofas covered in thick leather faced each other before a fireplace that possessed a unique fire screen made from tightly latticed metal to prevent accidental tragedies. The fire burned lowly as it always did—the animals preferred it a bit cooler than people would.

A full tea service rested on the table between the sofas—a table taller than was typical. The height helped keep twitching noses and sly little paws away from the refreshments.

"I don't know why he loves that spot so much." Jacqueline shook her head fondly at the hedgehog. "Heaven knows he's most in the way when he rests behind the door—he'd be much more comfortable in his nest."

"Perhaps he has a contrarian way of thinking and does it on purpose."

She arched an eyebrow. "Maybe. Or maybe he knows that's where visitors come in and he's waiting for his noontime feeding."

Vera chuckled, a low rasping sound that she kept

under control in the city but had learned to let loose in the countryside.

"Have you come to check on Marcella?" The baroness nodded toward one of the crates of shavings against the wall and it shivered as if in response. "She's quite well, only napping. Come, join me for some tea and we'll see if she deigns to grace us with her presence."

Vera smiled, scanned the leather sofa for other animals, then sat. "I'm glad to hear she's well, but it's you I've come to see, not the squirrel."

"I'm a better conversationalist, to be sure." The baroness poured a cup, doctored it just the way Vera took it, and pressed it into her hands.

Such a simple thing, but tears rose in Vera's eyes. She'd taken tea with her mother since she was a girl, and until the day she'd left London, her mother had to ask whether she took sugar or cream. Vera wasn't a dolt—she knew it was no accident that she cared so deeply for the baroness, a woman old enough to be her mother, when her relationship with her own was so fraught with disappointment.

"Are *you* well?" Jacqueline asked with a slight tilt to her head and a little smile.

"Yes, er…no. I mean, yes."

The baroness sipped her tea and arched a bold eyebrow.

"That is, I'm not quite sure at the moment?"

She laughed. "I appreciate your honesty. It's a rare trait in young ladies."

Vera wanted to wrinkle her nose. She wasn't young—she was quite firmly on the shelf. In fact, if one were to ask anyone in noble society, Vera Ashbury was so far on the shelf, she was toward the back of the bookcase.

"I've been thinking," Vera started, before faltering into a pause then continuing once more, "about going back to London."

She couldn't bring herself to call it *home*. Not after that dreadful letter.

"Oh?"

Vera nodded. "Do you know anything about how to obtain…employment?"

If they'd inhabited one of the silk-wallpapered drawing rooms of nobility that Vera had previously spent hundreds of silent, miserable hours in, she never would have mustered the audacity to utter such a scandalous question. But here, in the baroness's animal parlor, where there were no rugs because the formerly wild pets thought the world their privy, she felt it safe to ask.

"Why do you ask?"

It was an honest question, not an unkind one.

"I don't wish to return to my parents' house."

Vera winced at the lie. Half-truths *were* lies, no matter how often people employed them, but she'd used the majority of her courage in broaching the subject in the first place.

"Ah."

The baroness sipped her tea and seemed to consider Vera's question. It was one of the things Vera loved about her friend—there was no rush with her. If Jacqueline wanted a moment to consider something, she took it freely. She was firmly unconcerned with what others thought about her, and it showed—in conversations and in her appearance, all the way down to her well-oiled boots.

She finally met Vera's eyes. "A young lady like yourself would have several options for work, if you wanted. You might become a governess or a companion for the elderly."

Vera nearly snorted into her tea. That was what her mother had planned all along—that Vera would never marry, never have a family of her own, and never leave home. Lady Ashbury had deigned that Vera was to be *her* companion and caretaker as she grew old.

Never mind what Vera wanted.

Jacqueline continued, "Or you might support yourself by writing under a *nom de plume*. Do you have any special talent with the written word or the arts? Painting, perhaps?"

Vera wrinkled her nose, shook her head.

"That's probably out, then. I'm curious—when did you decide to take up a profession?"

*About an hour ago, when I received notice I'd been disowned.* Vera tamped down the hysterical laughter that bubbled in her throat.

"Fairly recently, but it's something I've considered in the past."

"Have you given up the thought of marriage altogether, then?"

Vera couldn't help it—she gave a little exhale of derision. As if marriage were an option, a selection upon the menu that Vera simply required the courage to order.

Whatever expression was on Vera's face, Jacqueline

read it. "Despite what the cotton-headed *ton* think, a lady's value doesn't steeply decline once she passes the threshold of twenty-two. There are many men who'd be honored to have a lovely, intelligent, kind wife like yourself."

"I've heard that, many times, but I've yet to meet one." Vera had aimed for breezy lightness in her tone, but had fallen far short and landed in a grumble instead.

"A pity that Canterbury's guests had to go so soon."

The Duke of Canterbury had recently hosted a hunting party with the thinly veiled object of inviting his single gentlemen friends to the countryside to meet Vera. Of course, he would never be so inelegant as to say it directly, but there was nothing a single lady could sniff out more quickly than a well-meaning friend trying to arrange a match.

"I'm not sure who wished for their departure more—Canterbury or the guests themselves," Vera said.

"Impossible to say."

"After all, no one wishes to share a roof with newlyweds," Vera said, thinking of her own predicament. She blinked and did her best to reroute the conversation, on the sudden fear that she'd perhaps sounded ungrateful. "Besides, I don't think that Canterbury's guests enjoyed their stay in the countryside."

Jacqueline arched an eyebrow. "I did hear that the Marquess Beaufort divested himself of his betrothed immediately after he returned to London. Perhaps *he's* in the market for a new bride."

"Doubtful. Daisy's such a shrew she probably put him off the institution forever. And if not, I'd only remind him of his inadvisable betrothal—he's better off looking somewhere else for marital bliss."

"What of Lord Cavendish? He was quite handsome and charming. I've heard whispers that he's scandalously wealthy, even if the source of said wealth is a topic of debate."

"How *do* you hear so much, all the way out here? Especially when you refuse to read the scandal sheets?"

Jacqueline smiled. "My Aunt Katherine is a terrible gossip and a much better source than those awful papers. She's sixty-four and sharp as a tack. She says that getting old is a double-sided coin—no one speaks much to you, as they assume you have nothing interesting to say. But everyone speaks in *front* of you. She says it's wonderful for gossip that everyone treats her like a geriatric statue."

Vera frowned. "Is she quite lonely?"

Perhaps this Aunt Katherine was in the market for a lady companion.

Jacqueline waved a hand. "Not at all. She lives in a house with four of her closest friends. They're all grand dames of society—invited everywhere for the prestige of their titles. Every evening they convene over gin and cards and tell each other the best bits of news."

"That sounds lovely, actually."

"It does. Though I wouldn't want to reside in London even for the sake of four close friends. Are you quite sure that you wish to return? I thought you were happy in the countryside."

"I am," Vera said honestly. "Exceedingly so."

Just then, a small brown face peeped over the edge of the leather sofa.

"Marcella," Vera crooned, setting her teacup and saucer down. "Would you like to come up?"

"Mind your biscuits. She's developed quite the taste for sweets."

Vera chuckled as the squirrel scampered up over the seat, then perched atop the sofa back on hind legs to survey the room.

The baroness shook her head ruefully. "I suppose I ought to hang some branches along the walls, as Benjamin suggested."

"For Marcella to climb? Your son's very clever to suggest it; I'm sure she'd love that."

"Why are you determined to return to London if you're happy here?"

Vera busied herself with taking up her teacup once more. "I wouldn't say I'm *determined*, but I am considering it."

"Do you think you'd enjoy having a position?"

"Possibly." She stared at a painting on the far wall. "But how does one *find* employment?"

"Typically, people advertise for such things in the papers."

"They do?"

Jacqueline nodded. "There's a section, usually toward the back, where people post advertisements of all kinds. Have you never seen them?"

Vera shook her head. "I suppose I haven't paid any attention."

She'd never had to before. Now it felt shortsighted—though no contortion of her imagination would have led her to expect *this*.

A knock sounded at the door, and Jacqueline stood to check that Sheldon hadn't wandered in the way before she called, "Enter."

Elda, one of the downstairs maids, entered the room. She surveyed their tea tray and, finding it adequate, picked up a broom and dustpan affixed to a stick in the corner and began scouring the floor for any sign of the pebbles that Jacqueline's animals regularly deposited upon the stone.

Vera watched her. Could she do the job of a maid if it were required of her? She didn't know the first thing about housekeeping, other than that it was hard work and plenty of it. But she supposed if she had to, she'd learn.

Vera lifted her chin. She would earn her own way. She may no longer be a daughter in her parents' eyes, but she still had her pride.

"Then there's the matter of references," Jacqueline said, once the maid had completed a circuit of the room and left to check the patio outside.

"References," Vera repeated, chewing her bottom lip. She had heard of the concept, certainly, but she'd given it as little thought as seafaring techniques or how shoes were cobbled.

Jacqueline nodded. "If I were hiring someone to perform a job, I'd want to see that they had excellent references. Especially if I were entrusting children or the elderly to their care."

Vera frowned. If one needed a position to have references, but needed references to get a position, how did one obtain that initial reference?

"Are you quite sure all is well?" Jacqueline peered over the rim of her teacup. "I certainly hope you feel you can confide in me."

"Of course. I'm debating many options, and I want to consider all of them before I make my decision."

Jacqueline nodded as if deciding something. "I suppose such a discussion of the future leads me naturally to a question I've wanted to ask you for quite some time."

Vera rested her teacup upon the saucer and gave the baroness her full attention.

"It has been a joy to me to have you so near, but I fear I'm selfish, as down the lane is not near enough for my liking."

Vera's forehead wrinkled and she tilted her head, trying to ascertain her friend's meaning.

"It gets lonely here with just Benjamin and the servants. While you're deciding what to do, would you consider staying here?"

"Here? At Bertforth House?"

Jacqueline nodded. "You were so helpful while we cared for the injured stoat. And you know that Benjamin adores you. Would it be too much of a bother for you to move your things into one of the guest rooms upstairs?"

Vera blinked, her eyes wide. It had never occurred to her that the baroness would extend such an invitation, but now that she had, it was the most marvelous gift. Would Vera rather live here with her friend in true comfort, or share a house with a pair of newlyweds? Newlyweds who hadn't even asked Vera to stay with them to begin with?

"Of course," she said. "It would be my pleasure."

"Very good, though Benjamin and I will be sure to give you your privacy as much as possible. We don't want to frighten you off too soon."

Vera shook her head. There was little chance of that.

She had nowhere else to go.

## CHAPTER 2 - STEPHEN

Stephen held a hand to his nose, but nothing could dampen the smell of the other inhabitants of the post chaise. His mustache bristled against his hand; his beard itched his throat. He hadn't shaved since Samantha had broken their engagement. He frowned at himself, but it wasn't his fault he kept thinking of her—the couple across from him were either headed to or from their wedding ceremony, judging by how they whispered and canoodled under her wide bonnet.

Stephen had once been in love like that—or at least he'd thought so. But two weeks after he proposed to Samantha, he'd told her of his intention to stay in India and practice medicine there. She'd balked. She'd wanted to accompany him back to England.

England—where the air was cold, the roads mostly decent, and comforts readily available. She'd envisioned herself as his wife, yes—but as a baroness of a large English manor. Not as nurse to the unwashed masses of Calcutta.

Perhaps it was his own fault—he'd spoken of home so often. He'd described the herds of deer, the summer picnics on the back lawn—he'd spoken of *ice*. In the sweltering crescendo of an Indian summer, how could talk of berry ices *not* be tempting? And it seemed that the thrilling thought had translated—to him.

He'd *kissed* her, heaven help him. Not that she'd been anything but willing. But she was a missionary's daughter who longed for cold fog. He was a child of England who dreamed of staying in the Indian heat.

After their abrupt parting, within a fortnight she'd married the captain of a schooner and sailed for Italy.

With her departure, Stephen suddenly noticed how his collars chafed with sweat after a day, how his eyes strained in the poor light of the finicky lanterns at night, how thick the swarms of mosquitoes really were. He finally saw India as Samantha had.

A desperate desire to escape had gripped him with an almost panic-inducing intensity.

Stephen finally understood Samantha's need to flee, and he almost forgave her. He booked passage on the next ship home. Heaven help him.

They'd warned him India would be hard. He'd believed them, but his own determination had been enough to see him through, until the debacle with Samantha.

It was cold comfort that a fresh-faced doctor arrived to take his place only days before Stephen left. Stephen had abdicated everything—his years of notes, his supplies, several linen shirts that would be ill-suited to England.

Under the condemnation of the new Dr. Jules's judgemental stare, Stephen packed his bag of physician's tools and a small knapsack and left. He did not know whether he wished the man well, or wished for some misfortune to fall so that Jules might not view Stephen so harshly.

The whole way home, Stephen wondered if he'd ever loved India, or only Samantha.

Certainly without her there, his passion for healing felt hollow. All the inconveniences that had once felt trivial swarmed him like a flock of street children. He was a fraud. His ideals—what he'd set out to do—nothing more than wisps of dreams that disappeared in the frothing wake of the ship ushering him back to England.

At the London docks, he'd hired a hackney. He delayed in the city only to visit a tailor and a bootmaker to place orders, then headed straight to the station. From there he took the stagecoach, travelling in increasing discomfort toward Devon.

Stephen could have sent notice he was coming. He could have hunkered down in a London hotel and waited for his mother to send their coach. But he'd spent six years in India—certainly he could handle a few days on a hard bench next to the good people of England. Besides, the entire trip home was a kind of self-imposed punishment for him. He didn't deserve comforts—not when he'd abandoned his post so abruptly.

Except, he'd forgotten how much the good people of England *stank*.

Just like the people of India, actually. Three months on a ship with nothing but crisp ocean breezes had cleared the memory of body odor from his sinuses. He'd also forgotten just how many good people of England they crammed into one coach. And how cranky he got, travelling without proper provisions.

The coach rocked, rapping his head against the window. Stephen barely refrained from elbowing the woman next to him. She was a tiny thing but had somehow managed to claim the lion's share of the bench seat, defending her space with scandalously spread knobby knees beneath worn muslin skirts and elbows that she wielded like vicious, pointy cudgels.

Stephen reconsidered elbowing her—he was certain he could get away with such a thing without being recognized. He was wearing worn black trousers and a formerly white shirt of dubious quality, and he hadn't had a proper shave or haircut in months. He looked as he felt in his heart—a wretched vagabond fleeing self-inflicted disappointment and failure.

An hour later, the stagecoach lurched to a stop. He grasped his belongings and nearly flung himself from the open door in his hurry to be away from people.

The manor was only an hour's walk if he cut through the fields. Fog hung low over the tall grass—the sun hadn't quite come out today. The thought of a cool mist brushing his face as he traipsed the familiar paths of his youth was too tempting to pass up.

Stephen picked a hedgerow and started down it. It was only when he got too far from the main road to go back that mud sucked at his boots with every step.

*If only Samantha could have seen* this *side of England*,

he thought bitterly. *Perhaps she might not have been so keen on living here.*

The stalks of wheat in the fields nodded their agreement. Stephen trudged further up the embankment where the ground was passably drier, hunching his shoulders against the chill. He'd been too long in India—his blood had thinned, and even a mild breeze like the one currently toying with his overlong hair was enough to set him shivering.

Not that his old coat was much help. He'd relegated the thing to the back of his cupboard when he'd arrived in Calcutta. Now it was frayed at the seams, and some insect had feasted holes in the thing.

An hour later, his stomach was lowing like a discontented cow, and he regretted attempting the walk at all. He should have travelled into town with the rest of the passengers, had a hearty bowl of stew at the inn, and sent a messenger to his house. He rounded a bend and the slate rooftops of Bertforth House appeared in the distance. He hastened his steps.

It was nearly strawberry season, and if the first crop had been a bit early, cook might have made those delicious glazed tarts. The hope was enough to galvanize him; he hurried down the lane, his boots eventually crunching upon the gravel of the drive.

Not much had changed in his six years' absence. The shrubbery was trimmed, the windows gleamed. Only the color of the shutters had changed slightly—when he'd last stood upon the flagstone steps, they'd been blue. Now, they were a crisp charcoal. He frowned, realizing the description he'd given his betrothed had been slightly wrong. The image that had stolen her heart had been partially false.

And Samantha...

She was here—in his house.

*Samantha.*

His knees locked. Through the wavy glass of the front door, he could see her long brown hair, the pleasant form of her hips, shoulders, and waist. She was humming something, swaying as she...

Was she arranging flowers? In one of his mother's vases? In *his* house?

Stephen thrust the door open so hard it slammed back into the wall, rattling the glass in the window panes.

"What are you doing here?" he roared.

She screamed, pitching the vase—flowers and all—at his head.

He ducked. The crystal shattered against the lacquered wall—right where his head had been. She was strong—and *not* Samantha.

The young lady ran into the nearest room—the front parlor. Mindlessly, he rushed after her, his hands held up in supplication.

"Help!" she screamed, picking up a Limoges clock and chucking it at him. "Vagabond! Miscreant! Intruder!"

The cricket pitchers at Vauxhall didn't have a thing on this woman. Stephen barely caught the clock (an anniversary present from his father to his mother the year before he'd passed—his mother would mourn its destruction) before she laid hands on the fire poker and took a mighty swing at his brain box.

"Murder!" she screamed.

"No, wait!" Stephen jerked backwards as the iron hook whistled inches past his nose.

"Help!"

There was a scrambling of footsteps in the hall. Stephen retreated behind the mohair sofa just as his mother darted into the room, her cocked rifle pointed directly at his forehead.

The sight of a gun pointed at one's head *was* alarming, even if said gun was wielded by a person who'd never wish one harm. It was an eight-pound trigger, and accidents happened all the time. Stephen could be forgiven, then, for his momentary distraction. A moment that the stranger took by hitting him full-force in the arm with the poker.

"Ow!" he yelped. "Stop it!"

But she raised the poker again, determined to finish him off. Her hair had come loose from its clip and was a riot of ash-tinged brown around her face. Her cheeks were pink with exertion, her straight nose flared in anger.

*Beautiful*, he thought irrationally, right as she wound up to take another swing.

"Stop!" the baroness cried. "It's Stephen."

The strange woman halted her assault and blinked. "Your son?"

"Hello, Mother." He gripped his bicep firmly, gritting through the pain.

Stephen was lucky she'd hit him with the broadside of the poker, or he'd be in need of stitches.

"That's him, under all that scruff." The baroness uncocked her gun and set it on the sideboard.

"Then why did he attack me?"

"I didn't *attack* you."

"You verbally assaulted me." The woman's lower lip jutted—not a pout, not even close. This was a stubborn rebellion. "There's a dent in the wall from you bursting through the door."

"Stephen," his mother chided, a sparkle of mischief in her eye. "I just had that lacquered."

The baroness crossed the room and hugged him, enveloping him in her unique scent—french perfume and snuff—and a lifetime of memories.

"How was your journey? Are you well?"

"I was better before I became so well-acquainted with the fire poker." He glared at the lady as she put the poker back in its proper place.

"This is Miss Vera Ashbury. She's staying with us for a while."

"What do you mean?" He frowned.

"How was your journey? I had no news of your arrival, but of course I'm delighted you're here. Have you come to stay this time?"

Her question brought him up short, as did the streaks of silver in her dark hair. Stephen blinked, and the memory of his mother as he'd last seen her disappeared, erased by this six-years-older reality before him.

Though she was easily recognizable, the lines of her face were deeper. The crinkles at the corners of her eyes spoke of grief and laughter in equal measure. The smile lines bracketing her mouth were fixed. She was still an exceptionally lovely woman, but Stephen had somehow forgotten that time had passed in England just as it had in India.

"Yes," he said. "I've come home. To stay."

Vera stood behind his mother, so Stephen was the only one who noticed her start a little at his words, noticed the momentary appearance of a line between her eyebrows. Who was this woman, and why was she displeased by his homecoming?

"I'll have the servants open your rooms and bring you a bath. Would you like to eat in the dining room, or would you prefer to have a tray sent up?"

"I'll have a tray," he answered, distracted by Vera's sudden departure through the far door. He frowned at his mother. "Who is that woman?"

The baroness tilted her head. "I told you—she's a friend of the family. She's staying with us."

"I hardly see how she can be a friend of the family if she's unknown to me."

"Very well. Vera's a friend of *mine*." She arched an eyebrow and straightened his coat. "Never thought I'd see this terrible tweed again. I'm amazed it made it through, though I suppose the pattern was so awful it put the moths off their meal, hmm?"

His mother moved to the archway and began issuing instructions to the butler and the housekeeper, who hovered unobtrusively in the doorway.

"Give them a few moments, then you can head up." She peered past him. "Where's your luggage?"

"I don't know." He glanced toward the entryway. "I think I dropped it when..."

"When you attacked Vera?" Her jet eyebrows were raised in censure once more.

"I didn't *attack* her. I simply inquired what she was doing here."

"At such a volume I heard you bellowing all the way in my back parlor?"

Stephen didn't have a good answer for his behavior, not without explaining how his mind had played tricks on him. He just shrugged.

His mother didn't notice—she was peering past him again. "Where is your betrothed? I'm eager to meet her, though I confess I'm shocked you were able to find a woman with that otter pelt on your face."

Stephen reached up and touched his beard self-consciously. "Did you not get my letter?"

"I've received numerous letters; you'll have to be more specific." She crossed to her desk, sat, and opened a ledger book.

"The one announcing my arrival home. The one telling you I'm no longer betrothed."

"Oh, dear." Concern furrowed his mother's brow. "Is the girl dead, then?"

"What? No. She ran off with someone else."

"That's even worse." She arched an eyebrow and licked the tip of her pen. "You probably wish she'd succumbed to fever."

"Of course not."

"Right, otherwise you would have mourned her.

Better for you to know who she truly is—it's an easier break. *Now* would be the perfect time for the fever to set in. Don't worry, son. I'll pray earnestly after her health."

"*Mother.*"

He'd forgotten how quick she was—how impossible. Even the old version of her—the skirts-wearing, house-managing, rule-following version—had run circles around him in conversation. On some level, it was comforting to realize she was, in many ways, unchanged.

"Yes, dear?" She blinked innocently up from the ledger she was filling in with deft strokes, using an unfolded letter for reference.

"I don't wish for Samantha to die."

"That's hardly up to me."

He closed his eyes and took a deep breath. He didn't know whether he wanted to yell in frustration or laugh.

"I'm glad it appears you're quite over her," she said, interrupting his thoughts. "Obviously she was just a distraction, not your true match."

Stephen sighed and rubbed his temple. There was an ache beginning there, and he mentally ran through the process of making a tincture to soothe it if it got any worse.

His mother continued, "A shame you didn't come earlier. Lady Candace moved in next door, but she's already married to the Duke of Canterbury, so that won't do. Unless..." She glanced up from her book. "How are you with pistols? A decent shot?"

"I'm not going to duel the Duke of Canterbury for his wife," he grumbled.

His mother shrugged. "She's quite a beauty."

"I'd rather discuss the young lady living in our house, if you don't mind."

"Why? Are you interested?" Her eyes were upon him once more, her expression intent and lively. "You could hardly do better than Vera."

"I'm not marrying *anyone*. Why is she here? How long will she be here? Who is she to you?"

"Miss Ashbury is a dear friend who is staying with us indefinitely."

"Where did she come from?"

"That's an odd question for a physician to ask his mother, and at such an age, too. But I will endeavor to answer, despite the embarrassment it might cause us both. You see, Stephen, when a man and a woman love each other very much—"

"Mother, stop! You're being purposefully obtuse."

"No, dear. I'm being purposefully *literal*. It's you who are asking all the wrong questions."

"What do you know of her family?"

"Enough. She's a friend of Lady Candace, and now she's my friend, too."

He sighed. "Have you grown bored with the frogs and the hedgehogs and whatnot? You've stooped to collecting *people*?"

The pounding at his temples had worsened considerably. It was possible that he hadn't had enough water that day—it had been a long journey with few stops, but Stephen was inclined to think that his mother's roundabout way of speaking wasn't helping in the least.

"Stephen, you look quite overwrought. Would you like

a fainting couch? Some smelling salts? I don't believe we have any in the house, as every lady here is of a firm constitution, not delicate in the least, but we can send someone to town to procure some right away..."

"Mother..."

She tapped her chin. "If only we knew a *physician*."

"*Mother*. Please, just stop for a moment."

"Very well." She turned back to her ledger entries as if they'd never started the convoluted conversation in the first place.

Stephen took a deep breath and forged ahead once more. "Why is the lady not at home, with her family?"

The baroness lifted her head slowly and examined him, giving him her full attention. She interlaced her fingers over her ledger. "How would you propose one go about *asking* such a delicate question?"

"You haven't even *asked*?"

"I know enough to understand that if her family home were a kind place to be, a safe place to be, then she would be there. She is not. That's enough information for me to make a judgement on the subject, and it should be enough for you, too. Do not go prying into piles best left undisturbed."

"She could be a thief, for all you know. She could be on the run from her *husband*."

She exhaled derisively through her nose. "She's never been married."

"How do you *know*?"

The baroness raised her head once more, this time to

scowl at him. "Tell me, Stephen, do you think I'm an idiot?"

"Of course not."

"Then why do you insist on asking me questions that infer that I am?"

"If her family isn't in the picture, certainly she must have *some* independent means. Her clothing is fine enough."

The lady had worn a lovely, light-blue muslin with narrow pleats stitched across the bodice. Stephen shook his head and reprimanded himself for noticing what she wore at all.

"Gifts, I believe, from the duchess." His mother licked her pen, turned the page. "They're quite good friends, you know."

Of course he hadn't known. But the weight of the implications tugged the corners of his mouth downward.

"*Gifts?*" he repeated. "Who gives a fine dress as a gift? It's excessive, is it not?"

"Oh no, dear. The duchess gave her an entire wardrobe. Vera was the only one who stood by her during that whole debacle in London. And then they travelled here, together."

Stephen didn't give a whit what the debacle had been. His mind whirred. He'd heard of this type of gambit—where an innocent-looking young lady would single out a wealthy mark, isolate them from family and friends, and bilk them for their money. It took a spectacularly talented actor to accomplish such a con, but if they succeeded... Well, there was hardly a bigger payout to be had.

Though his mother kept speaking—something about a scandal, a broken engagement—Stephen only listened to the broad strokes of the matter. That was quite enough to stoke his astonishment.

Reading through the lines, this Vera character had set her sights on a wealthy, lonely young lady, encouraged her to break her engagement—to a *marquess*, no less—and had neatly detached the lady from family and friends. Vera had gone so far as to relocate them to Devon, of all places!

This Candace had been culled from the safety of the herd and she hadn't even realized.

Miss Ashbury had done such a wonderful job with the ruse that Lady Candace had bought her an entire wardrobe—a very expensive wardrobe, by the looks of things—all to thank her for being such a loyal friend!

*Why,* Stephen thought, running a hand through his overgrowth of dark hair, *if it hadn't been for the Duke of Canterbury's timely intercession, the lady might even now be destitute, having spent her family's fortune feeding the insatiable pit of greed that was her "dearest friend."*

But the duke had wisely stepped in and married the girl—out of a charitable, protective nature, no doubt—and this Vera had set her sights on a new mark—his lonely, widowed mother.

Perhaps a dowager baroness wasn't *quite* as wealthy a target as this Lady Candace had been, but she would do just fine. Look at the progress Miss Ashbury had already made! Ingratiating herself to the family, moving in... Stephen shook his head once more. He suddenly believed that his arrival home at this precise moment was due to Providence, and Providence alone.

"Dear heavens, are you even listening?" His mother shook her head with affectionate wonder. "I thought you'd grow out of that habit well by now, but I see that hope was unfounded."

"Apologies, Mother. I was lost to my thoughts."

"You always did find your own mind the most interesting place to be. What were you ruminating upon this time? A new surgical process, or how to get out of a social engagement?" She waved her hand in dismissal. "The latter is impossible; you haven't been home long enough to be invited anywhere yet."

"Are you *quite* sure about this Vera character, Mother?"

He hoped she'd say no, or at the very least pause in reflection.

Instead, she snorted. "I'm more certain of who she is than of who you are, at the moment. But give it time; I'm sure we'll reacquaint ourselves quickly."

Stephen made a low noise of discontent in his throat. Her eyes narrowed. His mother's discerning gaze always had seen too much; Stephen did his best to clear the disapproval from his features.

She said, "Go see Canterbury if you won't take my word for it."

Stephen decided then and there that he would go visit the duke—as soon as possible.

His mother frowned. "Vera is my guest. If you do

anything or ask anything that makes her feel the slightest bit unwelcome, it is *you* who will be thrown out, not her."

He gaped. "You can't be serious."

Dear heavens, Miss Ashbury was further along in the process than he could have believed! His mother was inclined to choose her over her own son!

"Right on your travel-worn derriere. You may test me on this if you like, but you might want to ask the household staff about the last young man who gambled on whether I meant what I said."

"What young man? Who was *he*?"

"Really, Stephen, it's a good thing you've come home to give your poor nerves a rest—you sound as shrill and jumpy as Great Aunt Bertian, God rest her soul."

He gasped. "Aunt Bertian *died*?"

"It's not a requiem, it's a *request*."

"*Mother!*"

## CHAPTER 3- VERA

*Of all the dreadful luck*, Vera thought.

Then again, if it weren't for poor luck, she'd have no luck at all. A brass bell jingled merrily overhead as Vera entered the village inn. Beyond a large archway, small groupings of people sat at tables, eating the stew that the innkeeper's wife made fresh every morning. The smell of lamb and rosemary scented the air, setting Vera's stomach to grumbling. She'd avoided the breakfast table that morning, because she was avoiding *him*—the Baron Winthrop, returned home unexpectedly from India.

Though the smells were distracting, Vera's focus wasn't on the dining room but the small alcove she stood in, with numerous shelves and cubby holes behind a small counter where the post was kept. The innkeeper was assisting a customer, and Vera's mind slipped back to the baron.

The way he'd *looked* at her—the narrowed eyes, the

deep crease between his eyebrows that spoke plainly of distrust. The master of the house had returned, and he was *not* happy to find Vera residing in the guest quarters.

"Good morning, Miss Ashbury," the innkeeper said, rousting her from her unpleasant thoughts.

She smiled up at him, hoping her expression wasn't as pinched as her emotions. "Lovely day, isn't it? I've come to check the post."

"As you do nearly every day." His full cheeks bunched with his smile. "You must be keen for a certain letter, eh? Today, you're in luck. Post just came in, and there's a letter for you, along with the papers."

Vera took the stack of mail eagerly and nodded her thanks. She ignored the kind laughter that spilled after her into the street before she managed to close the inn door.

Somehow, the innkeeper and his wife had gotten the idea that Vera was conducting some sort of romance via post. They'd decided *that* was why she checked in for new letters almost daily.

Not that the truth was any less embarrassing, Vera thought. She rounded the corner and pressed her back to the stone building, using the relative privacy of the small alleyway to tear open the letter.

*Miss Ashbury,*

*I regret to inform you that none of the positions you inquired about are a good fit for one such as yourself. May I renew my suggestion that you reconsider Mr. Audel's offer? That position has not yet been filled. As you have no experi-*

*ence and therefore no references, another offer of employment will be difficult—if not impossible—to come by.*

Sincerely,
   *Mr. Bratton*

Vera pressed her lips together and closed her eyes. Dismay washed over her like a powerful ocean wave, threatening to buckle her knees.

Mr. Bratton was the manager of an employment agency, one that regularly posted notices in the papers. Vera had written to him directly, weeks ago, briefly explaining her situation and asking whether he knew of any positions that might hire a quality lady without references.

To her delight, he'd stated that he knew of such a posting and had put her in touch with one Mr. Audel, a wealthy merchant who was looking for a governess for his daughters.

She winced, thinking of the letter. She'd read it so many times that she could nearly recite the thing, but she was no more certain of it now than on the day she received it.

*My dear Miss Ashbury,*
   *Mr. Bratton kindly forwarded me your contact information, and it sounds like we might be an excellent fit. I am*

*in need of a governess for my two daughters, ages eight and eleven.*

THE LETTER HAD CONTINUED, describing the daughters and duties of the position. Nothing had concerned her until she reached the last few lines of the missive:

*My house is smaller than others you may be used to. Therefore, you will occupy my late wife's chambers. Do not be alarmed—though the room adjoins mine, I certainly will not use the door between if it is unwelcome.*

*Please write back with a description of your person. Mr. Bratton informs me you are twenty-four years of age, which is a bit older than I'd prefer. However, I am willing to make an exception depending upon your appearance.*

*I look forward to getting to know you better.*
*Sincerely,*
*Mr. Charles Audel*

IT WAS the only response she'd received, but she hadn't written him back yet. Instead, she'd shoved the letter into the desk drawer in her bedroom and prayed for something, *anything* else.

She'd written to every single job posting that had been

even remotely close to something she thought she could do. Most of the time, she'd received no response at all. But with every polite rejection, her despair mounted, weighing down her limbs.

Now that the baron had returned, her hopelessness threatened to crush her.

As she'd quit the room that first day, she'd heard the baron ask, *Who is she?* His question rolled around in her mind like an untethered barrel in the bottom of a ship. What he'd really been asking was: *Why is she here?*

When the baroness had swooped in to the rescue, inviting her to stay, Vera had gratefully accepted. Her intention was to trespass upon Jacqueline's good will just long enough to secure gainful employment. However, that had been weeks ago, and Vera was no closer to finding a suitable position for work than when she'd started.

With the baron returning, it was only a matter of time before Vera wore out her welcome and truly had no place to go. Perhaps she could ask Candace if she could stay with her, though her pride balked at the thought. That would be a temporary solution, unless she wanted to live off the charity of others for the rest of her days. No—this was no one's problem save her own.

Vera inhaled a shuddering breath, buried the letter from Mr. Bratton at the bottom of her market basket, and shoved away from the wall. She lifted her chin and stepped back into the sunshine.

Perhaps she might have asked Mr. Harris, the town shopkeeper, if he had a position available, but Candace's former maid, Hortense, had just married the man's son.

Besides, it had taken Vera some time to acquaint herself with the reality of taking employment—she'd rather not serve the people she'd once considered equals.

Vera didn't have much pride, but she was loathe to release the little she had left. Surely, there had to be *something* else.

"Miss Ashbury, wait a moment."

Vera paused, glancing over her shoulder. As if her fears and doubts had conjured him, the Baron Winthrop strode up the street behind her. Instead of the ragged clothes that had made her think he was some rambling vagabond, today he wore dark trousers and a charcoal coat. Though of fine quality, the trousers were belted tightly round his waist and the coat appeared to pinch his shoulders.

Vera pursed her lips, but if there had been a moment where she might have pretended not to hear him, it was long past.

"What are you doing in town?" he asked, gaining her elbow and peering down at her.

She longed to roll her eyes but settled for shaking her head. She'd never met a more boorish man than the Baron Winthrop.

"Good morning, Lord Winthrop." She gave him a sugary smile that she hoped would contrast his own frown and impress upon him how rude he was being.

If anything, his frown deepened. His silence demanded a response to his initial question.

"I was getting fresh air," she said. "And checking the post."

"Did you get any? Post, I mean?" He peered at her

basket, and Vera barely refrained from pulling it behind her back.

"What are you doing in town, Lord Winthrop?"

At her obvious refusal to answer his question, his frown ripened to something adjacent to a glower.

*Pity*, Vera thought. If the baron weren't stomping about, frowning like some terrible villain in a penny dreadful, he might be good-looking. He was tall with broad shoulders. Though his form was lithe and muscular, the hollows in his cheeks spoke of missed meals, and the dark smudges beneath his eyes inferred that he either had a drinking problem or hadn't slept well in over a fortnight.

However, even one night in a civilized house had served him well. His beard—though still far too long for the current fashion—had been trimmed a little, as had his hair. He no longer looked like a complete wastrel—he only appeared like a man with no concern for fashion or grooming.

Vera firmly told herself she didn't care what the churlish man looked like, and scolded herself for noticing any detail about him.

"I've come to order some trousers."

His words confused her momentarily—her thoughts had scampered well past the question she'd asked him.

"Ah." She nodded and turned to be on her way. "Best of luck to you."

"I'll walk with you."

She frowned. "What about your trousers?"

"I've already ordered them. Are you headed back to my house?"

The way he said it—*my* house—had Vera stiffening. She jerked a nod.

"Very well." He extended an arm toward the street with a mocking tilt to his head.

Vera suddenly wished she'd made up another errand to separate them. She set a brisk pace up the main street of the village, toward the road.

"How long have you been staying with my mother?"

*Ah, here it is. The inquisition.*

"A couple of weeks now." She kept her tone light.

It had actually been well over two months, but *he* didn't need to know that.

"And how long are you planning on staying?"

Though they walked quickly, the baron didn't feel the need to watch where he was going. Instead, he stared down at her as they went. Vera kept her face resolutely forward, tried not to let on how distracting she found his gaze. He was a full head taller than her, with sharp brown eyes that took everything in at a glance. If he were a kind man, and if he lost the beard and got a proper haircut, he might have been very pleasing indeed.

But he wasn't kind. Or welcoming. Or anything close to the sort.

"I'm not quite sure." Vera tried to sound carefree, breezy, as if she were the sort of fashionable lady who was often invited to stay in grand houses for indeterminate lengths of time. She thought her tone pulled off the illusion, even though she clenched the handle of her basket so hard it creaked.

Stephen's eyes flicked down and she loosened her grip.

She was unreasonably irritated that he'd picked up on the single detail that betrayed her inner turmoil.

"How long are *you* staying?" she snapped.

She regretted the words the instant they left her mouth. *This* was not the way to obtain his sympathy, his welcome. But there was something about him that she couldn't even bring herself to pretend to like.

"It's my house. I can stay as long as I like."

Vera coated her lips with another cloying smile and tried again. "I only meant that you're so dedicated to India. Surely you're going to head back soon?"

*Please*, she thought, desperately. *Please just go back to India.*

"No." It was a clipped, curt answer that left no wiggle room in interpretation.

"Why not?"

"I hardly see how that's any of your business."

She stopped in the lane, whirled to face him. "And yet, it's your business how long I'll stay?"

"It's my house," he repeated, doggedly. "Of course it's my business how long *guests* stay."

The emphasis he put on the word had her narrowing her eyes. He said it as if he doubted its truth, as if it meant something completely different than the traditional definition, but for the life of her, Vera couldn't figure out what.

What he said was true—it *was* his house. It *was* his business how long guests stayed. As the owner, he could see her out on the front stoop that very instant, and she wouldn't have anything to say about it.

Vera turned her face down the lane and began walking once more.

"Where did you say you were from, again?" he asked.

"I'm from London."

"You grew up in London?"

She nodded. It was mostly the truth. Of course, she'd been to the countryside a few times in her youth, but the bulk of her life had been spent behind the brick walls of the London townhome of her parents, Lord and Lady Ashbury, of middling fortune and even lesser fame.

Now, she didn't even have claim to that.

"How did you end up in Devon?"

"I came with the Duchess of Canterbury."

It was the truth, though Candace hadn't been the duchess at the time. Another story for another day—Vera certainly wasn't going to tell the baron the truth of *that*. He seemed to want to believe the worst of her for some reason; she wasn't about to tell him that Candace had been running from a scandal when she left London, and that Vera had been running from home.

"But she wasn't the duchess yet, was she?"

"What precisely is your point?" She stopped again, met his eyes again. She was tired, and if he had some charge against her, she'd rather he just spit it out and be done with it.

"Why aren't you staying with her, if she's such a close friend?"

"She's newly married."

"So?"

Vera's cheeks flushed. How to explain that Candace

had been so distracted with her whirlwind engagement, with all that had transpired, and then her new marriage, that she'd simply forgotten Vera, left her behind in her brother's house like a forgotten shoe?

Vera hadn't so much as seen her for more than a fortnight. They hadn't had a falling out or anything of the sort —Candace simply had different priorities now. She had a new husband, a new household, a new *son*. Of course she was busy. Of course Vera had slid far down the list of Candace's concerns.

Vera didn't blame her for that; there was nothing wrong or unseemly about it. But the way the baron said the words implied there was. The way the baron said the words, it sounded like he thought Vera was a liar of the finest order.

"The duchess is busy with her new household," Vera said, with all the patience she could muster—which wasn't much. "A houseguest wouldn't be welcome at the moment. I'd be in the way."

"Montclare is mammoth." He gestured wildly in the vague direction of the house, even though it was well out of sight.

"Perhaps once you are a newlywed, you'll understand. I have heard that congratulations are in order. Where is your bride-to-be?"

His expression iced over faster than a shallow puddle in winter. "You've heard wrong, madam. I am not betrothed."

Vera frowned. The baroness had been quite clear

about one of his recent letters. How could she have misunderstood so completely?

"My apologies."

"No need."

There didn't seem to be much to say after that. Vera set off again, the baron following at her side, frowning down at her every few moments.

Their footsteps were crunching across the gravel drive of Bertforth House when he said, "Why don't you return to London, if that's where your family lives?"

Drat—she had almost made it in the front door without another question. "Perhaps you've been so long away from England that you've lost all your manners. Is that it?"

"*Pardon* me?"

She gave him a dazzling smile. "You *are* pardoned. Thank you for asking."

Then she darted through the front door and up the stairs toward her bedroom without so much as a backwards glance.

## CHAPTER 4 - STEPHEN

Stephen wandered listlessly around the property of Bertforth House and found himself in the large greenhouse. It was mostly abandoned, save for the far section that the gardener used for kitchen produce.

The beds closest to the door were the ones Stephen had once used to grow the more common ingredients for his medicinal tinctures. Though the medical community had largely eschewed herbal remedies in favor of more precise compounds, Stephen still saw the value in having certain plants on hand. He didn't see the need to throw away two hundred years of herbal remedies because other things were *easier*.

He set to putting the beds to rights—pulling the dead plants, amending the soil with the dark loam in the bin near the door. All the while, he thought about his conversation with Miss Ashbury.

Regrettable—that's what it was. He'd acted like a lumbering beast. Yet there was something about her that provoked him—he'd found himself barking questions at her before he even knew what he was about.

She hadn't answered any of his inquiries to his satisfaction. Both his mother and Miss Ashbury had been remarkably cagey about the young lady's past and family. Which meant there was almost certainly something untoward that Stephen needed to discover.

Stephen didn't think his mother was intentionally keeping things from him; she was a remarkably straightforward, blunt kind of woman. The fault for the concealment lay squarely with Miss Ashbury herself.

What was the lady trying to accomplish? Who *was* she?

Stephen yanked at the stout stump of a rosemary bush and grunted. It seemed he had arrived home just in time. Vera had his mother's confidence—so much so that the baroness took her side over *his*.

*Unacceptable.*

He heard voices and paused his weeding to sit back on his haunches and listen.

Vera stood just on the other side of the garden wall, hidden from view, but her voice was readily recognizable through the open glass louver above him.

"I don't think I like him," a young boy said.

Stephen leaned closer, trying to hear better. Was this boy a contact of hers? Some runner in the network of criminals she was working with?

"It's far too soon for you to form such an opinion," Vera replied.

Their voices were clear enough that they must be

sitting on the bench just on the other side of the wall. Stephen crept closer.

"He *yelled* at you."

"He thought I was an intruder; I thought the same of him. It was all a misunderstanding, readily fixed. You cannot blame a man for being protective of his household and family."

The boy made a sound of derision. "The household isn't *his*. It's more *yours* than his. You've been here longer, as of late."

She chuckled. "That's hardly how things work, and you know it. Besides, it sounds like he was trying to help those less fortunate. Shouldn't his absence be at least partially excused for that reason alone?"

Stephen frowned. What angle was she playing, defending him? Did she know he was listening?

"No." The boy's answer was belligerent, absolute. "You're more my family than he is."

"Benjamin, that's not true," she said, gently chiding.

*Benjamin?* Stephen rocked backward on his heels with shock.

This was his *brother* who was speaking to Vera with such familiarity. Perhaps he'd been wrong all along—perhaps it wasn't his mother who was the mark, but his brother.

Though what she could hope to gain from a boy of eight, he didn't know. He racked his brain—what was his brother's allowance? Or was Vera playing a long game—hoping that the young boy might come into some inheritance?

Stephen's nose wrinkled. That made no sense. If she were hoping to gain something, a third son was a poor target. *He* would be a better mark—though Vera seemed to dislike him as much as he distrusted her.

"Listen," Vera said. "I know that you don't have a good relationship with him—"

"I don't have *any* relationship with him."

"Be that as it may," she said, her tone warning against further interruption. "Now is the time to remedy that. Family is important, and every relationship requires work. This world is a very lonely place without family."

She spoke as if from experience; Stephen's eyes narrowed.

"I have Mother. I have my brother Anthony. I have *you*."

"I might not always be here."

At least they agreed on one point, Stephen thought.

"Is *he* going to make you leave?"

"This isn't about me. Your older brother has returned home. I'm sure he loves you very much, and I'm sure you'll love him. You just have to try. Relationships are work, remember?"

Benjamin grumbled something too low for Stephen to hear.

Vera laughed. "I guess we'll find out at dinner this evening, won't we? Give him a chance. Now come along—Mrs. Portence baked jam biscuits. Let's find out if she's forgiven you for sneaking those scones last week."

Their voices faded into the distance, and Stephen sat there, blinking. So much had changed while he was gone.

He didn't even know his own brother. A great wave of grief threatened to drown him, but he pushed down the emotion in favor of thinking of Vera once more.

If anything, the overheard conversation only made him *more* curious. What was her angle?

THAT EVENING, Stephen frowned at his reflection in the mirror and ran a hand down his face. Perhaps his mother was right—maybe it was time to shave. Yet there was something that stayed his hand when he thought about reaching for the razor. Maybe it was the same something that had him choosing plain, simple fabrics when he'd visited the tailor, the same thing that had him skipping lunch in favor of mucking out the greenhouse.

*Penance.*

He didn't know if it was the guilt of leaving India so abruptly—of handing his patients off to another physician with as little care as he'd given the man his clothes—or if it was the pain of losing Samantha. Though "pain" wasn't quite the right word to describe it, not anymore.

Their relationship had been a brief spark in the pan—a flash of saltpeter. Sometimes, when his head was heavy on his pillow, he wondered if he'd been using the excitement of their romance to try to reignite his love for India.

Stephen adjusted his too-large shirt, tucking it in as tightly as possible before giving up and going downstairs.

The front parlor was awash in the glow of candlelight. The first thing he saw when he entered was the back of Vera's head. She was seated on a velvet sofa, her profile to him. Her hair was pulled up off her neck in a simple chignon, with sweeping tendrils left to curl against her cream-colored skin.

There was too much of that skin on display, Stephen decided.

Not that she was pressing against the bounds of propriety—far from it. The neckline of her blue-grey dress was modest in comparison to what many women wore to dinner parties. Yet the sight of that luminous expanse, of her collarbones...it felt scandalous.

He frowned and turned toward his mother. She wore a suit of black brocade that nipped in at the waist, with a large bow to one side. A profusion of white lace erupted from each arm of her jacket and around her throat. It appeared as if a great quantity of whipped cream was held in only by her trim jacket.

"Mother. Miss Ashbury." He nodded at each of them in turn as manners dictated. "Good evening."

"Stephen." His mother waved him over, and he deposited a brief kiss upon her cheek. "Allow me to introduce my friend, Mr. Hamish Thornton."

A man stood from the sofa where he sat next to Vera. It was a testament to Vera's lustrous skin that Stephen hadn't noticed him before.

The man was shorter than Stephen, but far broader in the shoulders and across the chest. Something in the way he moved reminded Stephen of a pugilist—but perhaps that was his physician's eye cataloguing that the man's nose had been broken at least once before. He had blond-brown hair, blue eyes, and lines in his forehead that spoke of a lot of time spent in the sun. He was thick, muscular—a former dockworker, perhaps?

The man stood and held out his hand to Stephen. He shook it by rote, his eyes flicking to Vera. Was this man connected to her in some way?

"How do you two know each other?" He nodded toward Vera as he addressed the man.

The man smiled, and Stephen didn't like the knowing little glint in his eye. "We don't, not really, except that Miss Ashbury is a friend of the Marquess Salisbury's family, and I'm the Marquess Salisbury's secretary."

Stephen frowned. The explanation left him more confused than he had been prior. What was the Marquess Salisbury's secretary doing at his mother's dinner party?

"I met the Baroness Winthrop at the Marquess Salisbury's estate here in Devon," Hamish said. "She and I have been working on a fox problem."

"It wouldn't have *been* a problem, if you'd left well enough alone," the baroness chided without any real heat.

Stephen instantly reevaluated. "A pleasure, I'm sure."

Benjamin stood stiffly at his mother's side, waiting for Stephen to address him. Stephen suspected the boy had been avoiding him on purpose until now. Benjamin was the spitting image of their brother Anthony at that age, though perhaps a bit taller and broader through the shoulders. He had their mother's dark hair, though there was something about the nose and mouth that reminded Stephen of their father.

"Hello, Benjamin." Stephen cleared his throat.

"Hello." The boy jerked a nod and regained his seat.

The room descended into a sudden, awkward silence that Stephen didn't know how to break.

In the end, it was Vera who came to the rescue. She leaned forward and asked the baroness, "How is Sheldon today? Is he feeling better?"

"He's eating well, which is a good sign."

Stephen looked back and forth between the two ladies. Who on earth was Sheldon? And why had no one asked for his assistance? He was a physician, for heaven's sake.

"Is someone ill?" Stephen asked.

"Not anymore." Jacqueline nodded. "Sheldon ate some cake, the little scamp. It upset his stomach."

"A servant's child?" he guessed, heading to the sideboard. "Mr. Thornton, would you care for a whisky?"

"Thank you, but I already have one." He lifted his glass of amber liquid as if to prove his statement.

"Sheldon is a hedgehog," his mother said.

"Are you still rescuing the wildlife?" He poured himself a tipple, then thought better of it and added another half-inch to his glass. "When will Sheldon be ready for the hedges once more?"

"Never, my darling. Sheldon is a permanent resident of the house."

His glass paused halfway to his mouth. "A *permanent* resident?"

Good heavens, he should have given himself a heftier pour.

Vera pursed her lips as if she were delighted at the direction the conversation was headed but didn't want to let on. He frowned as she laced her fingers together. There was something vaguely mocking and self-satisfied about her expression, but for the life of him, he couldn't figure it out.

"I've had Sheldon for well over a year now." Jacqueline nodded. "It's just luck that he and Clarence get along so well."

"Who's Clarence?"

Vera pressed her lips together as if she were trying desperately not to laugh. He frowned at her; she arched an eyebrow.

"My fox, of course."

"You have a *fox*? A fox who lives on the *property*?"

"In the house, dear. If it were safe for him outside, I would have kicked him out long ago."

Stephen looked around the room. "Where on earth is it?"

She waved a hand airily. "Heaven knows. Though lately he's taken to curling up at the end of Benjamin's bed, so it's possible he's there."

"He hogs the blankets," Benjamin added cheerfully.

"You allow him to sleep with your *son*?"

The baroness frowned, considering. "*Allow* is a strong word, Stephen. I don't know that one *allows* a fox to do anything. They're wild animals, after all. Very instinctual."

"Which is why they should remain outdoors, Mother."

"Don't be silly—Clarence is quite well-behaved. I've had him for years. He's not at all dangerous. Now, the badger was another thing altogether."

Vera exhaled something that sounded suspiciously like a snicker; Stephen ignored her.

"Are there badgers in the house right now?" Stephen blinked at the corners of the room.

"Of course not." His mother said it with the same inflection as one might say *Don't be an idiot*. "I've just told you—badgers aren't safe. No—all we have right now is Sheldon, Clarence, a raccoon, a squirrel, and three voles."

Stephen knocked back his drink and crossed to the sideboard to pour himself another. He'd returned to find his household gone half to Bedlam.

He glanced toward the far sofa. Hamish was grinning at his mother as if she were the most fascinating thing he'd ever seen. Vera was smiling smugly, as if the entire conversation so far had been of her design and was progressing perfectly.

Stephen rethought his second drink; he set his glass down upon the wood with a *thunk*. He'd need to keep his wits about him—he was vastly outnumbered and didn't understand the motley array of characters who'd infiltrated his house.

He aimed to get rid of them one by one—starting with this Hamish fellow, who was casting too-familiar looks at his mother, Miss Vera Ashbury, who had some nefarious design, and ending with every single rodent his mother had named in his absence.

"Shall we go through to dinner?" he suggested, offering his elbow to his mother.

THE TABLE WAS SET LAVISHLY. Crystal glimmered; china plates gleamed amid an array of shining cutlery. Stephen was relieved to see that not everything had gone awry in his absence, and that no one had been allowed to make off with the silver yet. He escorted his mother to a seat, but before he could react, Hamish took the place directly across from her. Benjamin claimed the spot to her right, which left Stephen to take the empty chair at the head of the table, with Vera on his right.

She didn't look any more pleased with the arrangement than he was—she frowned down at her plate before clearing her expression.

"What did everyone do today?" Hamish asked. Then he grinned across the table at the baroness. "Well, I know what *you* did. What did everyone else do?"

Stephen frowned—his mother had spent time with this secretary today? He opened his mouth to ask what, precisely, they'd done, but his brother beat him to the silence.

"Arthur and Seamus came over. We went for a walk to the creek."

Vera's smile was dazzling; Stephen tried very hard not to notice. Good heavens—who were Arthur and Seamus?

At this point, he wouldn't be surprised if they were two drunken louts who *lived* down by the creek.

"Who on earth are Arthur and Seamus?" he demanded.

Benjamin pressed his lips together and stared down at his plate.

His mother answered gently, "Arthur is the Duke of Canterbury's son. Seamus is his dog."

"Ah." He cleared his throat to cover his embarrassment. At least Benjamin hadn't fallen in with the wrong sort—yet.

"Were you able to trap the fox?" Vera asked Hamish.

The man smiled at the baroness again; Stephen stifled the urge to lob a butter knife at his head. "Not yet, though we're hopeful we've found what the bugger likes to eat."

"You're feeding him?" Stephen raised his eyebrows.

"In order to lull him into a false sense of complacency." His mother nodded. "Foxes are wily."

"Aren't they, though?" Hamish agreed, then nodded acknowledgement at the footman who set a plate before him.

"Of course, I would've had the animal weeks ago, if *someone* hadn't scared it off."

Hamish looked heavenwards. "I thought you were a poacher."

Vera and Benjamin both laughed, as if this were a running joke and they were all in on it. Stephen didn't want to admit how much that stung. He was the interloper here. Even this secretary seemed more comfortable in this house—*his* house—than he was.

"What happened?"

"As I said, I thought she was a poacher, so I hauled her out of the hedge by her arm. By the time I realized the true situation, the fox was long gone."

Stephen blinked, tried to absorb this information.

"You're truly lucky she didn't shoot you," Vera said, chuckling.

"Isn't that the truth?" The man sounded like the prospect would have been delightful.

"I came closer to shooting my son yesterday than I ever came to shooting this one." The baroness shook her head. "I still don't understand what you were thinking, busting in the door, yelling like that."

"I was mistaken," Stephen said, stiffly. "I thought..."

He trailed off, but the baroness raised her eyebrows expectantly. "You thought what? Vera hardly looks like an intruder; you looked far more frightening than she ever has. I don't blame her one bit for trying to brain you with the fire poker."

"Wish I'd seen that," Benjamin grumbled, so lowly that Stephen wasn't sure he was meant to have heard it.

"It's amazing she *didn't* shoot you, from what she told me," Hamish added with a knowing chuckle.

Stephen frowned at the knowledge that the man had heard a report of his eventful homecoming already. Just how close were his mother and this secretary?

"All's well that ends well," Vera supplied.

He pressed his lips together. Vera and Hamish claimed not to know each other, but what if that was part of the scam? What if his mother was the target, after all, but it was Hamish who was the main player, and Vera was just cast in a supporting role?

"How did you say you two met, again?" He waved his hand toward Hamish and Vera.

"We just met recently," Hamish said, slicing into his fish. "The first time Jacqueline invited me to dinner."

Stephen raised his eyebrows. Oh, it was *Jacqueline*, was it?

Hamish quirked a smile as if he'd read Stephen's mind and was replying, *Yes, what of it?*

Benjamin asked Hamish a question, drawing both the man's and his mother's attention away.

Stephen leaned toward Vera and murmured, "When's the last time you and the duchess spoke? If you're so close with her?"

"Not that it's any of your business, but I spoke with her last week." Vera flushed as if he'd caught her in a lie, but her chin jutted and she continued lowly, "I don't know why you're determined to find fault with me. I've done nothing wrong. I've no ill intent toward you or your family."

"If that's the truth, then why won't you answer simple questions about where you're from, who your family is?"

"I *have*. I've told you—my family is in London. My parents are Lord and Lady Ashbury—"

"And you've been gone from home for *how* long? Months, by my estimation. Why haven't you returned home to your parents? You aren't part of a grouping of young people, where your absence might be explained by general merrymaking. No—there's a *reason* you're still here, and I aim to find out what it is."

Her eyes were large, pleading. "It's nothing, I assure you. I'm here as a guest of your mother's because I'm fond of her and your brother."

Her fingers trembled as she picked up her knife, and he marked it as evidence of a falsehood.

"Perhaps I'm mistaken."

"That's what I'm telling you." She canted her voice low, to keep it private.

"Then you *aren't* staying with my mother because she's offering you free room and board?"

"What?" Her eyes were round.

The sight of her distress panged his conscience, but he soldiered on, determined to find the truth. "It seems to me that you've been moving from grand house to grand house as a guest. Is there any reason for it? One might think you have naught but charity to live on."

Vera blinked, her mouth agape. She set down her fork.

He leaned forward, trying to capitalize on her being flummoxed—perhaps she'd let something slip. "Who are you exchanging letters with, in the village?"

"Stephen." His mother's voice was sharp. "What are you two talking about down there?"

"Correspondence, Mother. How unreliable the post is these days."

He sipped his wine to settle his stomach. He wasn't sure if he was sickened or satisfied at the look of alarm that had crossed the lovely Miss Ashbury's features when he'd mentioned the letters. He didn't relish her fear, but there was something she was hiding—he was certain of it.

"I cannot help but agree with you," the baroness said, her voice still terse. "After all, the last letter I had from you stated that you'd bring a wife home. Was she lost in the post, as well?"

His eyes crawled up to meet his mother's narrow-eyed stare. *This* was why he had to find out what Vera was hiding. Because his mother cared so much for the lady that she was protective of her, even in defiance of her own son.

"It's as I told you, Mother. She and I parted ways. Amicably."

"Ah." She nodded. "That's right. Silly me—sometimes I forget that once a person has answered a question, it's rude to ask it of them again."

Though he doubted his mother had been able to hear what was said, apparently his exchange with Vera hadn't gone unnoted. The baroness turned back to her conversation with Benjamin and Hamish as if she hadn't just dressed down her eldest son in full hearing of everyone.

"Then tell me something I don't know about you." He smiled at Vera, endeavoring to make the expression reach his eyes; it fell far short.

"That won't be difficult. You haven't endeavored to get to know me. You've only tried to get to know *about* me."

He took a bite of his fish, pointedly waiting for her reply.

"I like to read. I've always wanted a dog, but my mother would never allow it. I'm not fond of swimming in bodies of water where I cannot see the bottom. Brown washes out my skin tone, makes me look sallow. I have two brothers and five nieces and nephews." She tapped her chin, looking toward the ceiling. "What else?"

"How about why you're really here?" he whispered. "Though you don't want to tell me, I *will* discover the truth."

She exhaled an incredulous gust, shaking her head. "Why on earth would I waste my breath repeating myself when you won't believe the truth when it's told to you?"

They were silent the rest of the dinner.

## CHAPTER 5 - STEPHEN

The next morning, Stephen rose before the sunlight had chased away the mist. It clung close to the ground and hovered near the hedgerows visible from his window. Fall would soon be underway, and the weather would require *all* denizens to wear a coat—not just those recently returned from India.

He took the back stairs at a trot, grateful to see that not everything had changed in his absence—the servants' stairwell was the same crisp whitewash it had always been, the edges of the stairs bent into smirks from the wear of a thousand feet.

The smell of roasted coffee and crisp bacon sent a wave of nostalgia rolling through him. His father had always preferred the bitter brew to the more traditional English tea. His mother had adopted the taste over time, though she still required a liberal dollop of heavy cream and a spoonful of sugar to drink the stuff. One wondered why she bothered with it at all now. Habit, he supposed. One couldn't be wed to another for twenty-odd years without rubbing off on one another.

"Good morning, your lordship," the cook said, drying her large hands on a soft bit of muslin she kept tied at her waist. "Come for a bit of breakfast?"

"Hello, Mrs. Portence." He crossed the room to grin up at her. When he was younger, he would have thrown his arms around her thick middle in greeting, but time sorted everyone into their roles, and such a display was no longer appropriate. "Just eggs and bacon, if it's not too early."

"'Course. I'm getting your mother's breakfast ready to send to the conservatory."

His eyebrow arched. His mother had traditionally been the last one up. It was just another thing that had changed while he'd been taking temperatures in Calcutta.

"Send mine along with it, if you don't mind."

The woman nodded. Stephen poured himself a cup of tea from the pot in the cozy on the wooden bench, added cream and sugar as a treat, and went in search of his mother.

The conservatory had once held flowers, but now the narrow rectangular planters ringing the round, windowed room were bare, save for a tuft of red fur that uncurled itself upon his approach. His mother sat at a table, head bent over the ledger open before her. A mug curled steam at her elbow.

"Good morning, Mother." He dusted a kiss across her offered cheek and tried to ignore the keen eyes of the fox in the planter.

"Morning, Stephen." She smiled, then blinked. "When did the tailor say your clothes would be ready? I didn't even like those trousers on your father."

He smiled and took the chair next to her at the round table, the one facing the fox. He wouldn't put it past the thing to nip him if his back was turned.

"Should only be a couple of days. Said he had several that could be altered; he'll send those along directly."

His mother hummed and turned back to her numbers. "Did you have a nice time at dinner?"

"The food was excellent, but I was confused by some of the company."

She gave him her eyes, waiting for an explanation.

"That man, Hamish. I don't like how he looks at you."

"I don't rightly care." She finished her entry and flipped the heavy book shut with a thud. "It's none of your concern."

"Of course it is. I'm your son, for one. The rightful owner of these properties, for another."

"Are you?" She leaned back in the chair and arched her eyebrow.

He glowered at her, letting his silence speak for him. His mother had always been different, but she'd never been difficult—at least, not toward him.

"You've been gone a long time," she finally said.

"Six years isn't such an absence."

"It is when both of your brothers and I were grieving. It is when the management of the estate was left to me."

"You're a very capable person, Mother." His brow wrinkled, trying to find the meaning in her words.

"I had no training, Stephen. I had to learn as I went. You might have helped me with that, shouldered some of the burden. You were the one your father taught to take it over, after all. A few months of your time would have been appreciated."

"I had a life back in India. People who depended on me." He threw up his hands. "I couldn't just leave them."

"Why not?" She tilted her head. "You left us well enough, and we depended on you, too."

Stephen sat, head bent, thinking. He was surprised at her words, and they rousted a deep shame and not a small bit of grief. He was ashamed to realize he'd thought of them less than he should have, worried even less than that.

Of course they'd been struggling—he had been, too. But he'd been an adult. His brothers were still children, and his mother had loved his father. Deeply. He shouldn't have left her to shoulder all of those burdens alone.

It had seemed so simple at the time—he'd stayed in India because he'd felt honor-bound to do so. Now, seeing it through her eyes, he wondered if he hadn't made a grievous mistake.

"I'm sorry," he said, lifting his head and meeting her eyes. "I didn't think. I didn't mean to abandon you—surely you must at least know that."

"I do. But your motivations hardly matter. It is done, and for better or worse, the experience of losing your father has changed me. I won't have you waltzing back in here and criticizing the person I've become—the person that loss forged me into—not after you weren't here to help."

"You're right. I'm sorry, Mother. I wasn't...I didn't mean to criticize." He ran a hand through his hair. "But please tell me you aren't cavorting with that secretary."

She tipped her head back and laughed. "No, he isn't one of my lovers."

"Your *lovers*?"

"And I know better than most the importance of following one's own heart," she continued, ignoring his outburst. "If you felt you needed to be in India for this span of time, I'm glad you were there. I'm even more glad you're home."

"Wait, Mother. Can we please revisit the fact that you have *lovers*?"

"We cannot. Besides, you know I just said that to shock you."

"You did?" he asked, relieved.

"If you like."

The lift of her shoulder wasn't convincing, but as the conversation was deeply unsettling, he didn't wish to pursue it further.

"I might understand your hesitation toward Hamish," his mother said. "But why on earth are you pestering Vera so?"

"I don't think she's telling the full truth about why she's here."

"Of course not," she laughed. "No one is ever telling the full truth about *anything*. That's the nature of human communication, dear."

He frowned. "That's not correct. *I* don't lie."

"Of course you do. Don't forget, Stephen—in order to

be fully truthful with others, first one must be fully truthful with oneself."

He rubbed at his temple. "And you're saying I'm lying to myself, is that it?"

"I don't know. Are you?"

He sighed and closed his eyes. "Please stop being purposefully difficult."

"Very well. Please stop hassling our guest. Vera may not have told you her entire life story, but it is the prerogative of a lady to have *some* secrets."

"Not if they're potentially damaging to you or Benjamin."

"She's a wonderful person, and my very dear friend. I trust her. Isn't that enough for you?"

It wasn't—not by a long shot. But he didn't know how to explain it to her, so he nodded.

Her eyes narrowed slightly, as if she read his falsehood. "At least tell me this...*why* do you think she's lying? *Why* do you think she's concealing something important?"

"I don't know."

It was the truth—Stephen had no clue where this sudden obsession with the young lady's past had come from. All he knew was that it plagued him, day and night. He'd puzzled it from every possible angle while he'd weeded his old herb beds yesterday afternoon in the greenhouse. He'd ruminated on it at length while soaking in a steaming bath before dressing for the evening. He'd studied the lady in question the entirety of that strange dinner.

He was no closer to finding out who she was or why

she was there. But the fact of the matter was, he believed with his entire heart and mind that she was hiding something—something big.

It was written in the small wince she gave when specific topics were brought up. There'd been a certain tone to her words yesterday when she'd spoken to Benjamin. Something was wrong with Miss Vera Ashbury, and he was determined to find out what.

"Are you sure you're not interested in the lady for *other* reasons?" his mother asked lightly, breaking the silence.

Stephen exhaled with the force of his derision. "Don't be ridiculous."

"She *is* quite pretty. And unattached."

A flash of ash-brown hair shone briefly in his mind's eye.

He leaned forward. "You forget that I was recently engaged to a young lady that fit those parameters exactly. She also was hiding something, and I took it on faith that her concealment wasn't harmful. I'm not keen on repeating that experience."

"Ah." She hefted the word as if it held all the weight of a mother's understanding.

Stephen found he didn't like the sound of that 'ah.' It was as if his mother had discovered something about him that he was trying to hide, but for the life of him, he couldn't suss out what. She couldn't believe that what had happened with Samantha was the sole cause of his suspicion of Vera...could she?

Stephen clenched his jaw. He wasn't crazy for thinking something was off with their houseguest. His suspicion wasn't because he was *damaged*. He was going to find out what she was hiding, from him and his mother, both.

He would do whatever it took.

His mother watched him with narrowed eyes, and Stephen had the inkling that she could read all his thoughts upon his face. He'd learned as a young boy that if in doubt, distraction was the best option where parents were concerned.

He pointed at the animal across the room. "Is that your fox?"

She clasped a hand to her elegant throat, her dark eyes wide. "There's a *fox* in here?"

Stephen refrained from rolling his eyes, but just barely.

"You truly have changed—you used to recognize humor."

"People grow up." He shrugged, trying not to let on that she'd echoed one of his own thoughts—it felt as if, since Samantha, the part of him that had once smiled and laughed easily had withered and curled in on itself like arthritic hands.

"I hope that you find that part of yourself again, Stephen. I truly do." She pressed her lips together, then asked, "What are your plans now that you're home?"

He was grateful for the change of subject, but the question caught him by surprise, like a cuff to the back of his head.

"I don't know what you mean. I'm going to run the estate, of course."

She frowned. "Very well. What else?"

"I imagine that will take the bulk of my time."

"What about medicine? Are you giving up the practice altogether?"

"I hadn't thought about it."

It was a lie. He *had* thought about it. All the way back from India, he'd thought about it. The truth of the matter was that he was tired. Exhausted. There were so few doctors and too many people to help. He'd run himself ragged until pieces of him frayed off at the edges and were just...lost.

She was studying him again, in that keen eye way of hers that made him think of falcons. "You know, India doesn't contain all the poor people who need a good doctor. England has plenty of those, too."

"Oh?"

"You don't have to choose, Stephen. It doesn't have to be 'India and being a physician' or 'England.' I can think of several people right now who could use a physician in town."

"What about Dr. Stanley?"

"He moved to be closer to his daughter, nigh on three years ago."

"And Dr. Roy?"

"That old drunk? I wouldn't trust him to treat a dog, let alone a person."

"In your case, you'd probably trust him to treat certain people before you'd allow him to treat your dog."

"True." She smiled affectionately. "But you get my point all the same. He isn't fit for practice. People have to call all the way to Exeter if they want a good doctor."

Stephen grunted, but only because his mind was too

busy processing her words. Perhaps she was right. He'd always loved being a physician, loved helping people, but he knew his title would get in the way. Most nobles thought that being a gentleman precluded one from being anything else. But perhaps the average citizen wouldn't care one way or the other.

"I'll think about it."

"And how are you planning on spending your day?"

"I thought I'd ask Benjamin to go fishing." He scratched at his chin. "I haven't spent any time with him since I've returned."

His mother nodded. "That's an excellent plan, but it might have to wait until tomorrow. Vera is taking him to Canterbury's this afternoon to visit Arthur and Seamus. He's been looking forward to the visit."

"Do you think it wise to allow her to spend so much time with Benjamin, when we don't really know her?"

"*I* know her, Stephen. That's enough for me. I hope it's enough for you, too."

## CHAPTER 6 - VERA

Sometime during the dinner last night, Vera's wariness of the baron had solidified into firm dislike. And she could pinpoint *exactly* when that happened.

*One might think you have naught but charity to live on.* His words stung her more than she wanted to admit. Perhaps it was because there was truth to them.

The animosity was clearly mutual, though Stephen didn't seem the type to be able to leave well enough alone—he insisted on pestering her with insipid questions that he'd already asked and she'd already answered. Vera wondered if the man was trying to catch her in a falsehood.

She'd answered his questions as politely as possible—a difficulty, as the scowling man could try a saint's patience—and exited the conversations quickly. Vera tried to remember that she was a guest of the baroness and that Stephen was her son.

The following morning, she did her utmost to avoid

the odious man altogether. Vera had tucked herself into an alcove in the library, an encyclopedia of flora and fauna open on her knees. It was a very convenient spot, as it was nearly hidden behind the open door. If one glanced into the room, it would appear empty.

The pedantic tread of Stephen's boots had passed the door several times already. Each time, Vera's shoulders twitched toward her ears and she hoped her hiding place would hold.

This time, the boots stopped. They entered. Vera sighed and turned the page. By now, she knew what to expect.

"What are you reading?"

*Why hello, Vera,* she mentally amended. *Lovely weather, isn't it? I confess I'm looking for a distraction—what's caught your interest?*

It was a game she'd taken up—trying to see if she could rewrite his words into some semblance of politeness. So far, she'd met with middling success. Vera couldn't even quite bring herself to like the pretend version of the man, let alone the real one.

"A collection of flora and fauna," she answered, then turned the page as if she were still focused on the book.

Every time he entered a room, she felt hunted, harangued. Vera suddenly had great compassion for a rabbit shivering in its den while a wolf dug at the entrance to the burrow.

He grunted to indicate he'd heard her. For one shimmering moment, Vera thought that might be the end of it.

"What of your parents?"

The momentary hope that he'd leave her alone popped like a soap bubble on the air.

"What do you mean?" she asked politely, turning the page once more.

*Mushrooms.* Vera enjoyed the taste of them, though she'd been a little fearful of them ever since someone had told her that there were poisonous varieties that looked just like benign ones. Now, whenever mushroom soup was served at a dinner party, Vera made sure she was the last one to taste it. She couldn't help but envision twelve guests keeling head-first into their tureens because someone had made a mistake at the market.

"Where are your parents?" he said, tearing her attention from creminis and death caps.

"London."

He *knew* this. She'd answered this question several times. Despite her determination to be nothing but kind and patient, to never show how much her host vexed her, she was very tired of answering the same blunt questions.

"So you say. Yet, you aren't in London with them."

Vera snapped the book shut abruptly. "What is it exactly that you think I've done wrong?"

"I'm not sure. Perhaps nothing, yet."

"Then why do you insist on asking me the same questions over and over?"

"I'm allowed to be curious about my mother's close friend."

"Perhaps if you paid the same close attention to your own affairs as to mine, your estate wouldn't be in the situation it is."

He reared back. "*Excuse* me?"

"No, sir. I will not. For while you were off gallivanting across the globe, your mother has been left to tend to your holdings, your inheritance. She's independent and capable, I'll give you that. But just because a woman *can* doesn't mean she *wants* to."

"My mother—"

"Is busy raising your brothers while doing your job as lord of these lands. Have you even tried to take back that burden since you've returned, or do you not care that the back fields lay barren and the eastern fence has a hole in it large enough for all the king's soldiers to pass through? These things are your responsibility, but you've been off playing martyr to all the desolate of India, romancing women along the way without bothering to marry them, and your mother has been left to keep everything afloat without you. These lands need a lord, sir."

His jaw worked for several moments, as if he were chewing on her words. "Are you insinuating that a lady isn't capable—"

She rolled her eyes. "Don't be daft. I wouldn't be so stupid, even prior to meeting your mother. But everything is much harder for her, as a lady. She can't even keep her own stewards from arguing with her—she has to tell them three times what to do, where they'd listen to you directly. If you'd bother to put your efforts toward anything but hounding *me*, you'd know that."

"That's quite enough," he snapped.

"Ah, my life must be a book open on a table or I'm

hiding something, but heaven forbid anyone turn the magnifying glass upon *you*."

He rounded on her. "Your life is open to inquisition because you're living beneath my roof, madam."

"It *is* your roof, isn't it?" Vera stood and reshelved the book. "Yet you know so little about it, content to abscond from the actual responsibility of the thing while still claiming all the benefits of lordship."

"That's enough."

"Very well. Then please excuse me, *Baron*." She gave a low, mocking curtsy and departed the room without looking back.

## CHAPTER 7 - STEPHEN

Vera was good, Stephen would give her that.

For several hours after they'd spoken, Stephen's focus shifted from his original intent to the content of the words she'd hurled at him. He'd locked himself in his father's study with the ledgers from the past six years, going quarter by quarter until he felt quite up to date with all the happenings of the estate.

In perusing the correspondence, he saw that Vera had a point—two of the stewards in particular seemed to take umbrage at receiving instructions from his mother. Stephen wrote several letters, informing the men of business of his return and telling them that he would be speaking with his mother to determine whether any changes in stewardship needed to be made.

It was only early afternoon, when he was relaxing in his bath, steam swirling about, the end of his beard damp upon his chest, that he realized the little minx had succeeded. Vera had completely distracted him with her words. He hadn't completed the inquiry he'd had in mind when he found her in the library. Instead, he'd spent all morning looking at ledgers.

Stephen snorted derisively at himself, sending little rings rolling across the water. Vera was a puzzle he'd yet to figure out, but he would. If his repeated questioning couldn't provoke her into changing her story—a true hallmark of a lie—then he would have to obtain the information elsewhere.

He stood from the bath, thinking of his new plan for the day.

The Duke of Canterbury's country estate, Montclare, hadn't changed much in Stephen's absence. The topiaries that delineated the front door of the grand house were a bit taller, perhaps, but that was to be expected of plants.

The Duke of Canterbury welcomed him in gladly. If he thought Stephen's appearance odd—his bushy beard and odd-fitting trousers—he was gracious enough not to raise an eyebrow.

Canterbury rang for tea and saw Stephen seated in a comfortable chair closest to the fire in the front sitting room—Stephen wondered if the man had noticed the thinness of his old tweed coat and wished he hadn't split the other at the shoulders the other day. If only his new clothes would arrive from the London tailors, but that would be another week at least.

The parlor was handsome and well-appointed, lacking the general fussiness of some homes. Stephen approved—he loved that country houses were often more practical than their city counterparts. Chairs were comfortable for sitting, not those terrible straight-backed carved monstrosities in London townhomes. Cushions and curtains were for comfort and lacked extra frippery and doo-dads. And walls were rarely upholstered in silk in the country. Paint or wallpaper or paneling, and that was all.

Stephen and Canterbury exchanged pleasantries until the tea arrived. It was the sort of conversation Stephen abhorred. His physician's profession fit him well—he could stride into a room and ask blunt questions, receiving blunt answers in return, before striding off to address the next problem.

Debridement of burns was a nasty business, but Stephen thought it vastly preferable to the art of polite conversation about nothing. At least with treating burns, there were clear instructions, clear steps.

"How was your journey home?"

"Altogether too long, though the weather was fine enough."

Canterbury smiled. "That's probably the sentiment of everyone on a sea voyage—except for those who enjoy the sea."

"True. No matter how many improvements they make in terms of travel, we'll always want it to be faster."

A maid bustled in with a tray, arranging it on the low table between them. Stephen caught the hint of a strong English blend as the tea was poured, and he sighed with pleasure.

Once they each had a cup in hand, Canterbury turned to Stephen with a smile. "What are your plans? Do you aim to stay in the countryside for awhile, or are you planning on returning to London once you've rested?"

"I'm not sure yet." Stephen fought the urge to tug at the ends of his beard—a nervous habit that had grown in right alongside the thing.

"I'm sure your mother enjoys having you home. Benjamin, too."

Stephen nodded and hummed, though he wasn't sure, if he were being honest. Things were strange between him and his mother—it was as if he'd left and returned to find someone so markedly changed, they had to get to know each other all over again. As for his brother, he didn't know him at all.

Stephen was casting about for something to say—it was his turn, after all—when a huge dog lumbered in and stopped, looking at the men in the chairs as if debating whether their presence should be allowed.

"My goodness," Stephen said, latching on to the possible topic with all speed. "What a magnificent animal."

Canterbury chuckled. "My son's dog, Seamus. He's come to find out if you're friend or foe."

"I certainly hope he decides I'm friendly. I wouldn't want a dog that size to be angry with me."

"Mastiffs are very even-tempered. You'd have to

provoke him to extremes before he took any umbrage. Although, he wouldn't like it if you bothered my son, Arthur, or his lady love, Millie."

"You have two of these animals?"

"Millie is a friend's dog, come to stay until she births Seamus's puppies."

"Ah."

"Now that the job is done, Seamus won't leave her alone. He's exceedingly protective—follows her around night and day. Only leaves her when she's napping in the kitchen—which she must be doing now. Reminds me a bit of Percy, actually."

"When do you expect the happy additions?"

"Percy's? Or the dogs'?" Canterbury's eyes twinkled. "You would know better than I when it comes to the Salisbury progeny, I expect."

Stephen sipped his tea, shook his head. "Actually, I haven't made it to visit him yet."

"He must not have caught wind that there's an experienced physician among us, then. He's been trying to bribe Dr. Halveston to leave all his patients in London and only tend to the marchioness. I expect you'll be hearing from him shortly."

"What of Seamus and Millie?"

The dog circled before them and lay close to the fire with a grunt.

"Well before Thanksgiving, best guess." He shrugged. "But I don't need to tell you how these things are—it's an imperfect estimate."

"Indeed."

Now Canterbury looked at him with patient expectation, as if he agreed they'd exhausted the need for small talk and could move on to the real reason Stephen had visited him today.

"This is a delicate matter," Stephen haltingly began. "But I was hoping that you might give me some insight as to the nature of one Miss Vera Ashbury..."

After his meeting with the duke, Stephen's thoughts were grim. He glowered all the way home, letting the horse take the lead, lest he put his boots to it or treat it harshly on account of his foul mood.

It wasn't as Stephen had thought—that the duke had seen Vera's destructive interest in Lady Candace and intervened on her behalf. No—it was far worse. It seemed this Miss Ashbury had deceived the entire countryside. Canterbury had cheerfully confirmed that Vera was all that was kind and wonderful. The man had even gone so far as to hint that Stephen himself could do no better for a wife!

Of course, the man hadn't come right out and *said* that, but the less-than-subtle signals were there. The duke had misread the purpose of Stephen's visit entirely. Canterbury thought that Stephen had been so charmed by the pretty miss that he'd started in on his due diligence before proposing.

Stephen rubbed the knotted bruise on this upper arm

and frowned. *Charmed, indeed.* He'd sooner marry his mother's hedgehog.

But Vera would be out of the house for hours this afternoon. It might just be the chance that Stephen was looking for...

## CHAPTER 8 - VERA

The day was cool and clear. The carriage swayed gently as they rounded the last corner that brought Montclare into view.

"What are you most looking forward to?" Vera asked.

"The biscuits." Benjamin grinned.

She shook her head, smiling. Boys had a close relationship with their stomachs, especially at this age. She remembered how ravenous her brothers had always been, from the age of eight until twenty.

"And seeing Seamus, of course."

Vera wanted to snort, but refrained. Benjamin was at an uncomplicated age—biscuits and a dog, and he was set to have a marvelous day. She envied him. The older she got, the more complicated things became. She would eat the same biscuits as Benjamin, pat Seamus's massive head, but she wouldn't derive near the amount of pleasure the boy would from either thing.

"Remember your manners," Vera said as the carriage

stopped in the grand drive. "No running indoors, and follow the lead of your host. Don't ask for things that aren't offered."

"Yes, Miss Vera."

She was satisfied—Benjamin was a very well-behaved boy, indoors. It was when he was set loose upon the countryside that she began to worry. And there were two of them—a set of diminutive conquerors, seeking to pillage the hedgerows for every scrap of mischief possible.

"Hello, Vera dear!" Candace rushed down the steps to greet her once she alighted from the carriage. "It's been far too long."

Vera smiled and agreed on the inside. They hadn't had a proper visit, just the two of them, since before Candace was married. Now, she wondered if they ever would again. There was either her husband or her new son-by-marriage present whenever they met.

Though she loved both of them in their own way, sometimes Vera longed for the intimacy that she and Candace had once enjoyed—sharing secrets and inner thoughts along with a tea tray.

But life was forever changing, and Vera thought maybe that was part of the lesson: never taking anything for granted, as it might soon be past.

*Even this,* she thought, reminding herself to be grateful. *Who knows how long I'll still be in the countryside?*

As Candace led her and Benjamin into the wide front hall, Vera's thoughts returned to the letter to Mr. Audel that she'd started only last night. Although she didn't want to take it, his was the only offer she'd received all these weeks she'd been looking.

With the return of the baron from India, she could feel her time in Devon growing short. It was as if she stood on the wet sand of a beach, and the tide was coming in. Even now, she felt the swirl of cold waters around her ankles; if she waited much longer, she'd drown. The baron was going to ask her to leave soon—she could feel it.

"I thought we'd take a walk through the gardens before luncheon," Candace said as Arthur stood from the leather sofa and Seamus lumbered up from his position in front of the fireplace, wagging his greeting.

Arthur was about the same age as Benjamin, but his frame was slighter, and he was half a head shorter. Candace had told Vera in confidence that her husband, James, wasn't concerned in the least—he'd been much the same as a child, only hitting a growth spurt when he arrived at the age of twelve.

"Sounds wonderful." Vera smiled, thrusting all her uncertainty about the future into a mental box. She'd lock it away for the day so she could enjoy this time with her dear friend.

Their steps moved from marble tiles out onto a flagstone patio, then crunched across gravel in the garden pathways. The gardens of Montclare were lovely. The late flowers of the season nodded their final farewell atop stems. Leaves were starting to turn—several trees adopting the new colors of orange and yellow first, as if they were adventurous young ladies trying the new fashions from France.

"How are you?" Candace asked, beating Vera to the question. "It truly has been far too long. Adelaide had to be the one to tell me you'd moved to the baroness's house."

*Because you were too busy to ask me yourself.*

Vera squashed the little bit of hurt she felt. Of course her friend was busy—a new husband, a new son, a new household, her brother and expectant sister-by-law returned from Greece. There was much to be going on with; of course Vera had fallen through the cracks a bit.

"I'm well. Helping the baroness with her pets." Vera smiled widely to cover her own fears and doubts.

"I hear the baron has returned from India. The entire town is talking of nothing else. How do you find him?"

"Between you and me?" Vera arched an eyebrow and Candace nodded. "He's a terrible grump. I daresay he's lost all conversational grace while he was away."

*If he had any to begin with*, she silently added.

"Shocking, indeed. Once he's rested from his journey, I'll invite the entire household over for dinner, so I can examine him myself."

Vera nodded, wondering if she'd still be in Devon when said dinner party took place. "We had a small gathering of our own yesterday evening. The baroness invited your brother's secretary to dine with us."

"Hamish?" Candace's eyes went wide. "What an interesting development. Do you think he and the baroness…"

She trailed off delicately.

Vera smiled. "I'm not sure about that, but I don't find the idea as shocking as some might. If Jacqueline were to settle down again, I don't really see her choosing someone *regular*, do you?"

Candace pursed her lips and looked toward the distance as if studying the birds winging through the sky over the far pasture.

"I see what you mean," she said finally. "I think you're right—if she *does* decide to dip her toe into the pool of romance, I can hardly see her in a London ballroom. She would prefer a different sort of hunting ground."

"Knowing her, she might find a match while hunting," Vera quipped.

Candace laughed, a wonderful tinkling of bells that Vera had always envied. Vera's own laugh sounded more like a low grinding. One of her brothers had uncharitably compared it to a carriage that had lost a wheel. Vera privately thought it was more like an elderly woman who'd smoked four pipes a day for nigh on thirty years.

"She has an excellent mind and she knows herself well," Candace said. "Wherever she finds someone, I daresay they'll be very lucky."

"Indeed. What man wouldn't enjoy a hunting partner as beautiful as she?"

They rounded the bend and caught a brief glimpse of the boys before they plowed through a hedge and scampered off.

"Poor Seamus." Candace reached down and patted the large dog on the head. "He doesn't even try and keep up when those two boys are running about like that."

"He stays in their general vicinity, though. That counts for something."

"It does. He's a very loyal dog."

"Has he tried swimming lately?"

The mastiff and Arthur had to be fished out of a lake only months earlier. The dog possessed fewer swimming skills than Vera did, which was saying something.

"No, thank goodness. We've kept him well clear of all water deep enough to drown in."

"Probably for the best. How is James?"

"Wonderful, as always. I am the luckiest of women." Candace snuggled deeper into her fine shawl and smiled.

"I've never heard of a better match. I'm so happy for you both."

She was, truly. James and Candace were meant for each other. Still, Vera ignored the little pang in her heart. It wasn't jealousy—at least, not the way she understood it. She didn't begrudge them for having found each other, and she certainly hadn't wanted to marry James. But she did want someone who fit her as well as James fit Candace—someone who was hers and hers alone.

That was a well-worn hope, a coin that had been tossed into a wishing fountain years ago and left to tarnish, forgotten.

"How is Adelaide feeling?" Vera asked, to draw her own attention away.

Candace looked heavenward. "I daresay she'd be feeling a lot better if my brother would calm down. He's far more nervous about the business than she is."

"A matter of personality, I suppose."

"He's always been a bit high-strung."

"They say that redheads often are," Vera said lightly.

Candace pursed her lips and narrowed her eyes. "Statements like that simply aren't fair. Now if I respond with anything other than perfect grace, I'll only be proving your point."

"That is the joke."

"What of the baron? Does he share his mother's hair color?"

Vera nodded, though she was perplexed at the conversation's return to Stephen. Though she supposed it was natural—the countryside only offered so many topics, and a newcomer would be high on the list for weeks.

Candace gave a sly smile. "Do you remember when we first arrived in Devon?"

Vera couldn't imagine what on earth had made her friend look so smug, but she knew better than to trust the expression.

"Are you referring to your brief, passionate affair with the gin?" Vera offered, trying to distract her from whatever mischief her mind had conceived. "Because I *do* remember that, yes."

She waved a hand covered in delicate white lace. "Not *that*. I'm speaking of that silly game I made you play—the one where you answered a series of questions about what you wanted your life to look like."

"Don't be ridiculous, Candace. And don't get any ideas into your head, I mean it."

For Vera *did* remember. Candace had pressed her into playing, guilted her into answering what kind of man she'd prefer to marry.

"You said he'd have dark hair and live in the country," Candace insisted.

"And you claimed you'd marry a blonde who lived in the city. We all know how accurate *that* turned out to be."

Candace just laughed—as a happily married woman, she was far past the point of injury when it came to previous speculation.

This was the problem with married people, Vera thought. As soon as they wed, they completely forgot the feeling of being unattached. It was as if a giant eraser moved over the blackboard of their mind, swabbing out all the fear, the uncertainty, all the little inconveniences and loneliness with which they'd once been so well acquainted.

They told their single friends not to worry, not to take it so seriously. It was as if they believed that since it had worked out for *them*, it would certainly work out for everyone, eventually.

That wasn't *true*. That wasn't the *reality* of things. But pointing that out to a happily attached person was pointless. They forgot that things didn't always work out so neatly for others as it had for them. They also forgot that a good match took far more than two eligible people living in the same general vicinity as each other.

"Very well," Candace conceded. "I just want to point out that the baron has dark hair and lives in the country."

"He also stomps around frowning at everyone who crosses his path." Vera nodded toward the hedgerow, where the boys' giggling could be heard. "Even Benjamin —his own brother—wants nothing to do with him."

Her eyebrows raised. "That sounds grim, indeed."

"That is precisely the word for it—grim. Speaking to him is grim. Being in the same room with him is *grim*. Looking at him is *grim*."

"He isn't at all handsome?"

Vera held herself back from rolling her eyes and settled on sighing instead—as if him being handsome had anything to do with it.

"Haven't you heard a word I've said? The man is a grump, a curmudgeon. I doubt he's ever smiled, or laughed, or so much as had a pleasant thought."

"I thought he was engaged."

Vera blinked.

Candace hurried to add, "I only mean that he must have been happy, at one point. Perhaps it's his failed engagement that's set him so low."

"I doubt the lady was any more cheerful than the gentleman. Most likely, she found someone even grumpier and decided to marry him."

The path narrowed, and Vera scooted closer to the large stone fountain to allow Seamus to squeeze through. It was terrible timing—just as she leaned, the huge dog bumped roughly into her hip. Vera was sent sprawling into the basin of the fountain. She was submerged for an instant in green-hued water.

Vera surfaced with a splutter, coming face to face with the massive face of Seamus. The mastiff tilted his head in gentle inquiry, as if to politely ask why Vera had chosen that moment to go for a swim.

"Are you all right?" Candace hurried over, her eyes

wide. She attempted to shove the huge dog over; he didn't seem to notice and began wagging.

"I'm...I'm fine." Vera sat up, sending another wave rolling across the surface of the fountain. "He bumped me."

"But you're not hurt? Are you certain?" Candace offered her hand and Vera took it gratefully.

Between the two of them, they managed to get Vera upright once more. Her dress was sopping; her bonnet was a sodden mess. Her hair clung to her face and neck like errant strands of seaweed.

"Truly. I'm unhurt. A bit surprised, is all."

"I'm so sorry." Candace helped her step over the wide rim and back onto the gravel path. "He's not a bad dog, I promise. He just has no concept of his own size."

"I know. No harm done."

Vera looked over at the dog. He'd somehow figured out that something was amiss, that perhaps he'd done something wrong, even if he wasn't quite sure *what*. He lay on his back, offering a meek wag and his stomach as a sign of goodwill. She couldn't help but grin and rub his belly, covering her wet fingers with errant fur.

"You're far more forgiving than I'd be." Candace shook her head. "That was a lovely muslin."

"It will be again." Vera rubbed the great abundance of luxurious fur at Seamus's neck. "The baroness is forever arriving home with grass stains and mud caked to her trousers. I daresay there's no house in all of England better prepared to deal with a bit of pond water."

"I *am* sorry. What a terribly abrupt end to a visit. I'll

call for tea and towels—I should have done already." Without another word, Candace hurried off around a corner in the garden.

Fifteen minutes later, Vera found herself comfortably bundled into the back of a carriage, headed toward Bertforth House once more. Benjamin had remained behind with Arthur and Candace, and Vera had promised to return for their picnic just as soon as she changed her clothes. If she hurried, they wouldn't even have to postpone the boys' luncheon.

Once she arrived at the house, she let herself in the front door and raced up the stairs, wincing at the water droplets in her wake. She'd have to alert the servants to the mess before she left—she didn't want anyone slipping and falling on the way down.

Vera yanked open her bedroom door, nearly catapulted herself inside…and froze.

Stephen sat at her desk, all of her carefully folded letters undone and spread out before him on the surface. He held two—one in each hand. It appeared he'd been reading them side by side. His wide eyes met hers—she didn't know which of them was more surprised in the moment.

"Get out," she snarled in a voice she barely recognized, slamming the door behind her. She didn't want anyone else to hear this outburst.

"Wait." He stood smoothly, his eyes still wide—whether at being caught, or because of her bedraggled, wet appearance, she didn't know. "Let me explain."

She tossed her ruined bonnet onto the wooden floor

with a wet slap and laughed mirthlessly. "Do you think me so idiotic that I *require* an explanation?"

"I just—"

"What?" She spread her hands on either side of her, bared her teeth.

It didn't help her temper that the two letters he held were the most excruciating of the lot of them.

One was the letter her mother had written, weeks ago, informing Vera she was no longer welcome at home. The other, Mr. Audel's highly improper job offer.

Maybe she'd gotten lucky, after all. Maybe Stephen still held those because he hadn't yet read them...

But her hopes were dashed when he held Mr. Audel's letter aloft. "You cannot possibly think of accepting this man."

"*Get. Out.*"

She whirled, looking for something, *anything* to launch at his head. All she found were pillows and similarly soft items. Drat her comfortable bedroom!

"I'm sorry." He pinched the letters between his pointer and thumb and held the other fingers up as if he were trying to calm a growling dog. "Forgive me, but I could tell you were hiding something; I needed to know what it was—"

"There is *no* excuse for you reading my personal letters! There is no forgivable reason for you entering my *bedroom*!"

"Of course not. You're right. I'm sorry."

She jabbed a finger toward the door, horrified to feel her rage pricking at the corners of her eyes. She always cried if she got angry enough—a terrible habit. Soon, she wouldn't even be able to snap at him; it would come out as a wet, pathetic warbling.

"Just, please. Let me explain."

Why was he still here? Why did he still hold her letters?

"Get out!" she yelled. "Get out! Get out!"

She strode for the fireplace and grasped the poker. If he didn't leave, she'd finish what she'd started the day he returned home. Vera half wished she'd killed him then and there. A tragic end, but everyone would have understood her confusion. This—this would be *murder*.

She found, in that moment, she didn't rightly care.

"You have been *awful* to me since the moment you stepped foot in this house," she seethed, rounding on him.

He nimbly stepped behind the velvet chaise, putting the sofa between them.

He held up his hands again. "Just wait. *Listen.*"

"I swear to you, if you don't leave, I'll do my best to brain you with this poker."

Something in her expression must have convinced him. He darted out, her letters still clutched in his hands. The slam of the door behind him broke the dam she'd held on her tears. She tossed the poker down onto the carpet with a thunk, threw her own damp person across her bed, and wept.

## CHAPTER 9 - STEPHEN

**O**h, *no*.

He'd been *so* wrong.

In fact, the only time he'd possibly been *more* wrong about a person was when he'd asked Samantha to be his wife.

His hands shook as he strode toward his bedroom. He needed to be alone. He needed to *think*. A crisp fluttering at his sides made him aware that he still gripped the terrible letters.

One from Vera's mother, disowning her.

The other from a man who'd offered a *very* improper position of employment.

Stephen had told himself he had no choice but to find out what Miss Ashbury was hiding.

He'd read everything—her letters, her journals, even the start of her response to the odious Mr. Audel—which Stephen couldn't help but notice had been dated only that morning. Which meant that Miss Ashbury had held off answering for weeks, but only started to agree once her position became truly untenable.

*He'd* done that.

Stephen ran a hand through his overlong hair. *He* had been the one who'd made her feel so unwelcome that she thought she had no choice but to write to that terrible man. Stephen doubted the man even had daughters—he'd certainly glossed over them in his letter.

It hardly mattered now. Vera certainly wouldn't stay, now that Stephen had invaded her privacy so thoroughly.

He closed his bedroom door behind him and leaned against it, letting his breath out in a huff of a sigh. He shook his head.

He wouldn't blame Miss Ashbury if she went straight to his mother and told her what he'd done. He might, if he were in her delicate little shoes. And his mother would be right to side with her against him.

Stephen collapsed into his desk chair and tried to think clearly.

He'd been correct in one aspect—Miss Vera Ashbury *was* hiding something.

But it was nothing close to what Stephen had suspected. She'd been disowned by her parents, for something as trivial as joining her dear friend in the countryside for a matter of months.

He'd found the stack of letters Vera had written to her parents—all of them drafts, all of them unsent. Stephen wondered if they were just for her own edification—some had begged for forgiveness, others had enumerated the terrible treatment she'd received at the hands of her own mother.

He'd also found neatly organized business correspondence. Vera was trying to find employment. She'd kept detailed records of every job she'd written about. There'd been dozens—she'd started out only inquiring about companions for the elderly and governess positions, but lately had been writing for all manner of jobs—maids, shop girl postings, *everything*.

A slimy thread of shame worked its way though his stomach. He groaned softly, dropping his head into his hands.

When he first decided to be a physician, it was because he wanted to help people. He'd prided himself on making the world better for those around him. He knew he'd done good for many people.

But not for Vera Ashbury.

For her, he'd made the world more difficult, made an already impossible situation far worse. He'd been all the things he prided himself on never being. He'd acted the part of the brute. He'd been *terrible*.

What could he possibly do to fix it?

He strode to the door, then jogged down the stairs. The housekeeper stood in the hallway.

"Miss Ashbury requires a hot bath and a full tea tray sent to her room."

"Very good, my lord." She nodded toward the door. "Does that mean she won't be returning to Montclare today?"

"I don't believe so. Will you send a servant back to wait

on Benjamin and accompany him on his return? Please give the Duchess of Canterbury Miss Ashbury's sincere apologies. Tell her Vera isn't feeling well enough to return."

"Indeed, my lord." She hurried to do his bidding.

Stephen took the stairs to his bedroom two at a time and shut himself in once more. As far as apologies went, offering a hot bath and some tea wasn't much, but it was a start.

By that evening, Stephen was surprised he hadn't worn a path into the thick rug in his bedroom with his pacing, but he had a plan. One that he'd already put into motion, as much as he could by sending off several letters.

He dressed for dinner far earlier than necessary and went to stand outside Vera's door. If he were her, he wouldn't come down for dinner that night. But he wanted her to. He'd been surprised to realize, sometime during that long afternoon, that he *wanted* her forgiveness.

He raised his fist and rapped it against the door.

"Yes?"

Her voice was clear, at least. It didn't sound as if she had been crying all day. That was something, he supposed.

"It's Stephen."

Her response was a whip crack. "Go away."

He'd expected as much, but it still made him flinch. He deserved it.

"I came to apologize. I'm going to stand here until you're ready to speak with me."

He jerked in surprise when the door flew open to reveal her scowling face. "This is your plan, is it? To hound me into accepting an apology, just to make *you* feel better?"

Stephen shook his head and handed over the letters, which he'd refolded. "Here. No. I need to speak to you. I... I'm sorry. I shouldn't have gone through your things. I shouldn't have gone into your room."

He kept his voice low in case someone was down the hallway, out of sight.

"No, you shouldn't have. But are you truly sorry that you did?" She lifted her eyebrows in challenge.

He thought about it, and his mouth twisted, giving away his honest answer before he could speak it.

"That's what I thought."

She went to slam the door, and he jammed his foot in the way. "Please, wait. Just wait a minute. *Ow!*"

Vera Ashbury rhythmically slammed the door onto his foot. Had he once thought this lady shy? She was disproving every part of that notion now, color high on her cheeks, her eyes flashing with fury.

Still, he kept his foot in the way. "You can't accept that horrible man's offer."

That was enough to get her to pause her relentless assault on his boot.

"You are not my father, or my brothers. You don't have any say in what I do, or for whom I work."

She pulled the door back, her face screwed up with the preliminary effort of her next slam, which looked like it was going to be a doozy.

"I'd like you to work for *me*."

"What?" Her hands dropped from the door in her shock.

Stephen tried to keep the relief from his face—his foot was *throbbing*. "You need references; I can give you one. As long as you earn it, I mean."

"Are you in need of a governess?" she snapped, rolling up on her tip-toes to jam her face closer to his. "Perhaps someone to teach you basic manners, fifteen years too *late*? It's too large a task for me, I'm afraid. Seek out someone with a bullwhip—that ought to do it."

Stephen couldn't help it; he grinned at her impertinence. Her eyebrows flew higher on her face; she gripped the door and wound it back once more.

"Wait!" He held up his hands. "I'm serious. I'm offering you a legitimate position, away from that dreadful Mr. Audel. Work for me for three months, and I'll give you a glowing reference. You'll be able to have your pick of any posting after that."

"What, pray tell, would the position entail? Say all you want about Mr. Audel, but there's only one man who's *actually* let himself into my bedroom uninvited."

Stephen's cheeks grew hot with his embarrassment. He prayed his beard covered most of it.

"Stop hitting me with your door for a moment, and I'll tell you."

"...And we had a picnic, and Seamus ate a plate of cheese when we weren't looking, and they're going to make him sleep in the stables tonight, for the smell."

The baroness looked heavenward. "Really, Benjamin. We're at the dinner table. If you want to eat with us, you must observe *some* propriety."

Stephen personally thought that a rich statement, coming from a lady who currently wore trim trousers and a pair of mud-splattered Hessians that rolled up to her knees, but he was wise enough to keep the thought to himself.

"Sorry. What about you, Mother?" Benjamin asked, carefully cutting into his fish. The tip of his tongue poked out the corner of his mouth in concentration.

"I went for a walk," she said. "Still looking for that fox."

There was something in her voice that had Stephen narrowing his eyes slightly. Something about her breathing or her octave was a bit strange. He glanced at Vera—her head was cocked, ever so slightly, as if she'd heard it, too.

"I certainly wish I'd seen Seamus push you into the fountain, Miss Vera," Benjamin added, eyes wide. "That is, I'm glad you're not hurt."

"I made quite a splash, I admit it."

Stephen tried to ignore the fact that Vera hadn't made eye contact with him once since taking her place. Even when she'd asked him to pass the salt, she'd addressed his earlobe. It hardly boded well for her accepting his offer.

He shifted in his seat and frowned. He *wanted* her to agree. Not only because the idea of becoming the countryside's physician had been nagging at him since his mother mentioned it, but because he wanted something good to come from his terrible mistake with Vera. This, he reasoned, was a prudent plan, where both of them could walk away feeling better about things.

And Stephen desperately wanted to feel better about things.

He didn't want to keep feeling like the kind of person who thought the worst of others, the type of person who broke into a young lady's bedroom and read all her correspondence to prove...to prove *what*?

He winced as he reviewed all the suspicions he'd had about Miss Vera Ashbury.

"Is it the fish?" his mother asked, peering over at him. "I keep asking Mrs. Portence to use more salt. Roland, please bring him the salt cellar."

The stoic butler did as she asked; Stephen had no choice but to sprinkle a small spoonful of salt over his already delicious fish.

"Have you given any more thought to what I said, Stephen? About going back into medicine?"

Stephen finished his bite and gulped water from his glass. "I have, actually. I ordered some supplies today, and I'm going to start replanting the greenhouse. Are you sure that there's truly a need in the village?"

"Once word gets out, you'll have more work than you know what to do with."

Stephen couldn't help it—his eyes slid to Vera, who was studiously ignoring him. "Well, I might have some assistance in that quarter. I'm thinking of hiring a nurse."

"Oh?" The baroness tilted her head. "Do you have someone in mind?"

Vera nodded at her plate as if coming to the decision right then. "Me, actually. I've accepted Doctor, er, Lord Winthrop's offer of employment."

Relief sliced through him—quick and pure, as if he'd jumped into a cool lake on a hot summer's day. It was all going to be all right. He could make up for his momentary lapse, for the injury he'd done the lady. This would work.

"Good heavens, Vera. Why on earth would you want to do that?" Jacqueline scrunched her face.

"Excuse me—" Stephen began, affronted.

His mother waved her hand at him, never once glancing away from Vera's face. "Yes, yes. You're excused. From this conversation, from the table altogether, whatever you like. Vera?"

Vera lifted her head, and for the first time since the blasted dinner began, she met his eyes. Hers were hazel, he realized, the colors the same as a canopy of fall leaves just turning color. Browns and greens, flecks of orange—all the colors of autumn collected in her pupils.

She swallowed deeply and Stephen was momentarily distracted by the motion of her throat. "It's a wonderful opportunity."

Jacqueline kept her eyes on Vera but said, "Benjamin, go to the kitchen and have Mrs. Portence cut you a big slice of cake. But you must eat it there."

The boy whooped and pushed back from the table so quickly his chair nearly toppled. The second the oiled hinges of the dining room door swung in his wake, the baroness turned to Stephen.

Her eyes narrowed; her lip nearly curled. His eyes widened in response—he couldn't remember his mother ever looking at him with such seething ferocity.

"*You* did this. *You* made her feel she had to earn her keep. Didn't you?"

Stephen leaned back. Guilt threatened to swallow him. He *had* done that. That, and worse.

"Not at all," Vera said calmly, surprising him. "He offered me an opportunity for gainful employment, and I took it. This cannot be such a surprise to you—I told you I was thinking of taking a position."

"As a governess or a lady's companion. Not as a *nurse*."

Stephen wrinkled his nose at the way his mother had spat the last. "What's wrong with being a nurse? It's an honorable thing to do, a wonderful way to be useful."

"Vera doesn't need to prove herself to you. She's my guest. She's *already* useful."

"I think it will be an interesting endeavor," Vera said.

"There's going to be blood, Vera. Other bodily fluids. Viscera." Jacqueline threw up her hands.

"It's rarely as dramatic as all that," Stephen said, his eyebrows high.

The ladies at the table both ignored him. His mother stared at Vera, eyes wide as if trying to impress her thoughts through expression alone. Vera's face was calm, but a tightness at the corners of her mouth spoke of her discomfort.

"It isn't a position a lady typically takes," his mother

pressed. "It will be difficult for you to overcome such a thing when it comes to society."

Vera's face flickered in understanding. "You're exceptionally sweet to be worried about such a thing, Jacqueline, but I fear such concerns are far behind me."

If anything, Vera's calm response seemed to infuriate his mother more. She sat up straight, her features smoothed into arctic rage that Stephen had only witnessed several times in his life.

"Vera, I think you'd better go ask Mrs. Portence for a piece of cake, too."

A sad little smile played at the edges of Vera's mouth as she picked up her plate and her wine goblet and headed toward the far door without uttering a word.

Once she was gone, his mother rounded on him. "What did you *do*?"

"Nothing." He spread out his hands as if to prove his innocence, but his single word of defense hadn't been quite as firm as it should have been.

She jabbed a finger in the air between them. "If she does this, it will be nigh on impossible for her to marry someone worthy of her."

"Good heavens, Mother. Was *that* your intention for the lady? She's not going to find someone cloistered all the way out here."

"That isn't for you to decide, Stephen."

"She hardly seems concerned with marriage; she's looking for employment. I heard it from her myself."

*In a round about way, of sorts.*

"Society looks down upon those in the medical profession—"

"I've survived their judgement."

"You're a *man*. A *titled* man. It's completely different, and you know it."

"I admit I'm shocked at your scruples." He twirled his fork in the air before cutting into his fish once more. "Aren't you always the one going on about following one's heart, one's passion, and that society can go hang itself?"

"This isn't *her* passion; it's *yours*."

He rolled his eyes. "If nursing is good enough for the sisters of mercy, I daresay it's good enough for Miss Ashbury."

His mother brought a hand sharply down upon the table top. His empty water glass jolted right along with him. "She is under my protection, and this will ruin her prospects."

"*What* prospects?" he asked gently. He canted his voice low so there was no chance his words would seep through the hall to the kitchen and injure Vera further. "The lady is unattached, as far as either of us know. As you've pointed out, if home were a safe place to be, she'd return there. As of now, she's being shuttled from friend's house to friend's house, but that cannot last forever, Mother."

Jacqueline chewed her lip.

"Will you really deprive her of the chance to gain a reference and secure her chance for future employment, over the scruples of a society that you don't give a whit about?"

She pressed her lips together and blinked.

"Besides, I doubt anyone will even find out. Who's going to tell them? You? Me?" He exhaled a scoff. "She'll work her three months and be back to London in a more genteel position before anyone has an inkling of what's going on."

"I want her accompanied." She lifted her chin. "Despite what you say, I won't have her traipsing all over the countryside in the company of an unmarried man. Regardless of her choice of employment, at least grant *that* would be inappropriate for both of you."

He sighed. "There's nothing less romantic than a medical setting."

"I won't hear otherwise. She'll take a maid with her."

"Which maid will you send to keep us from ravaging each other over pustulant wounds?"

"Don't you mock me at my own table, Stephen. And don't mock me for wanting to preserve what slim chance at a future Vera has. Just because her family's detestable doesn't mean *she* is. There are a hundred gentlemen who'd be lucky to have her as wife."

"So you say, and yet I look around and see none."

"I won't have you sinking her lower just because you don't believe someone would want her."

"That's not at all what I'm saying! She's pretty enough, I suppose, though she is well on the shelf—"

"You men and your *shelves*," she hissed, as if Stephen had been the one to coin the phrase.

He held up his hands. "I'm not the enemy here. She wanted gainful employment; I offered it."

"And how did you know she wanted a position, Stephen? You two aren't exactly close."

*The understatement of the century*, Stephen thought. His foot still throbbed from where Vera had slammed it in her door. Repeatedly.

"She's been sending dozens of letters from the village. It was only a matter of time before word got out. You know how nosy the innkeep is."

It wasn't quite a lie, but it was as close to one as he dared. His mother had a nose for such things. Even now, her slim nostrils flared as if scenting the half-truth on the air.

"Very well. I cannot stop either of you. However, she will travel in the company of a maid at all times. She's under our protection, Stephen, and even if that means little to you, it means a great deal to me."

"Fine—I suppose the maid can roll bandages or something."

"Oh no." She held up a finger and gave a brittle smile. "The maid is there for *Vera*. Not you."

Stephen recognized her expression well enough to know it was no use arguing. "Fine. The maid can follow her around and whack me round the head if we lose ourselves to passion in between emptying buckets of vomit."

## CHAPTER 10 - VERA

"Good heavens," Stephen murmured, three days later. "Where on earth did Mother find *her*?"

They stood on the front steps of Bertforth House, the sun dappling their shoulders while a cool breeze ruffled the trimmed hedges on either side of the door. The baroness had informed them that Vera's chaperone would arrive that morning promptly at eight. Stepping down from the plain carriage in the drive was a tall blonde woman who clutched a fearsome umbrella in one of her capable hands.

Vera smiled widely for the first time since she'd found Stephen rummaging through her correspondence. It had been three days, and three days without smiling was quite long enough.

"Hortense!" She ran forward and threw her arms around the woman. "How are you?"

"Very well, Miss Ashbury. And yourself?"

Vera held her at arm's length and beamed up at her.

"When Jacqueline said she was going to hire a maid to accompany me, I had no idea it was *you* she spoke of." She frowned. "But won't your husband miss your help at the store?"

Hortense's cheeks grew a bit pink. "Though my husband and I love each other dearly, it seems our relationship is best served with us working separately."

Vera laughed. "I can't claim that I'm not delighted. What about Candace—er, the Duchess of Canterbury? Won't she be upset that we've stolen you away for ourselves?"

"Her Grace already has a lady's maid. I believe she had to hire two to replace me, actually." The last was said with no small amount of pride.

"I don't doubt it. Candace always claimed you were the best lady's maid in all of England. It would follow that it would take at least two to take your place."

"This must be the doctor I've heard so much about." Her lips thinned as Stephen approached.

Vera cleared her throat. "Lord Winthrop, may I present Miss—er, Mrs. Harris?"

"Lovely to meet you, Mrs. Harris," Stephen said. "But it's Dr. Winthrop, actually. Especially when we're working."

"Of course, Doctor." Hortense held out a hand.

Vera couldn't figure out how such a small motion could convey so much challenge, but Hortense had somehow managed it. Perhaps it was because Hortense was only a couple of inches shorter than the man, though he was much broader through the shoulders.

Stephen took her hand and shook it crisply. "I think it's wonderful Mother has hired such a capable young lady to help us. If the cart gets stuck in the mud, you can help push it out."

With that shocking proclamation, he moved past both of them toward the cart. He gained the front seat easily, gathering the reins in his hands as if he'd done it a hundred times before. Hortense arched an eyebrow at Vera, who widened her eyes and gave a shrug in response.

"Well?" Stephen asked. "Are you ladies coming?"

VERA SAT on the front board with Stephen and tried to ignore how much she disliked him. Worse, it was like the man didn't know how she felt—he acted as if nothing unpleasant had ever transpired between them.

He held the reins with a quiet confidence that Vera couldn't help but envy. She sneaked a sidelong glance at him. Dark hair, curling at the temples, a dark beard that waved and still made him appear like a down-on-his-luck dockworker.

Stephen appeared a bit more civilized than the first time she'd seen him—but only by a small margin. It was the difference that a bath, a trim, and a comb made, nothing more. She tried not to cringe as she remembered the whistle of the fire poker as she'd swung it through the air. If she'd known what he truly was like, she might have tried harder.

He let the horses take the lead down the worn road that wound past the village and over a small river. The cart's wheels rumbled over the little wooden bridge, and Vera leaned to peer at the gentle eddies of water swirling over pebbles below.

"Milton's Creek," Stephen said, as if she'd asked.

Vera nodded stiffly, but she was determined not to relinquish her anger at him before she was ready. When that would be, even she didn't know.

"We're going to see Mr. Douglas," Stephen called, loud enough for even Hortense to hear over the crunch of wagon wheels and the clopping of horse hooves. "He's a widower who lives on a small farm. Mother says he's been feeling poorly, doesn't want to call for a physician."

"Is he not expecting us, then?" Vera blinked.

The idea didn't help the disquiet roiling in her stomach. Against all her well-reasoned arguments why she shouldn't be, she was nervous. She'd never held a position before, and despite the acrimony that lay between her and the doctor, she desperately wanted to do a good job.

It wasn't just the reference, either, though that was part of it—she longed for the day when she could put this chapter of her life behind her. She thought of it—envisioned a clear, bright morning not too long in the future when Stephen would hold out a letter he'd written that would give her the power to support herself, to never depend on anyone else, ever again.

"Not that I'm aware of." He shrugged as if the thought didn't bother him in the least.

Vera held the edges of her shawl even more tightly around her. Not only was it her first day of employment—ever—but they were arriving unannounced, uninvited. What did Stephen intend on doing—barging in and thrusting a tongue depressor down the man's throat?

She had a sudden, inappropriate image of the doctor and a faceless elderly gentleman wrestling over a thermometer, and she barely stifled a nervous giggle. It came out as a jarring hiccup instead.

Stephen slid those brown eyes toward her, then looked back to the road.

*Keep it together, Vera,* she chided herself. *The man already thinks little of you.*

She wished she didn't give a whit for his opinion—it was *he* who should be desperate for *her* good favor, after what he'd done—but wanting the approval of others was an ingrained habit she'd yet to break. Perhaps it was the result of growing up with a mother who was forever unsatisfied with her appearance, her manners, her words. Whatever the cause, Vera cared deeply about what people thought of her.

It was not her appearance or social standing she was concerned for—such petty cares had been eradicated by years of ballroom laughter at her expense. Perhaps it was because she knew she couldn't compete in those other arenas that made Vera value what people thought of her more important attributes all the more. She wanted to be seen as capable, intelligent, kind, reliable. With Stephen as her employer, it was doubly important he thought so.

Mr. Douglas's house was a small stone cottage with a freshly thatched roof. The yard was tidy, the fence that bordered the lane in good repair. A tuft of grey-blue smoke wafted from the chimney. Several chickens scattered when their cart pulled to a stop in the drive.

"I'll go first." Stephen slid a sardonic gaze toward Vera. "Don't want the man alarmed, thinking that a herd of noble do-gooders have arrived on his doorstep."

"Heaven forbid," Hortense murmured as soon as Stephen alighted from the cart.

Vera smiled to herself. At least she wasn't alone in this venture. She wasn't quite sure what Jacqueline had told Hortense, but there'd been an instant understanding between them, an expression Hortense had gifted Vera upon her arrival that told her that the maid was stoutly on her side.

After a moment where Stephen stood upon the doorstep, the front door was opened by a person Vera couldn't see. Words were exchanged, and Stephen ducked inside.

"Are you quite all right, Miss Ashbury?" Hortense said now that they were truly alone.

"Of course." Vera blinked with surprise that she actually meant it.

Other than Stephen being unwelcoming—other than him going through her private things, invading her bedroom, and reading her most embarrassing, most personal missives—she had little complaint at all.

"He reminds me of Shelbourne," the maid said, her tone dark.

"Does he?"

Vera thought for a moment, but she couldn't find any similarities between the man who'd publicly thrown Candace over and the doctor who'd just returned from India.

"Well, he reminds me of Shelbourne in that I don't like him very much," Hortense finally admitted.

Vera grinned and turned halfway in her seat to see her better. "It's wonderful to have you. Are you sure your husband approves?"

"Of course." Hortense waved a gloved hand. "As long as I'm home in time for dinner, there'll be no complaints."

"Are you...are *you* quite happy?"

"I am." She gave a smile and a nod that put an end to any doubt on the matter. "I'm far happier than I've ever been, which is saying something, as I quite enjoyed my time with Her Grace. I'm lucky to have married a man who loves me, whom I love back, and one who already had competent help on staff."

Vera grinned. "I'm happy to hear it."

"Well, come on then." Stephen suddenly stood, fists propped on his hips, next to the cart. "This isn't a tea party."

Hortense raised an eyebrow at Vera, but they each accepted his hand and clambered down.

"He's ill, then?" Vera asked.

"That *is* why we're here."

Vera stopped herself from sticking her tongue out at

his back as she followed Stephen up the walk; she settled for scrunching her nose instead. Hortense's smirk told Vera she'd seen it.

"I'll tend to Mr. Douglas," Stephen murmured. "You two see what you can do with the girl."

"What girl?" Vera stopped on the front step—he'd said Mr. Douglas was a widower of seventy with no children.

"The girl. The girl in the house." Stephen stalked in and Vera had little choice but to follow. "She's in the kitchen."

"What girl?" Vera repeated, to Hortense.

Hortense just shrugged, for of course she knew no more than Vera did.

Vera dithered for a moment in the small entryway. To her right was a small parlor with clean but worn furnishings that spoke of a lifetime of comfortable sitting. No fire burned in the grate, and she moved quickly through to the doorway that led to a kitchen with a stone floor. Here, at least, there was a fire, as well as the aforementioned girl.

She couldn't have been more than two years old, with deep blue eyes set in a face smudged with soot and dirt. Limp curls hung on either side of her face. Still, she smiled and held her hands up to Vera in a silent request to be picked up. Vera complied, finding the girl much too light for her liking. She was grateful that Hortense was at her back. Where had this child come from?

"What's your name?" Vera asked gently.

"Anne," the girl warbled.

Vera shot a glance toward Hortense for guidance on how to proceed, but she'd momentarily forgotten that

Hortense was only supposed to assist her and act as a chaperone. She had no more experience being a nurse than Vera did, and she'd not been hired to do so.

Vera straightened. "Hortense, please heat some water. If there's tea to be found, we'll have some."

"I believe Lord—Dr. Winthrop put some in the basket."

Hortense set said basket upon the kitchen table. At the fireplace, a heavy cauldron of water hung on an iron arm; the maid pushed it back so it would heat over the flames.

Vera turned back to the silent girl, who watched Hortense and Vera with wide, frightened eyes. Her grubby hands clasped the front of Vera's muslin. The girl's own dirty dress wasn't a dress at all; upon further inspection, it appeared to be a man's tunic that had been rolled up numerous times at the sleeves.

Vera frowned. There was so much she wished she could ask about the situation, but the girl couldn't answer. Besides, she shouldn't be the recipient of those questions. Perhaps Vera would have more answers when Stephen returned from upstairs.

"Well, let's get you clean," Vera said once the water over the stove began to steam.

There was a wide pot with a thick bottom in the corner that Vera suspected acted as a bathing tub for the house. Hortense set it on its side and rolled it to the center of the room, then went out the back door. Vera was left to stare down at the little girl she held. The little girl stared back, regarding Vera with patient interest.

When she returned, Hortense filled the bathing tub

with water and rummaged in a small supply cupboard before emerging with a large block of soap and two worn towels. Thus prepared, Vera attempted to set the little girl into the pot. But instead of frightened silence as she expected, the girl let out an earthly howl.

"I don't want to. No bath. No wash!"

Vera jolted from the sheer volume; she looked at Hortense for assistance, but Hortense wore a similar wide-eyed expression.

"Anne, if you behave nicely, there are muffins for after your bath. Won't it be nice to have a muffin with jam?" Vera asked soothingly.

"Want muffin *now*!"

"If you behave..." Vera began again.

"Where's *muffin*?" the girl shrieked.

"There's nothing to be afraid of. It's just a little water—"

But the girl howled, "Don't want bath. Don't *want*."

"I'm sorry, but you simply must. You're very dirty."

"*No!*"

"Anne," Vera tried again. "I'm sorry but –"

"Oh, enough of this," Hortense said briskly. She strode over to the squalling girl and, in one fluid motion, yanked the foul tunic from her body.

The howling didn't abate; it was only muffled for a moment while the tunic passed over the girl's face.

Vera was surprised to find the little girl naked beneath the shirt. She had no bloomers, no pelisse. Hortense lifted the girl and deposited her into the water.

Her yowling increased by what felt like a hundred decibels. Instead of one angry cat, now there was a chorus of them.

"Vera," Hortense prompted. "The soap, please."

Vera did as she asked—Hortense was in no position to reach for anything. She had one hand firmly on the wiggling girl's shoulder, and the other dumped mugfuls of water over the screeching girl's head.

Vera gathered the soap and a small rag and dunked them both into the water—which was already growing cloudy. She knelt and briskly chafed the soap with the rag. Vera took courage from Hortense's gentle but firm ministrations and soaped the girl's legs and feet. The little girl squirmed in their grasp—with the addition of the soap, Vera thought it was quite like trying to wrestle a greased piglet.

Hortense doggedly kept pouring mugfuls of water over Anne. The sheer volume emitting from the girl didn't seem to flummox her in the least. Vera wished she could say the same. Her heart pounded.

"Perhaps a toy—" she murmured to herself.

Her own governess had given Vera a rubber ball to play with in the tub, in order to distract her. Vera glanced around, but the closest thing she could find to a toy was a wooden spoon.

She lunged for it and offered it to the little girl. "How about this, then?"

Anne opened her eyes long enough to grab the spoon, then flailed and whacked Vera upside the head with it. Hortense let out a little huff that sounded suspiciously like a laugh—Vera frowned at her while she wrestled the waving spoon from the girl's strong grip. She finally succeeded and tossed it, clattering, against the stones.

In an instant, the girl's yelling ceased, replaced instead by deep, bone-wrenching tears. Vera looked at Hortense with wide eyes, but Hortense was determinedly focused on the task at hand. The maid's unspoken stance was clear—they would deal with Anne's emotional upset once she was clean.

Vera finished soaping her quickly from head to toe while the little girl sobbed. Unbidden, tears of her own pricked at the corners of her eyes. Who was this girl? How had she ended up here in the home of Mr. Douglas, who had no children of his own? And why was she so terrified of water?

Vera set to her job grimly as a new round of wailing began. She prayed that Stephen would ask the questions of Mr. Douglas that Vera could not ask the little girl.

When they rinsed her with a fresh bucket of warm water that Vera brought to sit alongside the pot, the girl began to scream again, but they persisted until her face and hair were as clean as the rest of her.

Vera unwrapped a worn, clean towel, and Hortense lifted her. Vera swaddled Anne tightly, took her upon her lap, and sat in the lone rocking chair that faced the fire.

There she rocked her, making soothing noises and offering encouragement. "See? That wasn't all that bad, and now it's over and you're clean. It's important to be clean. You smell nice and pretty and now you can have a clean something to wear and something good to eat."

As she rocked the girl, the crying tapered off into a sad

sort of hiccuping, then slid all the way down to a periodic sniffle. Vera ran her arms up and down the child's whole body, drying her as best she could while she was on her lap.

Hortense emptied the tub out the back door with a splash that sounded upon the stones. Then she bustled about, wiping up the deluge on the floor and cobbling together a tea tray from the mismatched pottery in Mr. Douglas's small kitchen.

"It isn't the royal silver, but everything's clean," Hortense said, finally setting the tray on the little table next to them.

Vera chose a biscuit and handed it to Anne. The girl gripped it with ferocity and began to gnaw it. Her eyes went wide. The crying cut off sharply, soothed by the alchemy of butter and sugar.

Now that the girl was dry, Vera realized that she and Hortense were both sopping wet. Vera's hair hung in limp ringlets on either side of her face. Her bodice clung and her skirts were far heavier than they'd been a half hour prior. Hortense's dress was splattered a darker blue.

Still, the little girl was clean and warm, and was now mowing her way through a ham-and-cheese sandwich.

Nearly a quarter hour passed before the little girl sniffled, looked up at Vera with her huge blue eyes and announced, "Don't like you."

Vera smiled. "I don't blame you at the moment."

Anne appeared to consider the words, her eyes serious.

Then she looked back up at Vera and grinned. "Muffin?"

Later, when the three of them were bundled back into the cart, their basket much lighter due to the appetite of the little girl in the kitchen, Vera waited only until they were a little ways past the house before she turned to Stephen.

"Who on earth is that little girl?"

"I don't rightly know," he admitted.

"You don't know? Didn't you *ask*?"

He shrugged. "Mr. Douglas said that he found Anne. He wasn't inclined to go into detail, but I don't think she was in a good situation."

"*Found* her? She isn't a dog."

"Indeed not." Stephen held the reins casually. "Most people care for dogs."

"You're being purposefully obtuse."

He arched an eyebrow. "If that's true, I hardly think that pointing it out will change my stance. Remember—you called it *purposeful*."

"What about her parents?"

"Dead. At least Mr. Douglas was forthcoming on that point. The girl has no family and neither does he. I think perhaps he saw an echo of his same loneliness within her."

Vera blinked and did her best not to let his poetic words soften her heart. "But you can't just *take* a child."

"Why not?"

"Because..." Vera trailed off, stunned by the realization that there was nothing truly in place to stop someone from doing so.

If the girl was an orphan, common thought prevailed that she should be in an orphanage, or a workhouse if she were old enough. Except Vera had brought soup to orphanages many times. They were the same as any other home in London—some were decent, some were awful.

*Much like families,* she thought.

She batted the errant thought away and tried to focus.

"But why would he want her?"

"I don't think he did," he said cheerfully. "But judging by what he told me, once he saw her plight, he couldn't just leave her there."

"I'm not sure that her plight is any better with Mr. Douglas."

Stephen's brown eyes slid over to her in that low searching way he had. "Did she seem mistreated? Did she seem hungry? Did you observe any marks that would speak to abuse?"

Vera considered for a moment. The girl had eaten every biscuit she could get her grasping hands on, but that wasn't altogether rare for a child of that age.

"No, but she hadn't been bathed in well over a week."

"Your parameters on judging parents are harsh—there isn't a family in Cheapside who would survive your examination."

"That's not the point—"

"I'm well aware of what the point is. The point is that people think when a child is born into a family, that must be the best place for them, no matter what. That's not always the case. You're judging Mr. Douglas far more harshly than you'd judge that little girl's parents, even though by the sound of things, the reverse should be true."

Vera watched the countryside pass by—a pleasant, living painting of pastoral green grass and gently waving tree branches. Stephen was right, and she didn't like it in the least.

"What I want to know," he said, breaking her reverie, "is how *you* ended up soaking wet? And why on earth did you put her in the brazier pan? Were you planning on turning the poor darling into a cassoulet?"

By the time they arrived back at Bertforth House, Vera was exhausted, and though it was a mild day, the gentle breeze from the ride back had chilled her thoroughly. She'd come to the realization that perhaps Anne living with Mr. Douglas wasn't what had bothered her. Maybe it was the fact that she saw part of herself in Anne's situation—without family, living on the charity of strangers.

She waved at Hortense as the woman departed. All Vera wanted to do was to have a bath of her own, to thaw herself before a fire and escape into a book.

Stephen turned to her with a grin and said, "Mr. Douglas needs congestion medicine. Tomorrow, we'll replant the greenhouse."

Vera was irritated that he looked energized by the thought. His broad shoulders were back; a smile lit his face. She felt bedraggled and tired in contrast.

She nodded and pulled her shawl more firmly around her shoulders. "Very well."

"I think this is the start of an excellent partnership."

Perhaps if he'd said the words in a more stoic tone, she wouldn't have taken umbrage, but he sounded far too cheerful for her liking.

"Let me make one thing exceedingly clear: I haven't forgiven you, not even a little. In your mind, you offering me a position, offering me the chance to earn a reference, to earn your *approval*, is sufficient apology. But you forced me into this. You're right—I have no other option available to me at the moment. The second I do, I'll leave."

Stephen frowned. Vera could guess at his thoughts—he probably didn't feel he'd forced her into anything. He probably thought he'd given her a chance at a respectable position, when all she had before was a letter from a dastardly man and no references at all. The truth of what she imagined Stephen thought angered her even more.

"I don't like you," she hissed.

His eyes snapped to hers, wide in surprise.

But she wasn't finished venting her vitriol. "I don't know what happened to you to make you such a distrustful, bitter person. I don't care. It's not my responsibility to understand or fix it—that's *your* responsibility. So yes, I'll be your assistant. I will do what is asked of me without complaint. But make no mistake—we're not in this *together*."

With that, she whirled toward the house with as much grace as she could muster in her sodden dress.

THE NEXT MORNING, Vera opened her eyes and groaned. The day she'd been dreading for weeks was finally here. It was her birthday, and no one within fifty miles knew or cared. Well, she thought, throwing back the bedcovers and sliding her feet into slippers, no one in a thousand miles cared. *No one* cared.

Back home, in London, birthdays were the one day her mother treated her nicely. Lady Ashbury deferred to Vera, allowing her to choose an outing—a trip to an iced cream shoppe, or luncheon at one of the grand hotels. There would be a present, and always a cake with dinner.

This year, there would be nothing.

She supposed it was appropriate. After all, what was the point of celebrating the birthday that put one firmly on the shelf? She was twenty-five today. No family, no employment—at least, not one that she'd been awarded honorably—and no references. A single man hadn't looked seriously at her since that Lord Whover-He-Was.

Heavens, she couldn't even remember his name—only that he'd been color-blind and hadn't minded her terrible-patterned gown at a ball her first Season. Lady Ashbury had quickly sussed the problem and rectified it with mounds of padding.

Vera sighed and scrubbed at her face. She slid on a dressing gown, cinched the sash around her waist, and slumped onto the padded stool before the vanity mirror.

She frowned. She certainly didn't *look* any different. Same ash-brown hair, same hazel eyes. Same straight nose and full lips. Vera had just unpinned her hair and picked up her brush when a bloodcurdling scream echoed down the hall.

*Jacqueline*, Vera thought, and lunged for the fire poker before running toward the source of the tumult.

## CHAPTER 11 - STEPHEN

Stephen hadn't slept well. He'd tossed and turned until early morning. Vera's words haunted him.

Sure, he'd overstepped, but he'd *explained* himself. Yes, he'd acted an insufferable brute, but he'd *apologized*, and he'd done it well, or so he thought. He'd also rectified the situation by offering the lady gainful employment, along with the opportunity to earn a glowing reference. Certainly that sufficed in terms of making amends... didn't it?

Doubts prodded at his back and shoulders like a lumpy mattress, and though his own bed was made of feathers, it felt as if he lay upon a burlap sack of rocks. With his mind in tumult, he'd marked the passing of one o'clock on his brass bedside travel clock before he'd been able to fall asleep. So it was well past his normal hour of rising when his bleary eyes blinked open.

Six inches from his face, a large pair of amber eyes stared back.

Stephen couldn't help it—he yelled. Well, calling it a *yell* wasn't the most accurate description, but he was a man, and men didn't *scream*. They certainly didn't do so in an octave that might have been described as *shrill*.

The fox—for that's what it was, curled on the pillow next to him—appeared as startled at his yell as Stephen had been to find the beast there. It jumped and flashed from his bed, disappearing through the open door to his wardrobe antechamber.

And heavens—was Stephen still making that noise? He clamped his mouth shut, embarrassed at his own reaction, when there was a sudden scrambling at his bedroom door. It flung open and Vera charged in, brandishing a fire poker.

Her voluminous hair was undone and spilled in ash-brown waves down her back. Her blue velvet dressing gown was tied at her narrow waist with a wide satin bow. Her eyes were bright and narrowed fiercely, her chin jutted in determination.

*Beautiful*, he thought wildly.

*That* disturbing thought was chased from his mind by a far worse one. Which was that the reason Vera had first reminded him of Samantha, he realized, was because he was *attracted* to her.

*Heaven help him.*

As Stephen had this startling, earth-tilting revelation, Vera lowered her poker and scowled. "That was *you* screaming murder?"

"I wasn't—" He shook his head, distracted as one of

her curls slid like a silken snake from her shoulder to rest upon her front.

"It *was* you, wasn't it?" She propped a fist against her hip and frowned, the poker held loosely at her side. "I never knew a man of your size could make such a screech."

"It wasn't a *screech*."

Perhaps it wasn't the most eloquent retort, but he'd never been forced to argue from such an unbalanced position. He'd never debated an opponent while he was bare-chested, wearing only his drawers. He'd certainly never debated someone who looked like Miss Vera Ashbury fresh from bed.

"I thought it was Jacqueline, though I should have known better. She'd never make a noise so piercing, not even if the house was burning down around her. Now—what's the matter? What on earth is wrong with you?"

*You*, he almost blurted. *You are the matter. You are what is wrong with me.*

It was because he was so stupefied that he gave her the truth. "A fox was sleeping in my bed."

"*Clarence?* You screamed like a ninny because of *Clarence?*"

Stephen did his best to give a dignified sniff. "I wasn't expecting him. He alarmed me."

"So I heard."

They stared at each other for several moments. He tried to school his features into mild indifference—he was frightened by the idea that she might see his thoughts on his face and sneer at him. Vera *was* frowning, but he couldn't read the source of her ire.

Stephen suddenly wished anew that he'd been kinder, that they hadn't started their relationship the way they had. Of course, it wasn't just his sudden realization of her beauty that made him feel so—he'd regretted reading her correspondence even before she'd caught him. From the moment he knew the truth of who Vera truly was, he wished he hadn't invaded her privacy.

But this moment certainly intensified his regret, for purely selfish reasons.

Vera suddenly broke his gaze and rocked backward on her heels. "I'd better go. It's a wonder no one's caught me here yet, and neither of us want *that* sort of scandal. Though I suppose the lack of servants running to your defense means that they're used to you yodeling at a high pitch whenever something disturbs your delicate nerves."

He spluttered.

*Delicate nerves?* He'd once amputated the forearm of a beast of a sailor who was awake and screaming the entire time. Stephen had been obliged to dodge a ham-sized fist swinging at his temple every time the man's cohorts lost their grip.

*Delicate nerves, indeed.*

His momentary distraction was all the time Vera needed to slip from the room before he could make a coherent reply. She snapped the door shut on her way out. He sat there for several moments, frowning in contemplation. Had she been *blushing* when she left him? For Stephen could have sworn he'd seen a dusting of pink along those alabaster cheeks.

*It was probably anger and disgust, nothing more,* he thought.

The entire interlude had been embarrassing at best. Not to mention highly inconvenient. What was he supposed to do, now that he'd actually *seen* her?

There was nothing for it—he'd have to treat her with professionalism. He'd offer her the same clinical detachment he gave every lady under his physician's care. After all, he'd handled many a lovely female form under the most delicate of circumstances, and he'd never crossed that great line that his profession dictated. Not once—not even in his mind.

But when Vera's hair had slid forward over her shoulder, when her insouciant shrug of derision had shifted her dressing gown, exposing just the end of her clavicle...

Heaven help him, it was only a *clavicle*. He'd seen a hundred of them, several of them broken, puncturing through the skin. *That* was what he should think of when hers made an impromptu reappearance in his mind. Gore. *Screams.*

*Like the one he'd made that brought her to his chamber in the first place.*

His eyes slid toward his dressing room. Doubtless, the fox was still somewhere inside. He threw back his bedcovers and went to dress, determined not to make so much as another peep.

Even if the blasted thing leapt from his armoire and latched onto his very head.

Stephen stared into his mirror for a long time, dithering. His mother had been prodding him to shave his beard ever since he returned home and he'd resisted. Now he wondered why. He didn't even like the thing, though perhaps that was the point.

Vera's words from the day prior came swooping back at him like deranged crows. She'd called him bitter and distrustful, and she had every right to think that. He certainly hadn't shown her a different side to himself.

*I don't like you.*

Such a simple statement, as blunt and effective as a sledgehammer swung at his stomach.

*I don't like you.*

But he wanted her to. Not just because he'd suddenly realized what everyone else in proximity already had—that Vera Ashbury was beautiful on the outside. No, it was because he was starting to suspect that she was beautiful *inside*, as well.

She hadn't seen him yesterday, lingering in the doorway of the kitchen, but he'd finished with Mr. Douglas well before Vera suspected. He'd seen the tail-end of the bath—how patient Vera was, how she'd borne the howls and blows of the child with nary a harsh word.

Stephen saw how she'd taken the squalling child onto her lap and murmured condolences, how she'd rocked little Anne into peaceful compliance. Her entire focus had been on comforting the child, not on her soaked dress or her ruined hair.

It was a shocking revelation. It was as if he'd bought a reproduction painting at a second-hand store and hung it in a back stairwell, only to be informed that it was the real thing. *Priceless.*

Hortense had glimpsed him there, staring. She'd arched an eyebrow with all the eloquence of her unsaid words, but she'd let him look all the same. It was as if the maid were saying, *Go on, then...really* see *her.*

And he had.

Now he stared at himself in the mirror, wondering if he was ready to shave off the beard that he hadn't realized he was using as a shield between himself and the world. He'd told himself that he couldn't be bothered to shave on the journey home, that it wasn't prudent to hold a straight-edge razor to one's throat on a rocking ship.

Now, he thought he might have been lying to himself. Perhaps his beard was born of more than convenience—perhaps he'd used it to keep people away.

It certainly was a fearsome amount of hair, he thought, tugging at the ragged ends. It made him look wild, slightly feral. It was a wonder that Mr. Douglas had believed he was a doctor at all, and not some brigand come to rob his house.

Stephen gave his beard one last glance, turned his back to the mirror, and pulled on his jacket. His unruly facial hair could wait.

When he arrived in the breakfast room, Roland

informed him that Miss Ashbury and his brother had already eaten and gone.

Stephen frowned. "What about my mother?"

"It's my understanding that Lady Winthrop hasn't yet been downstairs, my lord. Would you like me to inquire after her?"

He waved off the offer, even as he wondered at his mother sleeping so late. She was usually the first to rise, up at dawn with all those animals of hers. "No, let her rest."

After a quick breakfast of toast, eggs, and bacon, Stephen went in search of Vera. He found her in the greenhouse, bent over a raised gardening bed, Benjamin next to her. Their backs were to him. Once again, Stephen took the opportunity to study without being seen.

Vera's thick hair was pulled into an unassuming braided bun at the base of her neck. She wore a thick brown dress covered with an apron.

*It's hideous*, Stephen thought with a start. *It looks like someone skinned a sick oxen and draped her in it.*

"But why?" Benjamin was saying.

"Because you're far too young, and I'm far too old."

"I still think it could work."

Stephen felt he could hear the jut of the boy's lower lip from where he stood.

Vera laughed, a low, rough noise that slid down Stephen's spine and locked up his joints. Had he ever heard her laugh before? He suddenly couldn't remember, but then again, at this moment he couldn't remember much.

It was more effective than the medicinal brandy he

recommended for colds, that laugh. It did something funny to his stomach, was in danger of making him warm and languid.

"I cannot marry you," she said, not unkindly. "Though I thank you very much for the offer."

*Wait—what?* Stephen frowned.

"But *why*?"

"Because you are eight and I am twenty-five." She leaned a bit closer to the boy. "Can you keep a secret?"

Benjamin nodded quickly.

"Today is my birthday."

"Is it really?"

"It is."

"I haven't even got you a present!" he nearly wailed.

"This is my present—you helping me weed these garden beds. And once we are through, you can help me plant the seedlings, as well. That is all the gift I want."

"If you say so." Benjamin did not sound convinced. "I'd rather have a train set or a new pony."

"You might feel differently when you're as old as I am," she teased.

"Twenty-five isn't *old*."

"I pray you remember that someday when you're thirty and actually looking for a wife."

Though her tone was teasing, Stephen heard a very real thread of pain within it. He frowned. When his mother had insisted upon a chaperone to preserve Vera's honor in society's sight, he'd thought it ridiculous. Now, all he felt was guilt that he hadn't been the one to insist upon such a thing. His mother was correct—he had no right to put

Miss Ashbury into a situation that would damage her prospects.

How had he bungled their interactions so thoroughly from the start? Regret soured his stomach, and he quietly moved away from the door. He trudged back up toward the drive, his hands shoved into his pockets. He couldn't change what had already passed, but perhaps he could change their relationship moving forward.

And if that was too large a task, he'd settle for making life a little better for Miss Vera Ashbury.

## CHAPTER 12 - VERA

Vera soaked in her bathtub, enjoying the way the hot water softened the tense muscles in her back. Steam drifted upwards; the fire next to her crackled and glowed. She sank deeper into the lavender-scented water and sighed.

She'd spent nearly all day working in the greenhouse with Benjamin. Her eyes had often searched the far door of the glass structure, but to her surprise, Stephen never arrived to help them. It was just as well—thanks to Candace's recent obsession with gardening, Vera knew enough about planting to know how far apart to plant the herbs. It was a pleasant task without Stephen looming over her and frowning if she did something wrong.

Vera lingered in the warm bath as long as she dared, then hurriedly dressed, pinned her damp hair, and went down to dinner.

The evening meal at Bertforth House was usually as casual as breakfast, so Vera was surprised to see the flicker of candlelight over a beautifully set table when she crossed the threshold into the dining room.

"Surprise!" a chorus of voices called.

Vera jerked to a stop and blinked. Candace and her new husband, James—better known to society as the Duke of Canterbury—grinned at her from the sideboard. Jacqueline and Hamish stood at the head of the table; Percy, the Marquess of Salisbury, and his wife, Adelaide, stood nearby. Canterbury's son, Arthur, and Benjamin whooped their joy, too. And Stephen stood at the back of the grouping, studying her carefully.

Vera stammered, "This...this is for me?"

"I certainly hope so," Percy said. "Otherwise we've wasted a perfectly good bellow."

Adelaide jabbed him in the ribs with her elbow. Her soft-waisted gown barely hid the condition that had brought them back early from their honeymoon.

"Happy birthday, Vera." Candace rushed forward to kiss her cheeks. "I can't believe you never told me the date."

"Ridiculous girl." Jacqueline nodded her agreement. "Trying to keep such a thing from us."

Vera didn't have time to contest the statement—she was passed around and hugged and greeted. Even Stephen stepped forward to tell her happy birthday and give her an enigmatic look.

They were seated. Candace ended up on Vera's right, and by some odd twist, Stephen sat on her left.

"How did you know my birthday was today?" Vera murmured to Candace.

There was a foolish fluttering of hope within her heart that perhaps her mother had written to inquire after Vera, that perhaps her family was softening toward her.

Candace nodded toward Stephen, who was distracted by the footman serving the first course. "The baron invited us. I'm not sure how he found out."

"My brother told me," Stephen said a moment later. Apparently, he hadn't been as distracted as he appeared.

"Oh." Vera smoothed the linen napkin that lay over her lap. "Well, thank you."

"You're welcome." He dipped a nod and smiled.

Vera turned her head and blinked at her plate, discomfited. What was he on about, inviting people to celebrate her birthday? It was difficult to reconcile the action with Stephen—this was a decidedly kind gesture.

*Unless it wasn't. Unless he means to embarrass me in some way.*

Vera frowned at the thought, but it was impossible. None of her friends would agree to such a scheme. Even if Stephen stood, rang a spoon against his glass, and told the entire sordid truth—that her family had disowned her—Candace would still be her friend. So would Jacqueline. Percy would most likely toast her on principle—the marquess enjoyed anything that was a bit out of the norm, societally speaking.

"How did you find India?" the Duke of Canterbury was asking Stephen. "My friend Lord Cavendish spent a great deal of time there. I wonder if you ever met him?"

"Not that I recall, though that's not so surprising. The

Company has several physicians on staff in Calcutta. I mostly helped the natives of the country."

"Ah. How was your return home?"

Stephen answered the question, but Vera didn't catch it—Candace touched her arm to gain her attention and asked, "Have you heard that Dahlia is to come and stay with Adelaide for awhile?"

"Is she?" Vera smiled across the table at the new marchioness, who was listening. "You must be delighted to have your sister in the house."

Adelaide shifted in her chair. "I feel a bit guilty, pulling her from the society of town like this, but I'm thrilled to have the company. She's going to stay for at least a month."

"I'm sure she's happy to come. When does she arrive?"

"Within the week, if the weather holds. Percy's sent the carriage."

"What of Hannah and Rachel?" Candace asked.

"They've been invited to accompany the Duke and Duchess of Devonshire to their country estate. We truly thought they'd come and stay with us, but with the baby on the way..."

She trailed off awkwardly, and Vera understood. It was a rule of society that expectant mothers were shuttered away, closed off from all but their closest friends and family until their child arrived. It was a topic few felt comfortable speaking of, and even Adelaide's presence at dinner tonight would have raised more than a few society maven's eyebrows.

But Vera was very happy she'd come. "I'm sure they're excited to meet your child."

Adelaide nodded, the light returning to her eyes. "They are. Though I think at the moment, they're far more excited to see the duke's estate, Chatsworth. The duchess has promised they'll get to help her bake for the village, and Hannah is ecstatic to learn. Rachel's just excited about the library."

"I'm glad to hear she still enjoys reading as much as ever."

"I think our journey to London only intensified her love. Fed the flames, so to speak."

Suddenly, Stephen's knee bumped viciously into the bottom of the table, rattling the china.

He pointed. "Benjamin, remove him from the table at once."

The boy's chin jutted. "It's Vera's birthday; she'd want him at her party."

Vera blinked. Trundling down the center of the table, amidst the low bowls of draping flowers, was Sheldon. The hedgehog paused to sniff a leaf of ivy, then turned up his little nose as if finding the selection lacking.

Vera rolled her lips between her teeth to keep from laughing. Her thoughts were on the scream she'd heard only that morning—and the deep satisfaction she'd had when she realized it was Stephen squealing. It was the best birthday present she'd received in years.

"Our guests—the *ladies*—certainly don't want him on the table." Stephen's narrowed eyes were still focused on his little brother.

"Oh, Sheldon, you darling!" Candace gushed. "Have you come to celebrate Vera, too?"

Vera couldn't help it—she laughed. She doubted Candace had meant to contradict Stephen so directly—it was far more likely she hadn't heard him. When she glanced to her left, she was surprised to find Stephen staring at her, the expression on his face unreadable.

Though he didn't look precisely angry, she frowned at him. She'd done nothing wrong; he could turn that mysterious gaze upon someone else.

Jacqueline stood from the head of the table and rescued Sheldon. The hedgehog had been heading in Adelaide's direction, and Percy had a murderous glint in his eye. Percy had always been the protective sort, but it seemed having a little one on the way had stoked his instincts.

"Come along, Sheldon," Jacqueline crooned. "Let's get you back to your nest."

Hamish stood. "Allow me to accompany you."

Vera saw Percy's eyebrows rise, saw his mouth open—to say something smart, no doubt—but Adelaide applied her elbow to his midsection sharply. He pursed his lips in her direction, his expression a strange mixture of peevishness and devotion.

"Lord Winthrop," the Duke of Canterbury said. "How many creatures does your mother have now?"

"I'm not altogether certain, to be honest." He gave a rueful smile. "Her collection has grown tremendously in my absence, and I'm somewhat frightened to ask."

Chuckles around the table.

"The fox is his favorite," Vera found herself saying. "He absolutely *squeals* for it."

Vera felt, more than saw, Stephen turn his head toward her. She deprived him of her eyes and stared straight ahead.

"Is that so?" Adelaide said. "Is it quite tame?"

"So tame that it shares a bed with him," Vera said quickly.

"And how would you know that?" Candace murmured, only loud enough for Vera to hear.

Vera turned to her friend, shocked, but Candace's eyes twinkled in merriment. She waggled her eyebrows and Vera felt a reflexive blush heat her cheeks, though there was absolutely nothing of the sort going on between her and the baron.

"He more often sleeps with me," Benjamin said, recovered in an instant from having Sheldon taken from the room.

"Does he?" Percy asked. "Does he hog the bedcovers like some people?"

Adelaide jabbed him once more, and everyone else pretended not to see it.

*The man must have a constant bruise*, Vera thought.

"No, he's polite. Keeps to his own pillow."

"That's good, then," Percy said, his eyes sliding toward his wife. Adelaide's cheeks were ever-so-slightly flushed. "Some bedfellows snore and roll themselves into the covers so a gent can't find the end of the blankets. Or so I've heard."

Percy and Adelaide retired just after dinner. The last course had been punctuated with her carefully hidden yawns and apologies. Everyone else politely ignored her or assured her it didn't matter—everyone except her husband. After the third time, he began yawning loudly after her silent ones, and no amount of poking him about the midsection would stop him.

"Percy, *really*." Candace shook her head. "The only reason she's so tired is because she has a great lummox of a husband. The least you could do is be sympathetic."

"On the contrary, dear sister. I'm only showing my utmost support and solidarity."

Despite his shocking provocations, Vera had no doubt that the marquess was madly in love with his wife. She'd overheard Percy and Stephen deep in a murmured conversation in the hallway; the marquess had been questioning Stephen about his experience attending to expectant mothers during childbirth.

"If I need to, I can try to call Dr. Halveston away from London, but who knows if he'll consent? I'd much rather have someone nearby."

After dinner came drinks and cards. Vera somehow won every hand; she strongly suspected the other guests had conspired to make it so.

James and Candace were the last to depart, with

Candace hugging Vera soundly. "Happy birthday, dearest. I hope this year is your favorite yet."

Vera didn't have the heart to tell her friend her life was in a bit of a shambles. She simply hitched her very best smile onto her face and thanked them both for coming.

The door closed behind them, leaving Vera in that strange ennui that follows a night with loved ones; the house had gone from boisterous conversation and laughter to dim shadow and silence. Vera battled the strange, nagging sensation that perhaps she'd had too much wine and said something foolish.

She sighed and turned for the stairway.

"Did you have a nice evening?" Stephen asked from the darkness at the bottom of the stairs.

Vera whirled, a hand clutched to her pounding heart. She hadn't seen him there; she'd assumed he'd gone to bed when everyone else had left.

He waited for her to answer, his hands tucked into his pockets. His face was in shadow; she couldn't see his expression.

"It was very nice."

Despite the fact that Candace claimed it was he who'd invited them, Vera didn't believe the party had been his idea. Most likely the baroness had forced him into it.

"I'm glad you liked it."

"How did you know it was my birthday?" As soon as she asked the question she frowned. "Nevermind—I suppose you learned much about me when you read my journals."

He winced. "I wish...I wish we could begin anew. I

wish I'd never done that. I hope that in time, you'll see that isn't who I am. Not really."

"It may be that you wish that were the case, but our actions are far better proof of who we are than our words."

Stephen's shoulders rounded. He frowned and nodded. "You're probably right."

She sighed. "I don't wish to fight with you. I'll be your assistant, until such a time as I can find other gainful employment. Then I'll be away from here, out of your home forever. But as you've so stabbingly said, at the moment, I have little else but charity to live on."

Vera inhaled sharply through her nose—a poor attempt to stifle the tears that suddenly threatened to crest over her lower lashes. She had nothing except for her pride, and even that was bruised as of late.

"I *am* sorry," he said, his words as dejected as his posture. "I should never have said such things. If I...if I could take back the pain I've caused you, I would."

Vera peered up at him, trying to decide if his words were a trick. After a few moments, she was surprised to find she believed him.

"Very well," she said. "I accept your apology."

"You do?"

His relief was so palpable it nearly staggered her.

"Yes."

"Good. That's...that's good." He stood there for a moment as if he wished to say more, then gave a low smile. "Happy birthday, Vera."

## CHAPTER 13 - VERA

Two days later, she and Stephen stood in the bedroom of one Mrs. Edgar. The woman had been ill for a week, and her husband had called that morning, stating she wasn't feeling any better.

"Step back, Vera," Stephen murmured from the other side of the room.

Vera laid a damp cloth over Mrs. Edgar's forehead and pulled the blanket up to her chin. The poor woman was burning up, but still she shivered.

"Get *back*, Vera!"

Her gaze snapped to Stephen's, her face twisted in fury. She thought they'd gotten past this point, with the apology he'd given the night of her birthday. They'd both been exceedingly, cautiously polite to each other ever since. Vera was just getting to the point where she no longer tensed when he entered a room.

But now this. How *dare* he yell at her in such a way—

especially in front of other people? She might be his assistant, but she was still—

Vomit splattered the front of her apron and her shoes. Vera stared down with wide eyes, even as Stephen gently gripped her and firmly pulled her out of range of the second wave of Mrs. Edgar's retching.

"Go and get yourself cleaned up," he said, already stooping to throw rags over the dampness on the floor. He set a wide basin on top of the towels. "I'll take care of this. Ask Hortense to bring tea and some weak broth once she's finished helping you."

Dumbly, she did as Stephen said, holding the edges of her apron so the mess didn't drip onto the floor as she walked.

It was all Vera could do not to be sick. She kept her round eyes straight ahead, praying that Hortense wasn't the kind to be squeamish. Vera's own stomach roiled within her. She kept swallowing hard, all the way down the hall, where she backed through the swinging door into the kitchen.

Hortense glanced at her over her shoulder, then looked again. "Oh dear."

She hurried to pluck at the bows holding Vera's apron in place.

"My shoes," Vera lamented in a small voice.

"Follow me." Hortense stripped the apron and bundled it so all of the mess was contained, then led the way out the back door. Vera waited in a daze while the maid cranked the squeaky handle on the well. A full bucket appeared, and Hortense tossed it over the apron that she'd hung on the empty clothesline.

"It's not perfect, but it's a start," she said. Then she released the bucket down the well once more and went inside to grab a rag and soap.

It took no time at all for Vera to be set to rights. She was exceedingly lucky—none of the mess had sullied her dress or her hands. Hortense sent her walking through the tall grass at the edge of the garden to clean her boots, then wiped the remainder of the mess with a damp rag.

"Occupational hazard, I suppose," Hortense finally said when she was finished.

Vera could do little more than offer a weak smile and an insufficient thank you. She didn't know what she would have done without Hortense's help—most likely stayed frozen in her ruined state. At least she hadn't compounded the matter by being sick, too.

Hortense went to deliver the requested broth, leaving Vera in the kitchen with a strong cup of tea and her own self-berating thoughts.

*She should be the nurse, not me. She deals with this sort of thing so much better than I do.*

How on earth was she going to earn a reference if she couldn't stay in the room long enough to do her job? The only thing she seemed naturally good at was tending the herbs in the greenhouse, but those were *herbs*. She could probably neglect them altogether and they'd do just as well. They grew under almost any conditions—they were very nearly weeds.

Vera sipped her tea and straightened her shoulders. She

shouldn't expect to be good at assisting Stephen just yet. It was probably like everything else—it took time, patience, and *practice*.

At the thought, Vera gulped the last of her strong tea and retrieved a fresh apron from the basket. She would learn to deal with sickness with the kind of strength and calm that Stephen showed.

Even if she had to be thrown up on a hundred times.

In the end, she was able to avoid being hit again. Mrs. Edgar's stomach calmed enough to sip the broth, and when they left, she was sipping peppermint tea and looking a bit less pale.

"Idiot man," Stephen groused, steering the cart over a bridge. "Feeding her peppered mutton stew while she's ill."

Vera shook her head. "He probably didn't know any better."

He made a derisive sound in his throat. "Hopefully, we won't have to return. If he follows instructions, that is."

"I'm sure he will. He certainly looked sheepish when you told him the reason she hadn't gotten any better."

"Sheepish." He huffed a laugh. "It's a clever pun, considering."

"I'm...I'm sorry for before. For getting in the way."

He lifted a shoulder and smiled. "You'll learn. Hopefully you'll learn faster than I did—I think I got in the way of a sick patient a dozen times before I learned the telltale signs."

Vera nodded and watched the greenery go past.

"Do you enjoy it, though? The work, I mean."

"I think it's too soon to tell."

"Perhaps I shouldn't have asked you on a day when someone was ill upon your shoes."

She grimaced. "Please don't remind me. They're going to need to be polished."

"Leave them outside your door and I'll see that it's done."

"Thank you," she said stiffly.

Vera didn't know how to handle his kindness—it flew in the face of who she'd convinced herself he was.

After a few moments of silence, she asked, "Why did you become a physician?"

He lifted a shoulder. "I wanted to be useful. I know that some gentlemen find the same kind of satisfaction in the management of their estates, but I prefer to be closer to someone when I help. I wanted to make a tangible difference—not just a general, nebulous kind."

Vera twisted her lips, remembering the harsh words she'd delivered about how he'd neglected his duties as a lord.

Apparently, his own thoughts had wandered down the same lane, as he cleared his throat and said, "I've taken over the financials of the estate. You were right—my mother shouldn't have borne that burden alone all these years."

"I shouldn't have—"

"None of *that*." He frowned. "I hope that you won't start withholding truth from me just because we've come to a tentative politeness."

"Pardon?"

"We can be both—honest *and* polite. I shouldn't want a polite, dishonest relationship. You said things that I needed to hear. Though you said them harshly, I'm still glad you said them."

She blinked. "You are?"

He peered down at her. Whatever he saw on her face had him lifting his eyebrows, even as he returned his attention to the road. "My mother and I are very similar in some ways. Neither of us care for society as a whole, but for completely different reasons. She avoids them because she thinks the lot of them are judgemental nitwits. I avoid them because I detest maintaining the dozens of shallow or false relationships being part of society requires."

Vera thought about this for several moments as she watched the fields pass. The landscape was changing rapidly—the leaves were turning in earnest now, as if overnight, all the greenery had received a silent signal. Mornings had the sharp edge of a chill concealed within their misty cloaks. Fall was here.

Stephen quirked a smile and added, "I'd much rather us be true friends who are honest with each other than false friends who never move past shallow politeness."

Later that afternoon, Vera roamed the gardens with Benjamin, listening to him chatter about his day.

"...and Hamish is going to take me fishing tomorrow, can you believe it?"

"How lovely. You should ask your brother to go along with you."

She aimed her footsteps toward the greenhouse. She wanted to see if any of the plants had that special line of green at the edges of their leaves yet that spoke of growth. She knew it was probably too early to expect anything of the sort, but she still hoped.

Her thoughts were so consumed with the herbs that it took her a moment to realize that Benjamin was silent, that he hadn't offered an answer.

Vera came to a stop on the garden path and arched an eyebrow. "Benjamin?"

There was a stubborn jut to his lower lip. "I just don't think he likes me."

"Whyever not?"

"He's always snapping at me."

"Always?" She lifted the other eyebrow to join the first. "When did he last snap at you?"

"At your birthday party, and it was in front of *everyone*."

"You set a hedgehog loose on the dinner table in front of guests."

"It didn't bother *you*." His words were rebellion, but he jabbed the toe of his boot into the divot between two cobblestones and wouldn't meet her eyes.

"I'm used to Sheldon, but the other ladies aren't, and you know better than to do that. So why did you?"

His frown grew; he stared at the earth. Vera had two brothers—one older, one younger. She knew when to wait.

"Fine," he relented, kicking the earth once more. "I wanted to ruin his dinner party, all right? I did it on purpose."

"*His* dinner party?"

"It was his idea. To have all those people over."

This was information worth inspecting. Vera tucked it away for the future, when she was alone.

"Why would you want to ruin his party?"

*His party for you*, a small voice within reminded her. She shushed it and focused her attention on Benjamin.

"Because. Because I'm angry at him." His face grew red; his eyes screwed up at the admission.

Vera put a hand on his shoulder and rubbed it. "Why?"

"He *left* us. And we were all right. But now he wants to come back and pretend that he was never gone in the first place, that he's been here the whole time. And he *wasn't*."

"You missed him."

"No." But the answer came too swiftly to be anything but a lie.

"It's all right to miss people, Benjamin. It means you care for them."

"He didn't care for us, or he would have come home."

"That isn't true, Benjamin," a deep voice said as Stephen emerged from behind a hedge.

STEPHEN FOUND VERA LATER. She sat on one of the sofas that faced each other in the library, reading a book. At his approach, she hurriedly closed the novel and tucked it against her side, flipping her skirt to cover it. It was one of Candace's gothic romances—all sweeping misty moor and brooding hero.

This one was highly irritating—Vera didn't know why she kept reading it. She wanted to shake both of the main characters and plead with them to have a single, honest conversation before she had an apoplexy.

There was a hint of suspicion—there and gone—on Stephen's face as he slumped onto the facing sofa. Vera dearly wanted to know how the conversation between him and Benjamin had gone, but she didn't feel it was her place to ask.

She'd left them in the gardens immediately, only daring a single glance over her shoulder as she turned the corner.

Stephen had his hand on the boy's shoulder, speaking intently. Benjamin had swiped at his cheeks angrily.

"How long were you lurking behind the hedge?" she finally asked when it became clear that Stephen wasn't going to start.

"It wasn't my fault—I was checking on the mint. I heard what Benjamin was saying. I couldn't help but intervene."

"Was I not doing a good enough job?" she asked tartly.

"His grievance was against *me*. You can hardly blame me for wanting to address it."

"And?" It was all the curiosity she dared express.

He lifted an eyebrow. "I'll be joining Hamish and Benjamin on their fishing trip tomorrow."

"It's a start, I suppose."

"A start," he agreed.

Stephen crossed his arms over his chest and stretched out his legs, crossing them at the ankle. Vera noted the little lines at the corners of his eyes. He looked exhausted. She was tired, too, and she hadn't done nearly as much at the Edgar residence.

"We should go and visit Mr. Douglas the day after tomorrow," he said lowly.

"All right."

After a few moments, Stephen's eyes slid closed. With no one else in the room, Vera was able to study him as closely as she desired for the first time since they'd met. She'd dared not do so before—those eyes of his were sharper than any hawk's. They seemed to note every flicker of expression, every slight frown she tried to hide.

Stephen was tall, she'd known that, of course, but his current posture—long legs out before him—only accentuated the fact. His arms weren't as large as some men's, but they were in proportion to the rest of him and well muscled, with a dusting of dark hair along the forearm.

His face eased into sleep, and she was struck by how much younger he looked when he was relaxed. Thank goodness for that calamity of a beard, or the effect might have been overwhelming against her determination to keep the man at a distance.

Suddenly she was irritated at him for wandering in and falling asleep on the sofa across from her own. Didn't he have anywhere else to nap? It was *distracting*.

"Are you watching me sleep?" he murmured without opening his eyes.

Vera jerked. "What? No."

He cracked one eye. "Are you certain?"

"Yes."

"Good," he said, closing his eyes once more. "Because that would be strange."

## CHAPTER 14 - STEPHEN

Two days later, Vera and Stephen loaded into the cart. Hortense wasn't feeling well, but Vera insisted upon accompanying him to Mr. Douglas's anyway. Since his mother was out of the house on one of her infernal rambles through the undergrowth with the marquess's secretary, Stephen thought she perhaps had lost the ability to balk when it came to matters of decorum. Still, Stephen rounded up one of the downstairs maids to go along—a silent, trembling little thing that reminded him of a field mouse.

He frowned, staring off across a wild field and the stand of trees beyond. What *was* going on between his mother and that Hamish fellow? Stephen was so perplexed by the notion, he didn't have the courage to demand answers from his mother. Besides, he knew if he *did* demand answers, she'd deny him any on principle. Lady Jacqueline Winthrop was not the type to be bullied, especially by her own son.

"How was fishing yesterday?" Vera asked stiffly, breaking him free of his unwelcome thoughts.

"Well enough. We caught enough for dinner, but you were there for that."

In fact, she'd already sat through dinner, in which Benjamin regaled them with a detailed description of every hooked fish—including much conjecture on the three that slipped the line and escaped. Vera must want to know something different altogether, something that *hadn't* been answered yesterday evening.

Vera bit her lip. It was terribly distracting, those teeth sunk into that plump lip. Stephen frowned and averted his eyes, too. The horse plodded his way down the country lane, head bobbing to the musical tempo of his own steps. Birds twittered from the trees or flitted through the sky. It was a lovely fall day, the perfect weather—cool but sunny.

Stephen still needed a jacket, though it wasn't all that cold. He hadn't yet reacclimated to England's weather. This first winter would be brutal.

He turned and broke the awkward silence. "What do you know about this Hamish?"

Vera's eyebrows rose. "Your mother seems to approve of him. He's certainly a witty fellow."

Stephen's mouth twisted. He didn't need a reminder of the man's cleverness—not when he himself was the unwilling recipient of many of the man's rejoinders. In fact, that was probably why Vera had brought it up.

There was no easy way to ask what Stephen truly wanted to know: was the man courting his mother? The question was damned embarrassing, and the idea itself made the little boy within him want to howl, made the rebellious youth within want to smack the man in the nose.

That is, if he could land a punch on the fellow. Hamish looked like the type who was able to defend himself quite well. He was a solid man—not fat, but he had a presence about him. Plus, those eyes—they reminded Stephen of the one time he'd gone to see a boxing bout in London. One of the fighters was a short, swarthy fellow who wore down the favorite by simply absorbing blows and tiring the other man out. Then he'd landed one haymaker, and the thing had been finished.

Stephen had never returned, despite his friends' invitations. He found he couldn't enjoy a sport when he spent the entire time evaluating what had just been broken and what would be required to set the men to rights. There was something idiotic about the entire thing—two great lummoxes swinging their thick fists at each others' heads, for money, of all things, and not really all that much of it.

At one point, one of the fighters had broken a knuckle —Stephen was sure of it. He'd held out his own hands and tried to calculate how much his fingers were worth. Certainly far more than either of these men would win, and not just because he was a doctor.

He pushed the thoughts away and said, "I just wonder what his purpose is, in always being about."

Vera shook her head. "Are you really going to repeat the same behavior toward poor Hamish as you did with me?"

*Poor Hamish?*

He frowned. "I'm allowed to be protective of my family members—you've said so yourself."

"Are you even aware of how suspicious you are, or does it come so naturally that it doesn't even register?"

"I have the right to ask, don't I?"

"Yes, but once the answer is given, you're obliged to believe it unless you have evidence to the contrary. Or did you learn nothing from the...the debacle," she finished lamely, sliding a glance toward the silent maid behind them.

Stephen cleared his throat. Neither of them wanted the staff to know that he'd invaded Vera's bedroom and rummaged through her personal effects.

"Of course I have." He pulled the cart to a stop in Mr. Douglas's drive.

"Really? The situation with Hamish is an excellent chance to prove it," she said, her eyebrows raised in censure.

When they entered, Mr. Douglas was resting in the sitting room on one of the ancient upholstered chairs that faced the fireplace.

"I would get up," he said, by way of apology, once he'd successfully hollered at them to come in, "but I'm too lazy to be bothered."

Vera grinned at him and took his hand. "How are you feeling, Mr. Douglas?"

Stephen frowned. That was historically *his* opening line. Now he'd have to devise another.

"Better than I deserve, my dear. Better than I deserve."

His voice was raspy and weak, as if he'd used all his strength to welcome them in.

"Miss Ashbury, please make Mr. Douglas some tea. There's a satchel in the basket."

Vera nodded stiffly and took up the basket. She offered a final warm smile to Mr. Douglas and departed.

"Oof," the man said. "That was a cold front, make no mistake."

Stephen was suddenly grateful that the man's voice was weak, and therefore quiet.

"Never thought a ray of sunshine like her could have a bad side, but you seem to have found it, haven't you?"

Stephen didn't have an answer for that—the truth was laid bare in Vera's treatment of him. Under the circumstances, Stephen decided his opening line was sufficient, after all.

"How are you feeling?"

"Not too well. Getting downstairs just about did me in, it felt like."

"When did you do that?" He picked up the man's wrist and flicked open his pocketwatch.

"Only this morning. Before breakfast. Anne needs her meals on time. I had to boil enough water, make porridge to last the day. It's about all I can manage."

The man's pulse was slow but strong. Stephen kept his fingers on Mr. Douglas's wrist and secretly inspected his breathing. It was shallower than he would have liked.

Mr. Douglas continued, "She's a right angel, Vera is. If I'd met her forty years ago, I would have snapped her up. Wouldn't have ended up alone. You know, if you had half a brain, you'd be trying to marry that girl instead of angering her."

Stephen shook his head. Mr. Douglas wasn't the first patient to suggest he lacked in mental acuity, and he wouldn't be the last. He released his grip and rummaged in his bag, then unscrewed and assembled his brass and wooden stethoscope.

"Ah, brought the torture device back out, have you?"

"We both know it causes no pain."

"It's damned cold, is what it is."

Stephen resisted the urge to roll his eyes and chafed the edge against his hand until it warmed. Still, the old man gave a grumble of displeasure when Stephen set one end upon his bare chest and lowered his head to listen.

"Take a deep breath."

"They're as deep as I can manage," he argued, before taking a substantially deeper one than the last.

A distinct wet crackling sound met Stephen's ears. He didn't react, though the man's lungs still sounded too full for his liking.

"I'll prepare a steam bath," he said, rising to his feet. "Stay put."

When he went through to the kitchen, he brought his stethoscope. The maid was in the backyard, taking laundry from the line. Mr. Douglas was too ill to keep up with his housework.

Vera had put the kettle on, though it was not yet whistling. She held Anne on her lap, smiling down at her. The little girl had freshly washed face and hands, and Vera was brushing her hair with the set she'd purchased in town only days ago.

"How is he?" Vera asked.

"I want to prepare a steam bath for his lungs. Is there more water?"

She shook her head. "I used the last for the tea."

He nodded and went through to the well. By the time he'd retrieved a bucket, the teapot was singing its shrill aria. Vera pulled it, poured two cups, and set one far back from the counter's edge to cool.

"Will you mind her while I bring Mr. Douglas his tea?" Vera asked in a tone that insinuated he might not be equal to the task.

Stephen smirked—if only this lady knew he'd once overseen a ward of thirty sick children in the height of fever season, with only a single, elderly nurse to help him!

He wanted to tell her the story, or to point out that there was no possible way Mr. Douglas was minding Anne in his current state, but all he said was, "Of course."

He arranged the steam treatment—setting water in the pot over the fire, checking his stock of camphor and dried eucalyptus in his bag. Then he dug in the basket for the paper parcel he knew Mrs. Portence had packed before they left the house.

"Miss Anne, would you like a biscuit?"

Her eyes grew wide and bright. She outstretched her hand.

"Ah," he said, withdrawing the treat. "I am going to listen to your lungs first, and then you may have one."

Her chin jutted. "Hurts?"

"Not at all. Would you like to try it? Watch." He knelt beside her, put the large end to his own chest, and pointed. "You put your ear up to there."

She eyed him suspiciously, then bent her head, bringing her ear no closer than half a foot from the stethoscope. Then she raised her head and grinned.

"Did you hear it?" he asked.

She nodded, still smiling.

"All right, now your turn."

He slowly placed the flange upon the thin fabric covering her chest, waited a moment to allow her to get used to it, then bent his head and listened. It took mere moments for him to ascertain that she sounded perfectly healthy—her heart and lungs, both.

"Wonderful!" He grinned at her, more out of relief for her condition than anything. "When you grow up, I think you could be a physician, you did so well."

"Biscuit!"

"Very well."

He handed off the treat and turned to find Vera standing in the doorway, an odd look upon her face. Stephen couldn't read her expression.

He frowned and tilted his head in question, but she shook her head and ducked her face, smoothing her skirts.

STEPHEN SLID his eyes in Vera's direction. She sat next to him on the driving board, her back stiff, her mouth pressed into a line. He searched his memory of their time at the house, wracking his brain. How had he upset her this time? What had he done?

Perhaps Vera was upset that he'd asked her to make Mr. Douglas's tray, as if she were a maid. Yes, he thought, his eyes darting her direction once more, that was the most likely culprit. He frowned. Maybe he'd do it himself from now on, if the task offended her. He probably should have thought of that and done it today, as well.

"Mr. Douglas said something that bothered me today," Vera said.

Stephen jerked; he glowered, even as he searched her face. He hadn't thought the man was the type. Mr. Douglas was sarcastic, sure, and perhaps a bit uncouth, but Stephen thought the man was decent.

"What did he—"

Vera waved a hand. "Nothing like that. I can see it on your face. He asked me to take in Anne if he passed."

Stephen blinked in surprise. "What did you say?"

"I told him the truth—that I'm not in a position to care for any child. That I don't have a home or a husband, or even any family." She choked on the last, as if it cost her dearly to admit it.

He frowned. "I've told him he's not going to die—not if he takes his medicine, which he seems to be doing."

"He says this is how his father went." She watched him with large hazel eyes. "That he got sick, it went to his lungs, and he never recovered."

"He told me the same, but I see no reason why he shouldn't recover."

"Do you think that's all there is that's making him ill? Just the sickness?"

Stephen frowned. There was no way of being sure with these things. Medicine had made great strides the last couple of decades, but it was far from perfect. He himself had missed innumerable opportunities to learn from lecturers while he'd been away in India.

He'd consoled himself with the fact that he'd received thousands of hours of practical experience, but what if one of those lectures he'd missed was the difference between life and death for Mr. Douglas?

"I'll write letters as soon as we're home, asking for input on his case. I'm still in contact with several of my teachers; I'll ask them."

*And I will ask them to notify me of any classes I should take to hone my skills.*

"Thank you." She nodded. "For taking his fear seriously."

Stephen didn't have the heart to tell her the strange anomaly he'd seen play out a hundred times before. Often, when a patient claimed they were dying, they were right.

She said, "Perhaps it's the fear of aging that's making him nervous. He certainly took it very hard when I... declined his offer."

Vera's fingers tangled together in her distress; the sight made Stephen's stomach unsettled. He wanted to roll his eyes at himself. He'd worked through numerous bouts of the influenza without so much as a stomach turn. Now, this lady's emotions were a string whose end was tied to his intestines? Ridiculous.

"I feel very guilty about it," she admitted. "I wish I were in a position to tell him yes."

"You would take her in?" The idea brought him up short.

"Of course I would. She has nowhere to go—nowhere *good* to go, at least. If Mr. Douglas dies, she'll be trundled off to the orphanage. I've seen how those work. The good ones are full, and even those are very strict and afflicted with periodic poverty. Plus, all those children under one roof, and some of them traumatized..."

Vera trailed off and Stephen frowned. It had been even worse in India. There, orphans were left to the streets. The stronger preyed upon the weak, and none of them were ever safe. Disease ran rampant. Starvation nipped at their heels like the wild dogs that hunted in packs.

"I understand."

She looked up at him with hazel eyes swimming with tears. "I got the impression that he intends to ask you next."

Stephen frowned. He heard her unasked question. What would his reply be, if Mr. Douglas asked him?

"I'll think about it." That was all the assurance he could offer at the moment, but it seemed to be all that she needed.

She gave a sigh of deep relief, reached over, and briefly touched the hand that held the reins. "Thank you."

Stephen could only grunt a response—that simple touch, there and gone, had a strange effect upon him.

They were silent the rest of the drive, but Stephen's mind was whirring. He thought of Vera, and of Anne.

Mostly, he thought of Vera.

## CHAPTER 15 - VERA

"I'm sorry," he said. "Sometimes it's like this."

Vera nodded, swiped at her eyes with a handkerchief. It was full night, and two lanterns swayed from the poles above their plodding cart.

When the call came, they'd just been sitting down to an early supper. They'd run to the entryway and grabbed their supplies—Vera her basket, Stephen his handsome leather doctoring case. Elda, their silent shadow, had followed in their wake.

They'd been on the road within minutes, driving down the narrow lane at a teeth-clacking pace. They'd arrived just in time to give the family false hope, just in time to press bandages against wounds that had already bled too quickly and too much.

Then there was nothing left to do but to announce it to the family. The wife collapsed there in the yard with such alacrity, it was as if she'd been shot. Yet it wasn't a tangible wound to her heart, but an emotional one.

Mrs. May's husband was gone. He'd felled the tree and it had returned the favor on the way down.

"Those children," Vera managed to warble, then gasped an inhale.

"I know." Stephen nodded, his face grim. "It's the hardest part. It's easy to help, or even to walk away feeling like you've done all you can. But these kind of cases..." He shook his head. "These are the ones that keep me up at night. What if we had arrived even five minutes earlier? There's no way of knowing."

Stephen shrugged, and it looked like defeat. Vera rubbed at the ache in her chest. There were a few moments where the only sounds were the horse hooves clomping on the hard-packed road, the crickets' song, Elda's wheezing snore from the back of the cart, and Vera's periodic sniffling.

"That was the hardest part about India," he said, his eyes on the road but far away. "The children that I couldn't save. There was a boy, came in with a fever. I tended to him for two weeks."

"What happened?" Vera prompted when the pause grew too long.

Stephen gave a sad smile. "He got better. He went home. His mother brought me dinner to thank me, but it was too spicy—I couldn't eat it." His chuckle dribbled off into nothing. "Then I was called to an accident. That boy I'd spent all that time saving was crossing a road, talking to a friend. Neither of them were paying attention and a horse cart just..." He shook his head. "In my darker moments, I wondered if it wouldn't have been better for that boy to die of fever. If maybe, by saving him, I'd inadvertently killed his friend."

"Of course not. That's not how life works."

"I didn't say the thought was *rational*. But it's strange to think of how many lives were altered today, because we didn't get there in time. Those children without a father. That woman without a husband. And even the connections further back than that—someone in India hurt me, and I decided to leave. I'm still not certain whether I made the right decision."

Vera wasn't sure if she should ignore his broken betrothal out of politeness. In the end, honesty won out. "Your mother told me months before you came home that you were engaged."

He nodded, but there was no missing the tightness of his features. "Her name was Samantha, and I'm not sure she ever really loved me at all."

"You don't have to talk about it if you don't want."

Heaven knew there were so many things that Vera didn't wish to speak of—or to remember, for that matter.

"It's all right. She wanted England more than she ever wanted me." He gave a snorting laugh. "She settled for Italy—I guess it was close enough."

Vera cringed. "I'm sorry."

"The funny thing is, I don't think that I am. I would rather know—without a doubt—that my wife would choose me."

"But you regret coming to Devon?"

He shrugged, his eyes back on the dim road before them. "Do you?"

The question jarred her, until she remembered that he already knew her secrets. Ironically, he was the only one with whom she could freely discuss the truth.

*Did she regret coming here?* She thought about it.

The answer blurted out of her. "No. I don't regret it."

The admission made her feel lighter, somehow. She hadn't realized how much she'd needed to ask herself that question.

"Interesting."

"I don't think it was a mistake for you to return to Devon, either," she ventured. "I know you care about helping people, but your family needs you. Benjamin needs you."

"I'm realizing this." He cleared his throat. "My mother, too." He leaned over and bumped her arm lightly with his. "Hamish and Benjamin helped me replace the fence along the back pasture yesterday afternoon."

"So I heard."

Vera had seen Stephen return to the house, his tunic clinging to his skin, his beard wild down his chest. She'd felt *something*, but she'd looked away before she could decide what it was. Revulsion, probably.

"I'm going to hire some additional men to tend the back fields. It's my job to see to them, after all."

"And you're planning on being a doctor to the village, too?"

"You forget I have a new assistant who's going to be helping me."

"Well, this isn't the first time I've been strong-armed

into a position by a bully, but I do hope this time results in me receiving a reference."

It was as if her words drew a shade over his face—his expression dimmed in an instant.

"I'm not your mother, Vera." He scowled, as if the thought were abhorrent to him. "I'm not looking to trap you in a position you never wanted. I'm not trying to make your life miserable."

"I know." She was confused by the vehemence of his reaction.

"In fact, I'm very much trying to be your friend."

She blinked, frowned. "You are?"

"Yes!" he snapped, throwing his hands in the air. "And you're making it damn difficult!"

"Why shouldn't I? You were—"

"*Exactly.*" He jabbed a finger between them, as if she'd just admitted something that sunk her entire argument. "I *was*. I *was* awful to you when I first arrived home. I *did* do a terrible thing by invading your privacy and reading your personal correspondence. But I've apologized, and I thought you'd accepted that apology."

"I have." Her tone was defensive, nigh on belligerent.

"Then why are you treating me as if you *haven't*?"

"I'm not."

How had this gotten so turned around? *She* had every right to be angry with him... Didn't she? How was he making it seem as if *she* were the one in the wrong?

"You just called me a bully, Vera." He shook his head. "Name the last thing I've done that's actually been mean. Truthfully, what have I done *lately* to earn your ire?"

Her mouth hung open until she realized it and snapped it closed once more. Vera reviewed his actions and was shocked to find that, other than their first week or so, she came up with nothing.

Was he right? Had she been holding a grudge wrongly, viewing him through the lens of what he'd done weeks ago, when he'd apologized many times?

Stephen sighed as if hearing every word of her internal debate. "I know I hurt you, and I'm sorry. I wasn't—I didn't handle things in the right way, and I wish I could go back and change that, but I can't. All I can do is show you who I really am now."

"I can't forget what you did that easily."

He nodded. "I don't expect you to, but will you please —at the very least—give the same weight to my actions now that you do to those in the past?"

Vera thought about it. Could she do that? She thought that she at least owed him the courtesy of trying. She nodded.

"Good." His relief was evident in his voice. "Then can we please move forward as friends?"

Vera eyed the hand that he offered her, her lips pressed together. He kept it out, waiting.

Finally, she shook it. "Yes. Friends."

His answering grin startled her. He had straight white teeth. It was an honest smile, a nice smile.

"Good."

Vera went to sleep feeling more settled and secure than she had in a long time.

The feeling didn't last long.

She woke up the next morning, dressed in a simple blue cotton day dress, and went down to breakfast. As had become usual over the past couple of weeks, she and Stephen were the first ones downstairs. His back was to her; he was loading his plate from the covered servers on the sideboard.

"Good morning, Stephen," she said, smiling.

Vera felt lighter, felt as if their conversation the night before had cleared the last of the acrimony she'd felt from her mind. She felt as if they truly could be friends.

"Good morning, Vera." He turned, smiling, plate still in hand.

Vera's smile froze upon her face. "You...you shaved."

His wild, dark beard that only yesterday rested upon his chest had been replaced by a closely-trimmed goatee and mustache. The planes of his face were fully visible; Vera no longer had to wonder what the woolly mass was hiding.

In the earliest days of their acquaintance, Vera had uncharitably imagined the curling bramble hid some terrible or disgusting deformity—a jagged scar, perhaps, or a mole with a beard of its own.

The truth was far more difficult to bear. The beard had hidden a handsome face and a strong chin, with sculpted cheekbones that stood in masculine relief to the hollowed planes of cheeks below.

"Indeed." He smiled. "I just feel lucky you recognized me and didn't make a run for the nearest fire poker."

Vera felt she was in danger of some rash action, but it had nothing to do with impromptu weaponry. She could do little more than gawk as she retrieved a plate and began to move through the line next to him.

It wasn't that he looked like a completely different person; he possessed the same dark eyes, the same tidy eyebrows that were ready to wing into a sarcastic angle at any moment. No—the problem was that for the first time, he looked as he *should*. He was now the picture of an educated, cultured nobleman who'd run off to India to help the populace.

She'd privately hated that beard. She'd partially blamed it for the calamity that was the start of her and Stephen's relationship.

If he'd looked like this when he'd entered his familial estate and bellowed at her, she would still have been confused and affronted, but she wouldn't have tried to murder him with a poker. If he'd looked like this those weeks ago, she would have shown considerable more respect.

If he'd looked like this weeks ago, she would have fled to Candace's doorstep and begged to be taken in. For Vera would have known then what she knew now—that it was going to be nigh on impossible not to stare at the man like some kind of mute imbecile.

He was too handsome—a mind-muddling, slack-jawed kind of handsome. A kind of handsome that made a shiver of fear—it absolutely *was* fear, there was no possibility it was some *other* emotion—run up her back.

Worse yet, now she knew the man well enough to *respect* him. With attraction and respect, and friendship on top of it, how far would that mental scale have to tilt until she bore far more uncomfortable feelings?

Not far. Not far at all.

"Is something wrong with the bacon?"

He jerked a nod down at her hand, which limply held tongs over the platter.

"Of course not. Just deciding."

*Did* she want bacon?

Did she even *like* bacon?

Heaven help her, had she ever had bacon before?

Vera was so confused, she could barely focus on the task at hand. In the end, she scooped a huge serving of bacon onto her plate, then blinked at it in surprise.

Eight slices! How on earth was she going to eat eight slices of bacon? What on earth was she thinking?

"Ah, you have an appetite this morning. That's good."

A footman fled out the door to the kitchens, presumably to order more bacon.

"Pardon?" Vera blinked at him. Or rather, she blinked at those sharp cheekbones of his.

"Last night," he prompted, then raised an eyebrow.

"Mr. May? Some people cannot eat for days after such a thing. It bodes well that it hasn't affected your hunger."

"I hardly think I'll help the man by going hungry."

Stephen laughed, shook his head. Vera nearly reared back at the sight of his smile and wondered if it was too late to feign illness and flee to the safety of her rooms.

"I think you're perfectly suited to the medical profession, if that's your reply."

Vera scooped some fluffy eggs onto her plate, proud of herself when she discovered it was a normal-sized scoop and not a heaping one. She stepped closer to him and her eyes slid to take in his profile once more.

"Do you not like it, then?" He slid a hand over his face and chin, wincing.

"What?"

"My beard. Do you miss it?"

"Sort of," she croaked, then collected herself. "It's just different. It will take some time to get used to."

"So you *do* like it?"

"It's fine."

Fine? *Fine?* There was nothing about this situation that was *fine*. The word was an insult, for one thing—to his beard, to his *face*. Besides, Vera did *not* feel fine. She felt slightly queasy and unmoored, as if she'd been cast out to sea on a tiny raft.

What was she to do? How was she going to work with this man every day, *live* with him, while he looked like *that*?

"You and Benjamin planted the rosemary too closely," Stephen said.

He'd finished piling his plate and took a seat at the table.

*Ah,* Vera thought, relieved. *See? He's still insufferable.*

That was far easier to deal with—a handsome, insufferable man was no trouble at all. Vera took the chair next to him and plucked a piece of buttered toast from the toast rack.

"So I transplanted them," he added blithely, smearing strawberry jam upon his toast and passing her the jar. "Thank you for planting the herbs, by the way. It was helpful."

She took a huge bite of toast and nodded, wincing internally.

"You've actually been a great help to me these past few weeks," he continued.

Vera nodded again, but she had a sudden mental image of her throwing her plate in his face and shrieking at him to shut up. Intelligent, handsome, *and* appreciative? Heaven help her—this couldn't be happening. Maybe Candace would still take her in.

"I thought we'd go see Mrs. May this afternoon, or tomorrow. Check in, bring a basket. See how she and the children have been faring. If she's not sleeping well, I have a tonic for that."

Thoughtful, too?

Vera wondered if it was too early to request a brandy. She looked longingly at the far sideboard, but since the decanters weren't even out at the moment, she thought it best to refrain.

"Good morning, Stephen, Vera." Jacqueline paused in

the doorway, then offered Stephen a radiant smile. "You finally took my advice. I'm glad to see you're handsome as ever under all that fur. I will admit, I wondered."

"Good morning, Mother," Stephen said.

Vera was momentarily relieved that someone had joined them. Although, on second thought, she wished it had been Benjamin. Jacqueline had notoriously sharp eyes—surely she'd pick up on Vera's discomfort. Come to think of it, that was probably where Stephen had inherited his powers of observation. Their eyes and hair were the same, but everything else must have been inherited from his father.

"Did you sleep well, dear?" Jacqueline had bestowed a kiss upon Stephen's cheek and now paused to brush one upon Vera.

"Very well, thank you. And yourself?"

"Like the dead. Oh, pardon me. I'm sorry—I heard about that terrible thing with Mr. May."

It *had* been terrible, but Vera still found her first bite of bacon particularly delicious. Perhaps she could manage eight slices, after all.

Jacqueline's concerned eyes were upon Vera, but it was Stephen who answered her. "Don't worry—it seems our Vera has a firm constitution."

*"Our" Vera?* that stupid, hopeful voice in her head whispered. Vera chewed her bacon and slammed a mental door in the voice's face. It wasn't as if the man had said *"my"* Vera, after all. Not that such a sentiment would have been welcome.

"What are your plans for the day?" Jacqueline asked.

Vera was grateful when the conversation meandered on with very little input from her. She was even more grateful when Benjamin wandered down the stairs, got a plate, and sat next to her—it was far easier to sneak him her extra pieces of bacon without reaching across the table.

It was only later, when breakfast was finished and she stood, that she realized her mistake—she hadn't been paying enough attention.

"Vera, do you need some time to prepare, or are you ready to go now?" Stephen's face was expectant.

"Pardon?"

"To the village. To buy the ingredients for Mrs. May's sleeping tonic." He frowned. "Are you sure you're feeling well?"

"Quite well," she reflexively answered, then berated herself for not taking the opportunity to feign a small illness or headache.

"Do you need a moment?" Stephen took up his tea and downed the last of it in one go.

"Just let me grab my shawl."

## CHAPTER 16 - STEPHEN

Stephen gripped the reins and darted another glance at Vera. Her profile seemed backlit by the sun—a line of gold edged her delicate features, that set of overfull lips. In the light, her freckles looked like gold dust sprinkled across the bridge of her nose. Her ash-brown hair shone, several strands glowing like bronze threading fresh from a forge. For the life of him, he couldn't understand how she'd gone overlooked in all those ballrooms. For *years*.

Stephen frowned, shifted on the driving board. Perhaps there'd been an outbreak of early-onset glaucoma amongst the male nobles. Or maybe it was ocular presentation of syphilis.

Or perhaps it was as his mother claimed—that the whole lot of English nobility had but a few brain cells, and they used them all upon the wrong thing.

Stephen had told Vera he wished to be friends with her, and that was the truth. The problem was, he didn't know quite how to manage it. The only question he longed to ask her was an insipid, self-centered one—did she like how his valet had cut his hair? What did she think of how he'd carefully trimmed and shaved his beard?

It had taken him well over an hour to accomplish, and he didn't want to admit—even to himself—how often his thoughts had strayed toward Vera in the process. He smoothed a hand through his much shorter dark hair and frowned, racking his brain. *What did friends talk about?*

He and his physician friends spoke of medical things, but such topics would be abhorrent to a lady...wouldn't they? Then again, Vera had shown a remarkable aptitude for care. Though she lacked Stephen's education, she had an innate desire to help, to make their patients more comfortable. She hadn't blanched once—not even when Mrs. Edgar had been sick upon her shoes. Not even when they were tending to Mr. May.

Perhaps he shouldn't sort Miss Vera Ashbury into the same drawer as other young ladies. She'd surprised him, again and again. Which shouldn't be *that* shocking, upon reflection. His mother liked her, very much.

He decided to test his new hypothesis; he cleared his throat. "What are your thoughts on Mr. Cardwell?"

They'd visited the man only days earlier, at his wife's request. Vera had stood unobtrusively against a wall as Stephen performed a cursory examination of the man's vital signs and questioned him.

Vera slid him a glance and said in a dry tone, "I think he'd stop having such bowel calamities if he'd desist with the great quantities of bran."

Stephen laughed. He saw Vera studying him and wondered if she'd spied the lone dimple that peeked out from beneath his goatee. He was self-conscious of it—dimples, as a rule, should come in matched *sets*—but there was nothing he could do about it, save for growing his beard back.

"Why haven't you married? Before your betrothal, I mean," she said, surprising him. "Or was Samantha the first lady of your acquaintance?"

He chuffed a laugh. "I blame my mother."

Vera frowned. "I think she's wonderful. What's the problem—did she not approve of your choices, or did your choices not approve of her?"

"It's not that. When one is raised by a woman of such singular quality, it makes one realize that nothing less than a woman of singular quality will do." Stephen glanced out over the fields surrounding them. "I thought that Samantha was that person, but she proved me exceedingly wrong."

"Do you want to tell me about her?"

Vera's question was plain, honest, and Stephen was surprised to find that he *did* want to tell her about it. He hadn't told anyone before. Not even when his mother had asked a similar question.

"She was...in some ways, she was a lot like you, actually. In that she was helpful and kind." He winced, embarrassed by the admission, and plowed onward, hoping that Vera wouldn't focus on what he'd said. "She was the daughter of a missionary, and she and her mother helped in my clinic. Her parents were good people. I think she was, too."

Vera's eyebrows raised. "That's a very charitable statement, considering what she did."

"I know it would be very easy for me to cast her as some kind of villain, but at the time, I didn't see that she was truly miserable in India." He shrugged. "And not just in the general way that India makes all outsiders miserable—the heat, the smells, the great cacophony of it all. She wanted to leave just as much as I wanted to stay."

"Then why did you come home?"

"I think her breaking our engagement, marrying someone else—it stripped me of my idealism, in a sense. I hate to say it, but it helped me grow up. Even when I left, I was still very naive."

"How can you say that? I'm sure you've seen unimaginable things."

"Yes, but in some ways, I was still a little boy, running away from home." He glanced at her and admitted the truth. "You helped me see that, you know."

"Me?" She straightened, as if surprised.

"That sharp tongue of yours…" He shook his head. "It helped me realize that my priorities needed to shift. Back here. To my family."

Vera scrunched her nose as if she were uncomfortable with the notion. He wished he didn't find it so adorable, and decided to ignore it.

He continued slowly, finding his words as he went. "There is a strange kind of entitlement that is born from coming from a happy family. You begin to believe that they will always be there, that your family will always be all right, because it began that way."

"Your family *is* all right," she protested.

"Not because of me." Stephen straightened his shoulders as if to defend himself, but these words were true—they deserved to be said out loud. "I should never have left after my father died. I should have been here. I should have taken over the estate, helped raise my brother. Filled in for my father where I could."

Even he could hear the guilt in his words, but that was fine by him. He wasn't trying to hide it.

"They are happy. Whole. Healthy." Vera looked up at him, her eyes wide and earnest. "I was perhaps too harsh when you first returned. We didn't start well, you and I."

He grinned. "We certainly didn't, but that doesn't mean what you said wasn't true. Distance didn't absolve me of my responsibilities here. Though I am a physician, I'm also a title holder, which comes with a host of responsibilities—both of people and lands. Even before that, I'm a son, a brother. I don't...I don't think my father would have been pleased with my choices these past few years."

There it was—the deep, ugly fear that crept up to Stephen's bedside while he stared into the dark of his bedroom at night, beneath the weight of his bedcovers and guilt.

"I don't think that's true." Her gentle voice had him meeting her eyes once more. "Your mother is very proud of you. She was even before you returned home. By the tell of things, she and your father were nearly of one mind."

Stephen was grateful for her words; he smiled.

"There's no way for me to know. I simply must go forward in the way I think he'd be proud of, now."

She nodded with finality, as if he'd come to the most logical conclusion and she was proud she hadn't had to steer him there.

"What of you?" he asked. "What are your plans for your life? Did you want to become a governess, before...?"

He trailed off, trying his best to treat her situation as delicately as any surgery.

"No, I didn't."

Stephen searched her face for the telltale lines of pain with which he judged every patient. Surprisingly, all he found was a slight tightening around her eyes. Mild discomfort, then—nothing more.

Vera continued, "I wanted the same thing every young lady wants, I think. Well, most ladies of my acquaintance. I wanted a home of my own. A family of my own."

Stephen noticed that she hadn't mentioned a husband and suddenly wondered if *that* was her pain point. Had Vera had someone picked out—as he had—and the connection had gone wrong? Suddenly, it was all he wanted to know, but he didn't want to embarrass her, either. He'd done more than enough of that for a hundred lifetimes.

"You wanted love," he said carefully.

"I suppose I did."

"*Did*? Do you not still want it?"

Vera laughed, but he could hear the ache riding the low song. "I am twenty-five now. Such concerns are gratefully behind me. Perhaps if my mother hadn't been as she is, I might have had a chance, but it has been several years since I disavowed myself of the notion."

*Not completely,* he thought. *Otherwise, she wouldn't care at all.*

"One of my mentors—Dr. Halveston, in London—he didn't meet his wife until he was forty-four."

Vera smiled. "It hardly matters how old the gentleman is, in the eyes of society. Lord Fettiwig is still browsing for wife number three, and he's not looking in the appropriate shop, age-wise. Why, he made an offer to Candace only months ago, and she could be his granddaughter!"

"Some ladies might take him up on it," he teased. "They might do the calculations in their head and deem a year or two of misery a fair price for a lifetime of freedom and comfort."

"If the man were guaranteed to obey the laws of nature, perhaps. But he's outlived two of them, and both were much younger than he. I'm starting to think he might be killing them off, just for the thrill of selecting a new one."

"A shocking assertion."

She tilted her head. "But perhaps that will be my backup plan. Yes—I'll train with you for three months. Doubtless you'll teach me the recipe for a tonic that *could* be fatal. Then I'll write to Lord Fettiwig myself, see if he'll condescend to a wife as old as twenty-five."

Stephen laughed.

STEPHEN LEANED back against the gently sloped copper tub and sighed. His back and hips ached a bit from riding his horse, and the hot water felt wonderful. He'd been surveying the fence line of the property over the past few days if the weather was nice, noting repairs that were needed. Usually Vera or Benjamin accompanied him, sometimes both.

Today it had been Benjamin, and their time together finally felt natural, easy—as time between two brothers should be. They'd ridden to the far field in the morning, the one with the sizeable berm. Stephen was teaching Benjamin some of the basics of handling a rifle. They'd started with safety, naturally, and would proceed from there as Benjamin's responsibility allowed.

Overall, it had been an exceedingly pleasant day. Stephen tipped his head back and closed his eyes as steam wafted from the tub. His valet, Edwin, had drizzled a bit of oil over the top of the water that smelled of sandalwood and eucalyptus. Though Stephen typically eschewed all perfumes, this was the exception.

Stephen gave a small exhale of derision, remembering an instance some idiot had poured a great quantity of rose oil into his bathwater at a London hotel. Stephen had already been running late to the theatre; there was no time to request fresh water. His choice was to go smelling strongly of horse—and the whisky he'd spilled earlier—or to bathe.

He later wished he'd gone as he was. He'd stunk up the entire box; he'd reeked worse than Great Aunt Bertian's potpourri.

There was a tug at the bathing sheet near his feet.

He didn't bother opening his eyes. "Edwin, the water's fine; you may leave me."

Stephen froze as a sizeable splash sounded at the far end of his tub. He remembered his valet had *already* departed, as Stephen had instructed—the man was heading down to the kitchens, doubtless to flirt with the new parlor maid.

Stephen took a fortifying breath and cracked one eye. At the other end of the copper tub, half-submerged in water, was a raccoon. In that split second, Stephen couldn't help but notice that the raccoon had adopted a similar position to his own—on his back, leaned against the tub, and staring right back at him.

Though he'd sworn never to repeat the experience, Stephen gave an involuntary yelp that echoed through the chamber. He flailed and heaved himself from the tub, sending a wave of bathwater sluicing over the stones.

The racoon didn't seem at all alarmed by Stephen's reaction. Instead, it slid lower into the water as if settling in to enjoy the warmth. Stephen scrabbled for a towel and instinctively wound it 'round his waist, protecting the most vulnerable parts of himself.

"Stephen?" his mother called from his bedroom.

"Do not come in here!" he bellowed.

He checked the door to his bathing chamber, relieved to find it closed. He scowled—that meant the little bugger had been lying in wait, or had slipped in when the footmen delivered the water.

"Whatever is the matter?"

"One of your *creatures* has joined me in the bath!"

There was a moment's pause. "That'll be Hurbert. He dearly loves a swim, and I haven't drawn him a bath in ages."

"Mother," he snapped in exasperation, swiping at himself haphazardly with a towel.

He jerked his tunic over his head quickly, not wanting to lose sight of the raccoon. But the little beast spared him no attention—it was now lazily swimming laps in the copper tub.

"Yes, dear?"

Her voice sounded strange through the door—was she *laughing* at him? The idea of it only agitated him further. He yanked up his trousers, accidentally snapping his chest with his suspenders in his haste, and stomped to the door.

As he suspected, his mother waited with a brightness in her eye that could only be attributed to merriment.

He scowled. "I'd very much appreciate it if these animals were removed from the house!"

"I know, dear. But the fact is that most of them have lived here longer than you, as of late."

"Meaning that they take precedence over my comfort?"

"Their lives do; yes."

"I'm not saying you have to *kill* them, Mother. I'm

simply asking for them to be relocated. Don't the stables have room for some cages or whatnot?"

"Cages? Certainly not. They wouldn't be comfortable in *cages*."

Stephen opened his mouth to argue that it was now coming down to his comfort versus the animals' comfort, and he was *still* losing, but at that precise moment, the raccoon trundled out from his bathing room and shook himself dry on the carpet. Stephen was struck momentarily dumb by the sight and resisted the instinctual urge to punt the thing across the room.

His mother swooped down on the offending animal, picking him up and cradling him to her chest. "Did you have a good swim, Hurbert? I'm sorry if his yell upset you—"

"*Mother!*"

But she was already turning for the door. "Yes, dear?"

He slid a hand down his damp face and sighed, defeated. "Please keep your animals out of my rooms, at least."

"Of course, dear."

IF STEPHEN EXPECTED sympathy when he repeated the story to Vera the following afternoon, he was sorely disappointed. Vera laughed and laughed until he stared at her with exasperated patience.

A *little* laughter was to be expected—even he could see a *glint* of humor in it, now that he was nearly twelve hours removed from the experience—but this much? Certainly *this* much laughter was excessive. Still, Vera's laugh was that low rasp of hers that Stephen had come to love.

*Love?* What a shocking word to use in this context.

They were on their way back from Mr. Douglas's once more. Though the weather had turned cold, he seemed to be improving and was in much better spirits.

"Do you not like animals?" Vera asked after she'd recovered enough to speak.

This had taken some time, as she'd relapsed into laughter several times, with small breaks of hiccuping recovery between.

"I do. *Normal* animals, such as dogs and horses."

"Your mother's animals are so much smaller than dogs and horses. Why are you more frightened of them?"

"That's part of the problem—they give me the same feeling as a spider or snake. I'm half-convinced they'll charge me and scramble up my trouser leg."

"I'm the opposite. I can handle a hedgehog or a fox easily. The first time I saw the Duke of Canterbury's dog, I was petrified."

"Seamus?" Stephen grinned. "It's hard to imagine him frightening anyone."

"I know that *now*, and I adore him. But I was ill-prepared to deal with him when I first met him. It was a surprise, you see, and there he was, all six hundred pounds of him, stretched out in the foyer."

"He's only two hundred twenty pounds. Or at least,

that was the last measurement they had. The duke says Seamus has no concept of how large he is—the fellow is terrified of squirrels."

Vera laughed again. "So he's like you, then."

"I've been likened to worse, I assure you." His eyes slid to study her face in what he hoped was taken for a casual glance. "So are you saying you wouldn't enjoy having a dog like Seamus around the house?"

"Of course not! He's *such* a dear. It was only the initial shock of him that put me off, and only for a moment. Now I know what to expect and he doesn't frighten me at all."

"My father always had dogs around the house, but my mother prefers a wilder sort of pet, apparently."

"I doubt that dogs would appreciate a fox or a raccoon about the house," she admitted.

*Precisely,* Stephen thought.

## CHAPTER 17 - VERA

They were seated in the parlor. Stephen was trying to teach Benjamin the basics of chess. Vera pretended to read the medical textbook open in her lap while shamelessly eavesdropping on their conversation.

"That was an excellent idea, but remember that the king can only move one square." Stephen reset the board. "But look closely—there's another opportunity you might be inclined to take. Don't forget your pawns—just because they're smaller than the others, doesn't mean they can't be very effective."

Vera watched the ordinary scene—similar to others that had occurred a thousand times before in rooms much like this—and felt something within her shift. It might have been imperceptible had she not been paying attention, but as her thoughts were wholly focused on the physician with whom she shared a roof, she was able to discern it quite clearly.

Forgiveness—that was what the feeling was. *Genuine* forgiveness.

Vera forgave Stephen for what he'd done, for how terribly he'd treated her when he first arrived. She thought she quite understood it now. Though that understanding wasn't enough to excuse his behavior, he'd apologized multiple times and—more importantly—his actions proved that he meant what he said.

Even though she'd told him she forgave him, until this moment, she hadn't. Not fully, at least. There was still a shard left behind in the wound that kept it from fully closing, kept it from healing completely. Now, that little sliver of hurt had worked itself free.

"Well done!" Stephen exclaimed from the chess table. He grinned over at her. "Vera, come see. Benjamin has put me into check."

She obligingly set her book on the sofa next to her, a satin ribbon acting as her placeholder amongst a diagram of the organs.

"It hardly matters," the boy protested, even as his cheeks flushed with pleasure. "You're just going to get out of it again."

"Nonsense. I've been playing for years, and you've only been learning for a fortnight. You should never have put me in such a pickle—I think you have a natural aptitude for the game." Stephen beamed up at Vera where she stood at the edge of the table. "Look."

Vera smiled politely and nodded as Stephen showed her how Benjamin had accomplished the feat, but she heard very little of what he said.

Something had happened in that split second when Stephen had smiled up at her. It was as if that little shard had left a vacuum behind, and this new *something* had rushed in to fill it. Vera wasn't sure what it was, and that frightened her.

"My lord," Roland said from the doorway. "A servant has come from the Marquess Salisbury's house. It's the marchioness. They bid you come at once."

THEIR RIDE to Devon Manor was quick and tense. Thankfully, the road between the two houses was well maintained and there wasn't too much of it. Still, Vera glanced sideways at Stephen several times and his expression was the same—a grim clench of the jaw that spoke of his concern.

"Vera," he said, turning suddenly toward her when they were almost to the house. "In my experience, matters with pregnant ladies are either nothing at all or extremely grave. I don't know which this is, but I need your word that if I ask you to leave the room, you'll do it immediately without protesting."

She nodded and her eyes pricked with her worry.

*Adelaide,* she thought. *Please let nothing happen to Adelaide.*

Though she and Adelaide weren't nearly as close as Candace and Adelaide were, Vera still admired the lady for her kindness and quick intelligence. It was a rare combination in English society, where ladies usually demonstrated their wit by aiming slicing set-downs at their competitors.

When they arrived at the grand house, the mannerisms of the staff did little to calm Vera's worry. They were greeted in the driveway by a grouping of servants led by the housekeeper, who wrung her hands. Stephen rushed up the stairs behind a footman who took the stairs two at a time. Vera huffed in their wake, holding her skirts far too high for propriety's sake in her haste—but no one noticed or cared.

They swept through the door of the lord's suite. Vera nearly slumped into a chair—for there was Adelaide, resting comfortably in bed against a mound of pillows. She was nearly upright, an embarrassed little smile on her face, her eyes bright.

"Thank you for coming so quickly," Percy said, ushering Stephen to the bedside. "I was beside myself."

"Really, Percy, this isn't necessary." Adelaide gave a grimacing smile to Stephen and Vera. "I'm so very sorry. They shouldn't have called you at all."

"We weren't busy, were we, Vera?" Stephen smiled at her, as if checking that she'd made it up the stairs after all. "Now, since we're here, you might as well let me help you."

"I just had...I had a minor stomach upset." Adelaide's cheeks grew pinker by the second. "I feel much better now. There was no need to call the physician, as I told my husband from the first."

"Some mild stomach upset shouldn't be any cause for

alarm." Stephen frowned and looked back and forth between the married couple.

The marchioness was giving her husband a wide-eyed beseeching look, as if silently begging him for something. The marquess frowned implacably back.

"Are you sure that there isn't something else you'd like to tell me?" Stephen said gently.

Vera trusted his instincts—there was something they weren't privy to, some undercurrent here they didn't understand.

"Not at all," Adelaide said.

"Darling—" Percy tilted his head.

"I beg of you—please *don't*." She shook her head, her eyes wide.

"He's already here. We might as well *tell* him."

Adelaide still shook her head desperately, her eyes round.

Percy turned to Stephen resolutely, his back straight. "She belched."

Adelaide groaned and covered her face with her hands.

"Belched?" Stephen replied, his tone one of mild, professional interest.

Vera was impressed; she didn't know how Stephen managed it. She herself was struggling to gain control of her own winged eyebrows.

Percy nodded stoutly.

"Pregnancy can cause more eructation than normal—" Stephen began.

Percy threw his hands in the air. "You don't understand! It was the biggest belch I've ever *heard*!"

Vera choked back a giggle; she made little strangled noise, instead. Adelaide still covered her face, but her shoulders were shaking against her propped pillows. Vera desperately hoped the lady was laughing and not sobbing from humiliation.

"Oh, well—" Stephen said.

Percy kept on, waggling his finger. "And mind you, I went to *Eton*. Have you ever heard a bar room full of young lords freshly let loose upon society? It's crude and loud, and Lord Fergus could belch the entirety of 'God Save the King.' We used to have belching competitions, with points given for tenor and resonance and length of echo." He slashed his hand through the air for emphasis. "*This* belch left them all behind."

"I see." Stephen *was* smiling now, but it was still well within the bounds of politeness.

Adelaide peeked through her fingers. Vera was relieved to see that the woman was hiding embarrassed laughter, instead of tears.

"*Percy,*" Adelaide finally managed to gasp. "Please stop. I'm *mortified*."

"Well? The doctor needs to know." He turned back to Stephen, his eyes wide, intense. "I'm telling you, it was unnatural. *Cataclysmic.*"

Adelaide *was* crying now, but only because she'd been overwhelmed by her giggling. Vera had to hold a hand to her lips to cover her smile. She knew she had to strive to remain professional no matter the circumstances, but the sheer amazement in Percy's voice was difficult to overcome. The man sounded equal parts afraid and impressed.

"Lady Salisbury, did you feel better afterward?" Stephen asked.

"Much better."

"Then the emission served its purpose. If the condition persists, peppermint tea can be very soothing. I'd also recommend avoiding overly spiced or rich foods, as those can make the issue worse."

"Thank you." Adelaide nodded, wheezing through the residual laughter and swiping at her eyes.

"See?" Percy waved his hand. "I told you it wouldn't be off-putting. He's a physician; he's heard far more shocking things."

"Indeed," Stephen said. "Your husband was right to call—"

"See?" Percy repeated, his eyebrows raised.

"You should never hesitate to call. This is your first pregnancy, and it's natural that you'll have many fears and questions regarding your condition."

"I know *I* certainly do." Percy crossed his arms. "It doesn't help that we live mere miles from the Duke of Canterbury, who lost his first wife to childbirth. In your medical opinion, do you think there might have been environmental factors that contributed to the lady's death? Was it a mistake to bring Adelaide here?"

"Lord Salisbury," Stephen said firmly. "It isn't helpful, as a rule, to mention ladies who have passed in childbirth in front of your wife, who's on the cusp of such an experience."

Percy's wide eyes flew to Adelaide's alarmed ones. For the first time, he seemed to note how she'd gone a bit pale, how her fingers clutched at the linen sheets in distress. She certainly wasn't laughing anymore.

"Forgive me, darling. I'm frightened."

"No more than I am," she said. "If I can bear the fear—along with getting up a dozen times at night to relieve myself while you snore on, undisturbed—then I certainly expect you to do the same."

"Of course, darling. I am sorry."

"Very well," she sniffed. "You may make it up to me by allowing me to host a dinner party tomorrow night, to welcome Dahlia to the countryside."

"It's highly irregular to host a dinner in your condition."

"And calling our neighbor to tell him of my epic belch isn't?"

"He's a physician. It's not as if I wrote in to report it to the gossip rags. Besides, you must rest—"

"Percy!" She thumped the bed coverings. "If the physician says I'm able to sit at a dinner table—the same way I do *every* night, I might add—then you aren't going to be the one to tell me no."

All eyes in the room turned to Stephen.

Vera bit back a smile—she knew precisely the war that waged inside his head. If he gave the marchioness a clean bill of health, she was going to invite him to a dinner party. Stephen *detested* dinner parties, Vera well knew. Small talk was difficult for him—he'd rather discuss a new surgical technique in gruesome detail, rather than pretend to be interested in the hat Miss So-and-So had seen in the village shop only yesterday.

In the end, as Vera knew it would, his physician's ethic won out.

Stephen nodded. "You are quite able to *attend* a dinner party, as long as you leave every bit of the preparations to the staff and rest quite thoroughly before and afterward. I'd also recommend you don't serve anything too rich or full of spice, as that might cause you digestive upset."

Adelaide smiled triumphantly at her husband. "There, do you see? I'm perfectly able to attend, and we both know that is all I like to do when it comes to hosting."

"That's not true." Percy's chin took a belligerent stance. "You also like to tell the staff what kind of flowers you prefer."

"Then I shall give Mrs. Penn carte blanche on the matter, just to satisfy you. I won't even ask if the hothouse roses are blooming. Will that satisfy?"

"Very well, my dear. *I* will make all the preparations, including extending invitations." He abruptly turned to Vera and Stephen. "Lord Winthrop, Miss Ashbury, you are invited to an early dinner tomorrow evening. Please be here by five and be prepared to leave promptly at eight."

"You cannot instruct guests when to *leave*," his wife hissed, her expression appalled.

"On the contrary, my dear, I just did. And furthermore, you're already breaking the parameters of our agreement by trying to insert yourself into the planning. Perhaps we should just cancel the thing altogether." He turned back to Vera and Stephen and opened his mouth.

"No," Adelaide said. "It's quite all right. Five is

wonderful." She smiled at her guests. "Looking forward to seeing you both."

"A gracious invitation, indeed," Stephen said gravely, though Vera had to hide her smile at the slight quaver of his lips.

"Dearest," Percy said blithely, turning to his wife. "Do you mind if I send a rider to Kent? If you think you might have a repeat performance of today's intestinal upset at our dinner party, I'd dearly love for Lord Fergus to be able to hear it. Otherwise, he'll never believe me."

"*Percy!*"

The marquess neatly dodged the tasseled throw pillow aimed at his head. "Our marriage has improved your aim, my dear. I take all the credit, and you are very welcome."

# CHAPTER 18 - STEPHEN

Late-morning sunlight shone through the waving branches, dappling Stephen's and Benjamin's shoulders as their horses plodded along the fence line of the far pasture. A cool breeze brought the smell of moldering undergrowth and the faint scent of woodsmoke. Fall was well underway, and soon, grey clouds would cover the landscape like a lid placed atop a pot.

At least this fence line was in good repair, Stephen was relieved to see. He'd saved this parcel of land for last, as the groundskeeper had informed him it was the newest one, built only three years ago. This task had fallen to him, as the men of work were completely engaged with finishing repairs to the old groundskeeper's cottage on the property.

"Cottage" was a bit of a misnomer. It was a spacious two-story house—Stephen had played in it when he was young—though it had been in slight disrepair for some time. His mother had recently ordered it completely refurbished. Local craftsmen had repaired one of the exterior walls, and they were endeavoring to complete the roof repair before the first rain. If the weather held for two more days, they'd make it.

"Are you going to marry Vera?" Benjamin asked, jarring Stephen from his thoughts.

"What?" He frowned. "Why would you ask that?"

"Because she won't marry *me*." The boy shrugged. "I already asked."

Stephen chuckled. "When did you do that?"

"*Ages* ago." His shoulders slumped. "But she said she was too old for me."

"Did you even bring her a present? Flowers? Anything?" Stephen teased.

"No." He wrinkled his nose, looked up. "Was I supposed to?"

"Traditionally, a man gives the lady gifts to show his affection."

"Huh." He considered this for a few moments. "Well, are you?"

"Going to get her a present?"

"*Marry* her," his brother said, as if Stephen were the biggest idiot who'd ever lived.

"How can I, when you've already proposed? It wouldn't be fitting."

"I don't think she'd mind. I certainly wouldn't. I didn't even kiss her."

Stephen's eyes slid to Benjamin. "What do you know of kissing?"

"Not much. Arthur says he practices by licking the back of his hand."

"I don't think you should listen to him. It doesn't sound like he's ever done it either."

"That's the problem." Benjamin dropped the reins and flopped his hands down on either side of the horse. "Nobody who's actually kissed a girl will tell us *anything*."

Stephen stifled the urge to laugh at the boy's earnestness. "Because it's a private matter. A gentleman should never kiss and speak about it afterward."

"Then how is someone supposed to learn, if everyone's keeping it a secret?"

"It's not *secret*, it's—"

"Have *you* ever kissed a lady?"

"I have."

Benjamin frowned; his forehead wrinkled. "But you aren't married."

There was a time when the innocent statement would have set memories of Stephen's engagement sucking at his feet, memories that would try to pull him into a dark pit of depression. Now, Stephen was happy to realize all he felt was amusement at his brother's precious naivety.

"I'm not," he admitted.

They rode for some time while his brother pondered the possibility of that equation, the only sounds the muffled thud of their horses' hooves against the damp earth.

"Do you think you *will* marry?"

Vera's face flashed in his mind—there and gone like a firecracker.

He shook it away as best he could—she was his assistant, under his protection. "Perhaps."

That afternoon Mr. Douglas said, "Miss Ashbury, the gentlemen must be chasing you through the village. Good for you, telling them all 'no.' Tell me, how many hearts have you broken this week?"

Vera laughed in that throaty way of hers, and despite Stephen's resolution not to sniff in that direction, he couldn't help that his ears were tuned to her answer.

"None that I'm aware of."

"Humble, too. What a rare jewel you are."

From his vantage point in his armchair, the man could see Stephen through the doorway, but Vera could not. Stephen felt Mr. Douglas's eyes upon him and made a show of rummaging through his bag.

"You mark my words," Mr. Douglas said. "One of these days, some noble gentlemen will ride through this town, and he won't leave until he takes you with him. A man would have to be a right idiot not to see what a treasure you are."

Vera chuckled again. "No wonder I come here so often—speaking to you does marvels for my own esteem."

"Do you wish to be married, Vera?"

"Only if the right gentleman asks me."

"Do you have someone in mind?" he asked archly.

Stephen didn't even bother to hide the fact he was

listening now. He stood like a dolt and stared down into his bag.

"I haven't met him yet," she teased. "But you will be one of the first to know should that change."

"Don't settle for less than a viscount, my dear." The old man sounded satisfied. "Though I think you'd make a splendid duchess, myself. It's too bad that Canterbury's married, or I might suggest you trot on over there."

Stephen clenched his jaw. He knew the old man was needling him on purpose, but all he could hear were Vera's words. *I haven't met him yet.*

Why on earth should her statement bother him at all? It was the fact that it *did* bother him that was so very arresting.

"What on earth are you doing?" Vera said from his elbow.

Stephen jerked. "Looking for the camphor."

She frowned, glanced into his bag, and plucked a bottle from one of the fabric compartments. "It's right here."

"So it is. Thank you."

"Are you feeling quite well?"

Before he had the chance to answer, she reached up and placed a cool hand against his brow. His head swam. Concern flickered at the corners of her eyes.

He jerked away on reflex. "I'm fine."

"Are you sure? You look quite flushed."

"I assure you I know my own person."

But did he, really? For he felt with that single touch of her delicate fingers to his forehead that she'd bewitched him somehow. Or rather, that the innocent touch had been a key that unlocked something within him—something he might never have otherwise admitted to himself. Something he'd been actively avoiding and rejecting for weeks now.

Vera gave him a sidelong glance and frowned again. "Why don't you step out and get some fresh air? I can make the steam bath; I know how."

Stephen nodded and fled out the back door without another word. Behind him, he could have sworn that Mr. Douglas was laughing. At *him*. For the man had seen the whole exchange and surely knew what was running through Stephen's mind as he paced the small garden at the back of the house.

*Vera.*

She was amazing. Beautiful, kind. Compassionate. She was everything he'd *thought* that Samantha was. He groaned and rubbed at his temples. What a mess he'd made of things! If he'd started off right, she might have one day looked at him with something more than friendship.

Now—because of his own actions—friendship was all they would ever have. They'd made excellent progress these last few weeks, but their relationship was far from what it *could* have been. If only he hadn't acted as a paranoid lunatic!

If only he'd realized that the reason he'd been suspicious of Vera wasn't because of the danger she posed to his mother, but because of the danger she posed to *him*.

To his heart.

Some deep-down part of him must have realized it

from the beginning. And drat it all—how had Mr. Douglas figured it out well before Stephen had?

Stephen took a deep breath and tried to reorient himself to this new reality. It didn't change anything, him knowing what he knew. Just because he felt a certain way didn't mean *she* ever would. It certainly didn't absolve him of his duties as a physician.

On that thought, he took another deep breath, steeled himself, and ducked back into the house. Vera sat very close to Mr. Douglas's chair. The man had a steaming bowl on his lap and a towel draped over his head, but upon Stephen's entry, he looked up.

"All right there, Dr. Winthrop?" Mr. Douglas asked, a twinkle in his eye.

"Yes, thank you."

"How was that fresh air?"

Stephen frowned at him—how did the man make a mockery of such a simple question?

"Very pleasant."

Mr. Douglas nodded. "I bet that fresh air got you all sorted."

"Enough chatter," Vera chided gently. "You're wasting the steam, Mr. Douglas."

"All right, girl. If you say so."

He pulled the towel back over his head, and Stephen was relieved to be free of the man's cunning gaze.

"Are you *truly* feeling better?" Vera's eyes were wide, guileless. "You certainly felt a little warm."

A little chuckle from beneath the towel, which they both ignored.

"Much better. I think the kitchen was stifling."

"*Vera* certainly wasn't warm," Mr. Douglas said gleefully.

"Perhaps you should loosen your collar," she said. "I usually have to do the same when I'm near the fire."

"I doubt that thought will help," came Mr. Douglas's muffled voice.

"Pardon?" Vera said.

"Breathe the steam," Stephen ordered, perhaps a bit too loudly. "If you're talking, you're not breathing deeply enough."

There was a muffled grumbling from beneath the towel, but thankfully it was too low to hear.

On the way back to the house, it felt very crowded. There were now four passengers in the small cart—Hortense, Stephen, Vera...and his newfound knowledge of how he felt for her.

## CHAPTER 19 - STEPHEN

The dinner guests arrived in a rush all together at five o'clock sharp in the gravel driveway of Devon Manor. Perhaps their haste was due to the knowledge that they only had a few hours to spend together—Stephen had seen the gleam of crazy in the marquess's eye. He didn't doubt that the man would quite literally put his polished boot to a guest's backside if they dared stay too long and disturb his wife.

"Vera, darling," Candace, the Duchess of Canterbury said, rushing forward and kissing both of her cheeks. "You look radiant as always. That dress is simply lovely on you."

"How could it not be, when you were the one who picked it out?"

"Shh," she said, glancing around to make sure no one else had heard. She seemed satisfied that only Stephen was close enough, and he pretended to be engrossed in the other greetings taking place. "You must learn how to take a compliment for yourself, instead of perpetually trying to dodge them or fling them back on the giver."

Vera chuckled and Stephen smiled reflexively. Good heavens, he was no better than a marionette—there was an invisible string connecting Vera's laugh to the corners of his own mouth.

He hastily greeted their host to distract himself. "Good evening, Lord Salisbury."

"Please, everyone here must call me Percy. Certainly we are close enough for that if my lovely wife insists you come to our house in her condition."

"Her condition seems to be happiness and beauty," Candace chided, embracing her sister-by-law.

"Pretty sure it was her beauty that helped get her into the condition," Percy murmured.

Thankfully, only the gentlemen were close enough to hear him.

Canterbury raised an eyebrow in dry humor. "I hardly think jokes of that nature are appropriate, considering our relation to one another."

"Why on earth not?" Percy frowned.

"Don't host a party if you don't want others to attend, is all." He nodded at his wife, Percy's sister.

Percy's face screwed up into blatant disgust. "Really, Canterbury. You say the most shocking things."

"*I* do?"

"Besides," Percy continued. "*This* entire party is one where I would have preferred if all of the guests had sent their regrets. I believe I specifically suggested you all do so, in fact."

"Apologies," Stephen said, even as his eye traced Vera's progress across the room. "Mother wouldn't hear of it."

"And I must blame my wife." Canterbury nodded.

"Bunch of cowards," Percy groused. "Not even willing to stand up to the females in your family."

"Percy?" Adelaide called from the other room.

"Coming, darling!" He rushed in the direction of her voice, leaving his male guests to chuckle in the hallway.

"Good evening, Hamish." Stephen offered his hand.

Hamish grinned and took it. "Lord Winthrop. You're looking much different since the last time I saw you."

Stephen rubbed his chin. "Perhaps I'm a coward as our host suggests—Mother hounded me for weeks."

"She said you'd shave it when you were ready, and I guess you finally were."

Stephen didn't quite appreciate the tone Hamish used—it reminded him too much of Mr. Douglas—nor did he appreciate the fact that Hamish looked at Vera as he said the words. Canterbury half choked, half coughed, and Stephen frowned.

Percy appeared in the archway, his hands upon his hips. "Well? Are you gentlemen coming?"

THE GUEST OF HONOR, Miss Warrington, was one of the marchioness's sisters. Introductions were made all around. She was pleasant enough; Stephen paid attention long enough to note that she was blonde, of average height, wore a purple dress, and was decidedly not Vera.

That was how Stephen was starting to look at all ladies these days. His interest was like one of those decision trees he'd made as study aids in his medical education.

Was the woman Vera? Yes? *Interested.* No? *Only interested enough to fulfill societal duties.*

Still, as he was seated next to Miss Warrington, he was obliged to speak with her a little. At least Vera was directly on his other side, so he could split his attention to her. Lately, he'd become singularly charmed with her laugh—or more precisely, interested in *what* made her laugh.

Stephen had noticed that she rarely laughed at the expense of others. Even the teasing little jokes that the marquess and marchioness lobbed back and forth with love in their eyes—Vera only smiled or grinned. She preferred a clever, dry wit, which he was glad of, as he thought he possessed just such a sense of humor.

"Miss Warrington," Stephen began, once the first course was served—it was a single round bite. He blinked at it and prayed the serving size wasn't indicative of the courses yet to come. "How are you finding the countryside?"

"It's lovely, although I confess I've yet to see much of it. Devon Manor is situated so charmingly, and the company within so pleasant that I haven't stirred once since I arrived days ago."

"I'm sure that your sister and your brother-by-law are delighted to have you visit."

On his other side, Vera was saying something to the

Duchess of Canterbury—something about a luncheon Candace was planning.

Stephen mustered the energy to say to Miss Warrington, "My mother tells me that your brother-by-law has performed quite the renovation on Devon Manor the past year or so, and that the Duchess of Canterbury worked on the gardens while she was here."

*There.* That should be enough to keep Miss Warrington talking long enough for him to eat...well, whatever this was on his plate. He'd given the lady *two* topics to address. He stabbed the bite with his fork, popped it into his mouth. *Delicious.* He blinked and stared at his plate. He'd like an entire platter of...*that*. Whatever it was. He suddenly wished he'd paid more attention to what he'd just eaten.

"...she even went so far as to invite the townspeople for a picnic to allow them to see it. Have you had the chance to see it yet?"

Stephen hadn't the faintest idea what Miss Warrington was on about. He'd been trying to decide if the flavor still lingering upon his taste buds had been lamb or a very fine roast beef. Or was it possibly venison?

Still, he saw Vera's head inclined toward them and decided she might be able to help him limp through the conversation.

"Er...I haven't," Stephen said, then turned to Vera. "Have you had the opportunity to see it?"

"Pardon." Vera blinked. "I'm not certain of what we're speaking."

She looked at him expectantly, but Stephen shook his

head. "Miss Warrington will describe it far better than I ever could."

"The garden folly." Miss Warrington leaned past Stephen to smile at Vera. "Though you were staying here with Candace at the time, so I'm sure you saw much more of it than I have."

Vera nodded, her eyes bright. "It's lovely, isn't it? So strange that a sculptor of that skill would have consented to carving statues situated all the way out there."

*Had the topping been pickled onions?* Stephen surreptitiously sucked his teeth. *And there was definitely horseradish in the mix.*

"...you should ride out and view it." Miss Warrington's eyes were upon him once more, and Stephen tried to pay better attention.

With those waving doo-dads atop her head, Miss Warrington reminded him strongly of the *monal*, a small, pheasant-like bird native to India. It had a sprout of feathers growing out of its head that bobbed when it walked, just like that. Stephen found it very distracting.

"Thank you. I might just do that." He turned to Vera. "Would you like to come with me?"

"Ah, but she's already seen it so many times," Miss Warrington interjected smoothly. "I'm happy to accompany you, if you'd appreciate someone to show you the way. I'll be sure to wait to see it again until you can join me —to better replicate your own experience of seeing it for the first time."

There *had* been pickled onions atop the dish, but that

wasn't all. There had also been an earthy sweetness in the dish.

*Beets! It was absolutely beets!*

"A very kind offer." Stephen nodded and smiled, thrilled with his discovery.

Who knew that beets could lend such a depth of flavor to a meat dish? It was a revelation, of sorts. Stephen listed the ingredients to the dish as if it were a tonic that could cure all disease. *Lamb, roasted beef, or venison. Horseradish cream sauce. Pickled onions, roasted beets, atop a small toasted square of bread.*

But it would be much better if Mrs. Portence could just make him a sandwich with those ingredients. Consuming the thing one bite at a time was unnecessarily fussy.

Stephen turned to Vera, intent on asking her if *she* liked roasted beets, and noticed a little frown upon her lovely lips. Thankfully, Miss Warrington's attention had been claimed by the Duke of Canterbury, who sat on her other side.

"Did you not like that, then?" he leaned toward Vera and murmured.

She jerked, her eyes wide. "Pardon?"

"I'm very intrigued, myself."

"*Are* you?" She seemed disturbed by the idea.

"Indeed. I'm going to sample that delicacy again, as soon as possible."

"That's quite an ungentlemanly sentiment," she spluttered.

"On the contrary." He frowned. "It's how things are

done among gentlemen. Once you try something you like —even in someone else's dining room—there's no need to wait to have it again. I was thinking of doing so as soon as tomorrow, but if you don't like it, I can wait for a day where you're otherwise occupied."

"It hardly concerns *me*," she stammered, leaning away from him.

*Had the pickled onions turned his breath sour?*

Stephen mimicked her, leaning back to not blow foul air into her beautiful face. "Very well. Perhaps Benjamin will join me."

"You're going to introduce Benjamin so soon?"

Stephen frowned. "You act as if there's some sort of waiting period with these things, but unless societal rules have markedly changed in my absence, I don't see any point in *waiting*. Once I've decided I like something, I aim to figure out if I want to add it to my regular rotation."

"Your *rotation*?" Vera's mouth dropped open; color rose in her cheeks.

Stephen's forehead creased. "Every lord of a manor has his preferences. It shouldn't be a shocking assertion in the least."

"What about commitment? What about love?"

Stephen frowned and eyed her wineglass, wondering how many glasses she'd had. He knew she felt things keenly, but this was a bit much. "Those are strong words to use for—"

"I think they're *appropriate* words," she snapped.

"Why on earth does this bother you? I assure you— Mrs. Portence doesn't mind—"

"Mrs. Portence?" Vera hissed, her eyebrows flying upward. "*Mrs. Portence?*"

"Vera, calm down. Just because I like something, doesn't mean I expect *you* to partake. Everyone likes different things. Everyone likes *variety*—"

He was cut off when he was forced to lean back to let a footman place a bowl of soup before him. Stephen was momentarily distracted by the relief he felt when he saw it was a normal-sized portion.

Vera whispered, "Temperance and steadfastness are important characteristics in a man."

"You certainly don't have to *join* me," he replied, flummoxed. "Though I think if you just *tried* it—"

"Certainly not!"

Stephen doubted Vera could have looked any more shocked if he'd suggested she wore a bedpan as a hat. He was stunned dumb by the anger flashing in her eyes.

She leaned forward and bared her teeth, hissing, "This conversation is *over*. I don't want to hear anything further on the subject. Frankly, you've disgusted me."

*Dear heavens, the lady must be drunk.*

Stephen had known some gentlemen of this sort in his youth—the kind who had a drink too many and became enraged at the world for no reason—but he hadn't thought Vera the type. He quickly ran through the recipe for a tonic to ease the effects of overindulgence—one that had been very popular during his college years at Eton.

"I think you'll feel much better about things in the morning," he finally said.

Stephen was embarrassed for her, but part of adulthood was knowing how much one could imbibe before turning into a blathering imbecile. He'd had to learn that lesson himself, more than once.

"I doubt my opinion on the matter will ever materially change."

"We'll just wait and see."

## CHAPTER 20 - VERA

Vera woke the next morning feeling sick to her stomach. She blinked up at the canopy for a few moments, praying that the memory of what had transpired the night before would fade, that it had been some sort of nightmare.

But it wasn't. It had truly happened. Vera groaned.

The dinner party had started well enough. Vera thought she looked nice in her blue-grey gown. She'd taken extra care with her hair, having a maid curl several long pieces to drape against the bare skin at her neck and decolletage.

Of course, her opinion of herself took a direct hit when she glimpsed Dahlia Warrington in that stunning aubergine dress. It had a daringly wide neckline that just exposed the tips of her shoulders and all of her long, alabaster neck. Next to her pale perfection, Vera couldn't help but notice that she'd grown quite tan—probably from all the time riding in an open cart on the way to medical calls.

Delicate purple beading along Dahlia's bodice shimmered in the candlelight, drawing every eye toward her. Her shining blonde hair was swept into a complicated arrangement that would have impressed even Hortense, and several dyed feathers were tucked in amongst the golden curls and braids.

Dahlia had dressed as if she were meeting the king in London instead of attending a dinner party among friends in the countryside. Then again, Dahlia always looked as if she were ready to meet royalty. It was almost too unfair, that a lady as naturally beautiful as Dahlia Warrington also possessed such a knack for dressing herself.

Dahlia's large blue eyes were fringed in thick, dark lashes that contrasted perfectly with her honey-golden hair. Her eyebrows were combed and waxed; her full lips perfectly showcasing her cupid's bow beneath a delicate, straight nose. She was flawless, the pinnacle of everything a young English lady should be.

Vera stifled the urge to squirm in discomfort. She knew very well that Dahlia outshone every other lady in the room, but why should she care? Vera was used to being on the sidelines of things. She'd spent many a miserable hour pressed against the wall of a ballroom, praying that her drab, bulky gown would disguise her as one of the pillars. Even then, she hadn't been bothered as much as she was now.

*I've never been tempted to hate anyone for being beau-*

*tiful before,* Vera thought when Stephen was introduced to the lovely young woman. *I certainly shouldn't start now.*

They were seated; the first course served. Vera admired the stunning tablescape. If the marchioness had no hand in it, she should definitely commend her staff for rising to the occasion.

The china was ivory, lined in gold dots. The crystal goblets sparkled in the candlelight thrown by the chandeliers above and the silver candelabras on the table. Low silver bowls held stunning arrangements of flowers that spilled over their edges to kiss the fine lace tablecloth.

The first course was a beautiful amuse-bouche, as had become the fashion adopted from the French. Vera examined the layers carefully—a delicate shaving of roast beef atop a slice of roasted beet and some cream-based sauce. Pickled onions dusted the top.

*Interesting,* she thought, before carefully cutting the tiny square in two.

Though amuse-bouche was supposed to be a single bite, it wasn't proper for a lady to ever have a full mouth. Vera refrained from rolling her eyes when she glimpsed Stephen spear the entire thing with his fork and eat it in one go.

On his other side, Miss Warrington was being her typical charming self. Vera ignored the sad little flip of her stomach and did her best to contribute to the other conversation at the table. She tried not to notice how very *interested* Dahlia sounded when speaking to Stephen. He chatted with her, and why wouldn't he be interested right back?

Why, at one point, Stephen had been so overcome with Miss Warrington's beauty that he'd completely lost the thread of conversation! He'd been struck dumb by the loveliness of her face paired with those charming feathers she'd pinned in her hair.

Had she been alone, Vera would have put her face into her hands and groaned.

But then Vera's suspicions were confirmed when Dahlia all but outright asked him to accompany her—*alone*—to the garden folly, which the lady had already seen. There was only one reason a lady like that would ask for male company—she was *interested*.

Vera felt a sharp pinch somewhere in the vicinity of her chest, though she did her best to convince herself that it was her stomach, nothing more. She frowned. Perhaps beets didn't agree with her.

But then—*calamity*. Vera pressed her hand to her head, remembering that terrible conversation.

Stephen wasn't at all who he thought he was. He was a degenerate knave with no honor at all! Vera remembered all the times she'd been alone with him and wondered that he hadn't attempted anything untoward. If he were trying to put Dahlia Warrington into his "rotation," as he called it, why hadn't he been improper with *Vera*? She was far less protected than Dahlia was; far less desired, too. The only explanation for it was that Stephen wasn't interested in Vera at all—not even as a matter of convenience.

Vera flopped her covers back and shoved her feet into quilted slippers, then grabbed her velvet dressing gown and threw it on. Winter was creeping ever closer, there was no doubt of it. The chill of the mornings afflicted the large house, only chased away by the fires the maids woke early to light. Thankfully, there was one already burning in her fireplace. Vera sat close to it, staring into the flames.

Even now, even though Stephen himself had said such things directly to her, she didn't quite believe it could be true. She'd never been so wrong about someone, not ever.

Vera had thought he was a good man. Brusque sometimes, but that was perhaps to be expected, given his profession. He treated his mother with affectionate respect, his brother with care and kindness. Even though Vera and Stephen had certainly started off on the wrong side of things, relationally speaking, there had been a marked shift as of late.

Vera enjoyed working with him. She respected him, admired how tactful and competent he was as a physician. They were friends, and if Vera were being honest with herself, there was a small voice inside her that had started to whisper that they might someday be *more*.

Now, that part of her was crying.

How could a man who showed so much restraint and intelligence in his work be so debauched and cruel in his private life? One moment they were enjoying the food and the wine, and the next he was stomping everything she thought she'd known about him to pulp.

*The wine.* Vera sat up straight. They'd been drinking!

Of course that was it—the man had been drunk! He'd been *so* drunk that he'd made a highly inappropriate joke that hadn't been at *all* funny. Vera knew how witty her brothers fancied themselves when they were too deep in their cups. Granted, most men of her acquaintance had long grown out of such a phase.

Vera felt relieved that she'd arrived at the truth of the matter. Stephen hadn't meant a single word he'd said. In fact, he was probably in the privy right now, casting up his regrets of the night before. Doubtless, when they had a moment alone, he'd apologize for his awful, untrue joke. He'd beg her forgiveness, and all would be mended.

Of course, Vera's realization did little to dampen her ire. Too much wine was no excuse for behaving in such a manner—for saying such things! Even her brothers had never gone *that* far with their joking—at least not in her presence. Though there *had* been a great deal more flatulence, but that was another thing, altogether.

Stephen was most likely mortified. He'd beg her forgiveness. She wondered how long she ought to hold on to her anger for this terrible offense. A week ought to be sufficient. Four days at the very least. For she *was* quite hurt by the entire thing—she was a lady, and he shouldn't forget that, no matter how close they'd recently become.

Vera wondered what lengths Stephen would go to, to make amends. Would he bring her flowers? Would he bring her a gift of some kind? Perhaps he would get down on his knees and beg for her pardon. Here, she slipped into a little daydream before she shook herself out of it. Whatever he decided was worthy recompense, she would be magnanimous, but firm.

Thus bolstered, Vera got ready and went down for breakfast.

## CHAPTER 21 - STEPHEN

The next couple of days were very trying for Stephen's patience. It was like he and Vera had gone back to the beginning of things. Every time he entered a room, Vera left it. When they shared a meal, she sat as far from him as she could manage. She ignored him completely, except for when he caught her scowling at him for no reason at all.

At first, he thought she was embarrassed at her own behavior and didn't want his presence as a reminder of it. He was the only one who'd heard her ridiculous outburst, after all.

Stephen was willing to give her a bit of distance. He thought she'd find him and apologize for her unreasonable behavior when she was ready. Then perhaps they'd have a slightly awkward conversation about knowing one's limits while drinking wine, and that would be the end of it.

But time and his gentle patience did little to mend things. In fact, the longer he gave her to process her own feelings, the angrier she seemed to become. She fairly snarled at him when he'd politely asked for the salt at the breakfast table the second day.

She even had the temerity to turn her back to him while he was speaking, in front of Mr. Douglas, that afternoon.

"What on earth did you do?" the old man asked, grinning. "I didn't think anything could make Vera that angry."

"Nevermind," Stephen had said, and Mr. Douglas laughed.

Stephen would have been far more embarrassed to admit that he had no real idea *what* he'd done, especially when the man looked positively delighted at this turn of events.

In the end, Mrs. Portence *did* make the sandwich—she'd gone so far as to write the marquess's cook and request the recipe—but though it was as delicious as he remembered, he enjoyed it little, remembering that it had been the start of the strange rift between him and Vera.

Mid-morning on the third day, he'd had quite enough. He waited until Benjamin and his mother left for a ride, then cornered Vera in the library. She was sitting in her customary perch upon a leather sofa. Her eyes went wide and darted toward the door when she noticed him looming before her.

"Are you ready to speak with me yet?" he said.

"No."

Stephen sighed. "Vera, this has to stop. I know you're angry with me, but we have to live together. We have to *work* together. And frankly, I think this whole thing is quite ridiculous."

She stiffened, her chin lifted. "That's possibly the worst part—that you don't see anything wrong with it. I gave you time to apologize, and you haven't."

"Why on earth should *I* apologize?" He reared back in surprise.

"I thought perhaps you'd been drinking too much," Vera plowed on. "I thought that perhaps you'd made a terribly off-color joke that you'd regret in the morning."

"I thought the same of you—that perhaps *you'd* had too much."

She narrowed her eyes. "Oh, I assure you—I was perfectly sober—"

"So was I!" He flopped his hands in the air.

"—I meant every word I said. The fact that you see *nothing wrong* with your...your desire for *variety*..." She spit the last word as if it were a foul thing.

Her chest heaved. Stephen had never been more perplexed in all his life. On one hand, Vera had never looked more beautiful. Her anger lent a lovely clarity to her eyes, an animation to her stunning face. Her cheeks were flushed, and every golden freckle stood in stark relief to her luminous skin.

But no matter how gorgeous she was in the moment, she was acting like a crazy person. No matter how he felt for her, he wouldn't consign himself to a lifetime of living through random tirades such as this one.

Vera took advantage of his stunned silence and continued. "I've barely been able to look Mrs. Portence in the eye since you told me."

"I hardly think it's *her* fault." Stephen frowned. "She's just performing the duties Mother hired her to do."

"Your mother *knows*?" Vera's mouth gaped.

"Of course! Mrs. Portence has worked here for nigh on fifteen years. She did the same for my father, when he was lord, and probably for my mother, too, when I was away."

Vera appeared to be choking against a sudden bout of tears. Stephen hated the sight, no matter that this whole thing was outrageous and completely of Vera's own design.

"Look, I don't know how things were done in your household growing up—"

"Certainly not like this," she snapped.

"—but if you don't like a meal, you certainly don't have to eat it. Mrs. Portence will be happy to make you something else."

She reared back. "What?"

"It doesn't matter to me if you didn't like the amuse-bouche, but I shouldn't be punished because I *did*. We don't need to enjoy all of the same foods to get along, Vera, and it's quite controlling of you not to allow for a difference in our tastes."

"*What?*" Her hands dropped, her mouth gaped, her shoulders went back as if bracing from a shock.

"The amuse-bouche! I liked it. You didn't. Why on earth is that such a big deal to you?"

"You were talking about the *food*?"

"Of course!" Stephen's head drew back. "What on earth were *you* talking about?"

"Miss Warrington. And...and other ladies." She snapped her mouth shut, as if she hadn't intended on saying the words.

"*What on earth does Miss Warrington have to do with roasted beets?*" he fairly bellowed.

Vera covered her face and her shoulders began to shake.

"Oh dear." Stephen ran a hand through his hair. The other fluttered next to her shoulder then dropped to his side. "I'm very sorry I yelled. I'm exceedingly frustrated, but that's simply no excuse."

"You were talking about the *food*," she sniffled.

"I'm very confused," he admitted. "Were you upset because Miss Warrington liked the dish? And I did too, and you felt...left out, somehow?"

Vera just cried harder. He was trying to sort through the puzzle carefully, trying to slot things back into place as if someone had upended his medical bag.

He lay a hand on her shoulder. "I assure you, Vera, I don't mind in the least if you don't care for beets."

## CHAPTER 22 - VERA

Midmorning the next day, they were heading home from Mr. Douglas's. It had been a quicker visit than usual—Mr. Douglas had mostly slept, even when Stephen listened to his lungs and heart with that stethoscope device of his.

Today they'd taken the carriage. It was raining, and Stephen informed her that they'd be taking it more often because of the weather. Drops pelted the roof—Vera felt as if they sat in the bottom of a drum, with a giant tapping his fingers above them.

"So what did you think of Dahlia?" she blurted.

"Miss Warrington?" Stephen tilted his head, frowned. "Why are you asking me about Miss Warrington?"

"I thought she was very kind."

Of course she didn't have the courage to ask the question she really wanted to, so she'd come at the subject sideways. Internally, she shook her head at herself. Even after they'd resolved their misunderstanding the day before,

Vera desperately wanted to know if Stephen had noticed how exceptionally pretty Dahlia was. She was the type of lady a man would look at and think, *she'd make a fine baroness*.

"She was pleasant enough, but I thought you'd met her before."

"Well, yes. I have." Vera bothered the trim on the edge of her cloak and avoided his eyes.

"If your opinion of the lady is set, it hardly matters what *I* think of her." He stretched his long legs into the space between them, crossed them at the ankles, and folded his arms over his chest.

Vera recognized the posture—it meant he was thinking of having a little nap. On the tail of the thought was the realization that she knew him well enough to recognize his habits.

"I was making conversation, is all. It's what people do on carriage journeys."

His eyes were already closed; he arched an eyebrow. "More small talk? No, thank you. I've already had quite enough after that dinner the other night."

There it was—he didn't think of Vera as a regular young lady. Why would he? He'd made the effort to be pleasant over dinner for the people he didn't know well, but now he and Vera were alone and he'd rather not speak at all.

Vera set her features into a mulish expression. "Very well—we may be silent. You know, I've never known a man your age to sleep quite as much as you do. Perhaps it's *you* who should call a physician."

Stephen cracked an eye. "Excuse me?"

"You sleep more than my Great Uncle Bertrand used to, and he was nigh on eighty before he passed. Bumbling Bertie, my brothers used to call him, behind his back."

Both Stephen's eyes were open now and fixed upon her, but Vera pretended not to notice.

She looked out the window instead. "He used to sit in front of the fire all day and night, with a little knitted blanket tucked over his knees."

"As a physician, I learned quickly to get sleep wherever I can."

"Have you ever noticed that whenever someone points out a quirk of your personality, you blame it on being a physician?" she said archly.

He stared at her; she couldn't read his expression. It wasn't energetic enough to be called exasperation, but it might be a duller distant cousin of the emotion.

She continued, "Bertie blamed all *his* quirks on his age. He used to sit just like you're doing now. Perhaps I will knit you a blanket to tuck over your knees."

Stephen closed his eyes and settled further down against the seat. "A knitted blanket would be lovely. I'd like it in green, if you don't mind."

"Whatever you like, Bertie."

There had been a new sense of ease between Vera and Stephen the last few days. It was as if by settling their strange misunderstanding, the final piece of their friendship had been slotted properly into place. She felt more comfortable in his presence than she ever had before.

Vera had never experienced that with an unmarried man before—it was a novelty. With every other man of her acquaintance, she'd sorted them into two distinct categories—attached, and therefore easy to be around—or unattached. The unattached ones were difficult, as Vera was always aware of the fact that they were options for marriage, and she knew that *they* were aware of it, too.

Vera never wanted single men to feel as if she might have ulterior motives for speaking with them—as if she might be trying to coax them into matrimony. She'd once overheard the Marquess of Salisbury liken the feeling to a fox being pursued by hounds. Vera never wanted to act like a dog. Yet a distinctly canine growl threatened to build in her chest when she lingered on thoughts of Dahlia and Stephen too long.

Though she now understood that the man had been thinking of the amuse-bouche that evening at dinner—thank goodness—there was no mistaking the interest that had lit the young lady's eyes when she'd looked at the baron.

The worst part was that Vera couldn't blame her. Stephen was intelligent, handsome, and, once you got past the exterior gruffness, very kind. He cared for his family, his estate, and those who depended upon him for their well-being. He was titled, eligible, and possessed a remarkably fine set of teeth.

Miss Dahlia Warrington could do far worse. Vera nibbled her bottom lip with her teeth, concerned at the emotions roiling in her stomach. Truth was, if Dahlia cast her interested glance upon Stephen, she was sure to succeed. The only reason the man hadn't noticed her properly the night of the dinner party was because he'd been thinking of roast beef.

Typical of him, perhaps, but Vera could hardly expect his distraction to continue. Not when Dahlia was so pretty, so charming. Not when they'd surely meet again. So Vera was relieved when an invitation *did* arrive and it was only for her.

Though it was Candace who'd invited Vera, the tea party was held in a windowed, second-story room at Devon Manor.

"My husband has become quite insufferable," Adelaide said, easing herself slowly into a chair. Her tone and her smile negated any sting in her words. "He won't let me out of the house. In fact, he's probably lingering just outside of hearing distance as we speak."

"I've suggested she make a game of it." Dahlia leaned forward to pour tea on behalf of her sister. "That she should call for him and time his response with the mantle clock."

Candace selected a tiny scone from the tiered server. "Be careful in playing games with my brother, Dahlia. He has no qualms about playing them back. I speak from experience."

"A pity it's far too cold to be in the gardens," Adelaide said. "They're still so lovely, even though all the blooms have gone."

"The grounds are beautiful," Dahlia agreed. "I'm so glad I came in time to explore them while the weather was still nice."

"Percy and I can't claim any credit for how wonderful the view is—that's all thanks to Candace."

"Vera helped," Candace said.

"Hardly." Vera smiled. "You're only being charitable. It's true I planted some bulbs, once, but past that one small tuft of tulips, I can't share in any accolades at all."

"The tulips were stunning." Adelaide's eyes were wide with sincerity. "Simply lovely."

Vera nodded her thanks as Candace hid a smile behind her gold-rimmed teacup. "Have you refurbished the nursery yet?"

Adelaide looked heavenwards as Dahlia snickered. "Percy has taken management of that room firmly in hand. He won't let me so much as adjust the arrangement of the room without his assistance."

"You were trying to move the bassinet from one side of the room to the other." Dahlia shook her head. "Even I thought it was foolhardy."

"I'm with child, not an invalid."

"It's probably for the best," Candace said. "Percy is always better behaved if he has a project. The last project he took on was wooing you."

Dahlia grinned. "Indeed. The nursery is just a reasonable byproduct of those efforts, so it's understandable that he feels some ownership over that as well."

"I suppose I should be shocked that my unmarried sister speaks candidly about such things."

"I may live in the city now, but I grew up on a farm."

"How was London when you left it?" Candace asked, her green eyes round and guileless. "Have you seen any mutual friends lately? Daisy Knope, perhaps?"

Dahlia's smile widened. "She's been markedly engaged in the social whirl. Rumor has it she's planning a grand voyage to America at the end of the year in search of a wealthy husband. Apparently gentlemen there aren't as finicky about broken engagements."

"Gentlemen there aren't even gentlemen," Adelaide said.

Dahlia canted her head. "I'm not sure it's such a bad idea. I think more young ladies might have a chance at happiness if they were willing to take such a trip."

Adelaide blinked. "Certainly you aren't considering such measures."

Candace laughed. "Why on earth would she need to? She's had—how many proposals by this point?"

Dahlia sniffed. "It would be gauche to keep count."

"A baker's dozen, last I'd heard."

"It hardly matters, as none of them were proposals worth accepting."

"What are you looking for in a husband?" Candace tilted her head.

"She has a *list*." Adelaide wagged her eyebrows.

"I hardly think that's any of your business, as it's *my* list."

Adelaide's eyes narrowed. "One wonders what could be on the list, if Lord Stanley didn't make the cut. He's wealthy, titled, and very handsome."

Candace tilted her head. "Perhaps a full head of hair is on her list."

Dahlia turned to Vera, shaking her head. "Do you see why I find reason to escape this house and go riding every day?"

Vera smiled. "Where do you ride?"

"There's a lovely path out to the garden folly; I usually find myself there."

Vera frowned. "Oh? I thought you wished to wait and view the garden folly with the baron."

"Oh, not at all," Dahlia waved her hand gracefully. "I was only testing a running theory of the household. It proved quite correct."

"Theory? What theory?" Vera looked around the table, trying to meet the other ladies' eyes. Unfortunately, they'd found other places to look at the moment. Candace inspected her teacup, a little frown upon her lips. Adelaide was gazing at the chandelier, her cheeks pink.

"What theory?" Vera demanded.

Dahlia sighed and shook her head. "Honestly, you two." She turned to Vera with a gentle smile. "About you and the baron, of course."

"What of him?"

"These two pea-hens have a wager going on whether you'll be married by Christmas."

Vera felt heat crawling up her neck and suffusing her cheeks. "You can't be serious."

Candace plunked her teacup into the saucer, her eyes wide. "We're not *betting* on it. There are no *stakes*."

"But you're talking about it?" Vera shook her head. "The entire thing...it's preposterous."

"Is it, though?" Adelaide inspected her over the rim of her teacup. "You two are very close."

"We *work* together."

Vera felt a yawning pit open within her stomach. She'd never thought that Candace and Adelaide would be so cruel. Of course such a rumor would mean nothing to *them* were it to get out—they were both happily settled. *Richly* settled.

But Vera had to make her own way. If people began to whisper about what was going on between her and Stephen—and there wasn't *anything* going on, no matter how she wished the opposite—then she might be cast out of this job, cast out of the baron's *house* before she could so much as earn a reference. Then where would she be? Homeless, jobless, with no prospects.

"Vera, dear." Candace was studying her, a little crease of concern lodged between her eyebrows. "What's the matter?"

"I'm sure this has been an enjoyable pastime for you all, but there is nothing untoward occurring between me and the baron."

"Of course not—" Candace said.

"And forgive me for saying so, but you should remember how damaging such a rumor could be."

"We'd never tell anyone—" Candace began again.

"You told *her*." Vera jerked her chin down in Dahlia's direction.

Vera knew she was now the one being rude, but she couldn't help herself—she felt tears burning behind her eyes.

So typical of married women to make light of the single state. So typical of them to sip their tea in their comfortable sitting rooms and titter about it, to go so far as to make a *wager* on it.

She'd thought that Candace would be different, that she wouldn't so quickly forget the feelings of uncertainty, of trying to navigate society's tightrope in the fine balance between snobbery and propriety. Apparently she was like all the others—the moment someone slipped a ring onto their finger, she *forgot*.

"Oh, Vera. I'm so sorry—" Candace began.

Vera saw open compassion on the faces of Adelaide and Candace; Dahlia looked cautious. She was ashamed to feel wetness in her eyes. Vera stood abruptly, jostling the table so that the china rattled right along with her nerves.

"It's I who must apologize," she said. "If you'll excuse me; I'm not feeling well."

Vera walked briskly out of the room and straight out the front door, not bothering to request the carriage. She set off down the driveway, the crunch of the gravel beneath her boots sounding almost as quickly as the beating of her heart.

Vera knew she'd made a fool of herself in there; she

knew she wouldn't be invited back, but she couldn't help it.

Candace had hurt her. Vera had felt mocked, belittled. The fact that Candace had been discussing her private business with Dahlia only added more disinfectant to the cut. Dahlia, who'd haunted her thoughts. *Dahlia*, whose beauty mocked Vera in her dreams.

Vera had sincerely believed that Dahlia Warrington was interested in Stephen. She'd ruminated over those smiles, those glances, for well over a week. She'd braced herself against the inevitable—that once Stephen realized he could have Dahlia Warrington, he'd never look at Vera again.

Vera had gone so far as to imagine their wedding! She'd practiced her smile in the dark of her bedroom; she'd greeted the newly married couple with joy and grace. She'd thrown rice with a smile upon her lips.

To find out it had all been some sort of test, some sort of cruel *joke*—it was difficult to bear. Vera felt small, humiliated. She told herself that none of the ladies in that house could possibly understand her situation.

*Because you haven't been honest about it*, a small voice within her whispered. *Perhaps if you'd told Candace from the beginning—*

Vera shook the thought off and walked faster to outpace the reasonable sentiment. If Vera had told Candace that she'd been disowned, her friend would have felt sorry for her. She would have tried to fix things. Candace had already done too much for her, by Vera's accounting.

*It's your own foolish pride that's caused this whole mess.*

Vera stopped in the center of the lane, arrested by the realization.

Vera *should* have told her the truth of things. If she had, if Candace knew the full ramifications, the true *stakes* involved in the matter, she never would have made light of it. Vera could hardly blame her for misunderstanding the situation when Vera had worked so hard to keep the truth of it from her.

Her shoulders sagged. She was only a bit down the lane from Devon Manor; she could still see the roses covering the front of the house. Perhaps she should turn back and apologize. It would be humiliating, but far less so than the scene she'd just caused. What use was there in holding on to pride when it was false?

As Vera dithered in the lane, a carriage emerged from the driveway and headed her direction. It pulled to a stop before her, and the door was opened.

"Vera." Candace stuck her head out, even as a footman hurried to let down the stairs. "Will you please speak with me?"

She nodded.

Once inside, the door closed, the carriage rocking slightly as it headed onward toward Bertforth House, Vera bit her lip. She didn't know how to begin.

"I'm so sorry—" Vera began, right as Candace blurted, "I apologize—"

They shared an uncomfortable kind of smile.

"Truly, Vera," Candace said. "I'm so sorry I hurt you. I certainly didn't mean to, but I understand that it must have felt as if we were laughing at you. That isn't the case in the least."

Vera shook her head, mortified to feel tears pinching at the corners of her eyes once more. "It isn't your fault. I...I fear I haven't been honest with you."

Vera proceeded to tell Candace the entire sordid tale, beginning with her climbing down the elm tree all those months ago in London.

Halfway through, the carriage had jostled to a stop and the door was opened.

"Absolutely not," Candace said, her wide eyes never leaving Vera's face. "Take us for a short drive until I tell you to stop."

"Your Grace." The footman bowed and relayed her instructions; moments later they were off, and weren't disturbed again.

"No *wonder* you were upset with me," Candace said when Vera finished speaking. She leaned back against the padded seat. "I assure you, Vera—I had no idea and I meant no harm. I didn't know you'd taken the position from *necessity*; I thought you'd done it as a lark."

"I don't blame you. I'm sorry I didn't tell you the truth."

"But why did you not come to *me*?" Candace asked, perplexed.

Vera lifted her chin. "I don't want charity. You've already been too generous."

"Not for charity. For a *reference*. You were my companion for *months*. It matters not that the position was unpaid, that you did it out of friendship. You still travelled with me, lived with me, kept my spirits up. Surely you know that not every reference must be a *professional* one."

Vera blinked. She hadn't known that, actually. She'd certainly wondered how people started, since no one was born with references.

"If you don't wish to work for Baron Winthrop any longer, I'm happy to provide you with a glowing reference. I'm certain James would do the same. With a reference from the Duke of Canterbury, you could be happily settled in a position anywhere."

Vera swallowed back her shock. She hadn't thought of asking Candace for a reference, but that now seemed very foolish, indeed.

Candace frowned. "Though I must admit I'd much rather you just make our home your own. And if it's too much of a bother to live with us—though that's what I'd prefer—you must know that James has several houses. You could make a tour of them, if you wanted, check that they're all being run well in our absence."

It was thrilling and depressing, all at once. Vera suddenly had options, where only moments ago, she'd felt she had none. At the outset of her bargain with Stephen, she'd told herself she had no choice.

Somehow along the way, that sentiment had faded, replaced by a feeling of purpose. Vera liked helping him with patients. She found fulfillment in making people feel better. There was a sense of accomplishment and joy in it, even when she had to rinse her boots off at the hand pump.

"What a boorish knave." Candace frowned at the

passing foliage out the open window. "I have half a mind to set Seamus on him for how he treated you."

"It was all a terrible misunderstanding at the outset. Though Stephen acted beastly, he's apologized several times and his actions prove his sincerity. I assure you, things are much different now."

"They must be." Candace arched her eyebrow. "'Stephen,' indeed."

"It isn't like *that*."

"I truly think you believe that, which is going to make this all the more enjoyable to watch."

"Candace, *really*. If there were something of the sort between us, do you think I would have felt so jealous toward Miss Warrington?"

"Of course you would. It's the manner of things, before one is fully settled. Why, before James and I had an understanding, there were several times where I thought of drowning you in the well."

"*What?*"

Vera didn't know what shocked her more—the violence of the imagery, or that Candace could ever have been insecure where the duke was concerned. The man had followed her out to the countryside not two days after she left London—how could Candace not have seen how he felt?

"I suppose I should apologize for it now, but at the time, I thought it was *you* he was after. Very inconvenient, those feelings, as I adore you. I assure you, Vera," she added solemnly, "I would have found a way to be happy for the two of you, even if it took my entire life."

"This is a ridiculous conversation. You and James were made for one another."

"It's always more difficult to see such things from the inside, I think."

"It hardly matters now. You're happily settled."

Vera found it very easy to smile at her friend now. The momentary anger, those feelings of betrayal—those were gone, washed away by honesty and understanding.

Candace met her eyes, her expression solemn. "Vera, no matter what happens with your current situation, I hope you know that you are always more than welcome with me and James."

Vera nodded her thanks. She *was* grateful. She just still couldn't help but wish that she didn't have to be.

## CHAPTER 23- VERA

When Vera came down to dinner several nights later, there was an odd current in the room. She paused upon the threshold, her eyes narrowing slightly. Benjamin shifted in his chair, refusing to meet her eyes. She wondered if he'd snuck a lizard into his trouser pocket again, or perhaps he had Sheldon clasped to his chest beneath his shirt.

But that didn't explain why the baroness had a pleased lilt of a smile on her face. *Smug*—that was the word for how Jacqueline looked. Vera's gaze swept the table. Everything appeared much the same as any other night—the plain stoneware service that the baroness preferred when it was just family, as Benjamin and china were a combustible mixture—though the only empty chair was the one right next to Stephen.

As for him, Stephen looked...nervous. Which made *Vera* nervous. She scanned the room again. Perhaps she'd interrupted an awkward family conversation.

Yes, that must be it. For there was no other reason she could think of that would produce this strange tableau of expressions.

"Good evening," she finally said.

Stephen stood from his chair with alacrity. "Good evening, Vera."

Benjamin began to giggle. He clasped his hand over his mouth. His mother shot him a quelling glance that did little good.

"What on earth is going on here?" She paused, her eyes warily travelling across the tabletop again.

Had Benjamin put a small creature upon her chair? If so, why were the two adults acting very nearly as strange as the child?

"Nothing," Stephen replied, just a bit too quickly to be convincing. "Here, come have a seat."

He gestured at the chair next to him. Vera rounded the table and stopped with a gasp. Her eyes went wide at the large, lidded picnic hamper atop her chair. The *moving* picnic hamper.

As she stared, a distinct, high-pitched whimper rose from the basket.

"Is that..."

"Please open it. I think she's frightened of the dark."

Vera rushed to flip the lid back; she gasped. A puppy stared up at her with soft brown eyes. Her coat was a beautiful black with tiger stripes of reddish fawn. Vera bent and lifted the puppy from the basket, noting the pale pink ribbon tied in a bow at her neck.

Vera grunted under the puppy's solid weight. "She's huge."

"It's Seamus's daughter; of course she's huge. Happy birthday, Vera."

"I don't understand." Vera's words were momentarily muffled by a pink tongue licking at her chin. "My birthday was weeks ago."

Stephen frowned. "You can hardly fault me that your present wasn't finished on time. I wasn't the one in charge of making it."

Vera laughed; the puppy snapped playfully at one of her dangling curls. "Thank you, Stephen. She's wonderful. Does she have a name?"

"Not yet."

Vera frowned suddenly. She'd never heard of a governess who brought a dog with her. What would happen when she got a position elsewhere?

"But..." she started.

She looked to the baroness for support. Jacqueline was a supremely practical woman—surely she'd sussed out the problem with this arrangement already. The baroness was studiously ignoring her, going so far as to examine the chandelier to avoid Vera's eyes.

"I cannot possibly accept," Vera finally said.

"Whyever not? Do you not like her?"

"Don't be daft. She's *gorgeous,* but I can't take her with me when I go."

Jacqueline gave a delicate cough, then quelled the tickle in her throat with a sip of water, still avoiding Vera's eyes. When Vera looked back to Stephen, he was frowning.

"She'll always have a home here."

Vera couldn't read his expression, but his tone was grave, as if he were making a solemn oath.

Vera smiled. "Thank you."

"I thought we'd call her Miss Beets."

"Miss Beets?" His mother wrinkled her nose even as Vera's eyes went wide and her cheeks flushed. "What an odd name for a dog. Besides, it's traditionally the owner who gets to choose, and you've given the dog to Vera. I think it ought to be her decision, don't you?"

"Yes, of course," Stephen turned to Vera; he appeared to barely be able to keep a straight face. "My apologies, Vera. What would you like to name her?"

Benjamin leaned forward, his eyes bright. "I would name her Pickles."

Vera laughed and looked at Stephen. "I like Miss Beets."

VERA HAD SLEPT LATE, owing to her new roommate, Miss Beets. Though she'd insisted that the puppy sleep in her room, the poor thing had cried piteously from its basket half the night. Vera thought that perhaps the dog's distress was a warning of impending bathroom needs— during that time, she and the pup made several sojourns to the cold back garden. Vera, bleary-eyed and wrapped in her robe, started to suspect that the puppy hadn't been intended as a gift at all but was some sort of recompense for a perceived slight.

At one in the morning, Vera finally pulled the large puppy onto her bedcovers, desperate for sleep. Miss Beets briefly snuffled her cheek, turned several times upon the blankets, and curled into a warm ball. The puppy's sigh a moment later as much as said, *Finally.* They both slept quite soundly until the puppy placed a subtle paw on Vera's forehead at eight o'clock.

It followed then, that Stephen and Vera arrived at Mr. Douglas's house later than usual. Stephen frowned up at the house and leapt down from the carriage.

"Stay here," he said, trying to shut the carriage door on Vera.

"Why?"

He was already striding for the front door. He knocked, then entered, closing it behind him. Vera searched the house's facade, wondering what on earth had made Stephen act as he had.

*There's no smoke from the chimney*, she thought.

The implications dashed over her like a bucket of cold water, and she was running for the front door before she realized she'd exited the carriage.

*Anne,* she thought. *Mr. Douglas.*

She didn't know who she was more concerned for—the small girl or the elderly man. *But he'd been doing so well.*

Stephen was climbing back down the stairs, a large bundle in his arms, by the time she stood in the front doorway. Vera could see her own breath in the cottage.

Vera's chest kept ratcheting tighter and tighter, then the bundle moved and Anne peeked out at her from beneath a thick blanket.

Vera wanted to collapse with her relief, but she was afraid that would frighten the girl. "Mr. Douglas?" she asked.

Stephen's grim expression, the shake of his head, told her all she needed to know. "Take her to the house. Run her a bath and feed her. Get her warm."

"Come, Anne," she said, pulling the girl—blanket and all—from Stephen's arms. "You and I shall go for a little carriage ride and have some biscuits on the way."

Within minutes, Vera and Anne were heading back toward Bertforth House. Stephen had taken the two footmen back inside the house. Vera distractedly plied Anne with biscuits, trying to ignore how her throat felt like it was closing around her grief.

*Mr. Douglas, gone.*

Never again would she hear him tease her in that chiding way of his. Never again would he complain half-heartedly about the floral steam she made him inhale, about how the towel over his head was just so she could have a laugh at his expense.

Vera sniffled and swiped a tear from her cheek. She must be strong, for Anne's sake.

"Miss Vera sad?" The girl patted her cheek.

"Yes." Vera smiled through the tears that she was doing a poor job of hiding.

The girl offered up her half-gnawed biscuit, and Vera

smiled. "Thank you, but I'm full. You'd better eat that one."

Anne promptly complied while Vera murmured to her about all the things they'd do once they arrived at Bertforth House, about all the things they'd see there. She told her about her new puppy, Miss Beets, and of the hedgehog, the fox, and the raccoon that were friends.

If Anne had seen anything she shouldn't, she didn't seem all that disturbed. Vera fervently hoped that if Anne *had* seen Mr. Douglas's body after he'd departed, that the girl thought he'd only been sleeping.

"Did you and Mr. Douglas have supper last night, Anne?" she finally thought to ask.

"Yes."

"But no breakfast?"

The girl shook her head, her golden curls bouncing. "Mr. Douglas tired."

It had probably happened sometime in the night, then. Vera prayed it had been quick, that the old man hadn't suffered alone with no one to help him.

*What would become of the girl?*

Vera thought back to all those weeks ago, when Mr. Douglas had asked her to look after Anne once he was gone. If she had the means to do so, she would do it without a second thought. But as it was, the house she resided in wasn't her own. She could hardly presume to advise Stephen on the subject.

When their carriage wheels crunched upon the gravel of the driveway, the front door opened and Jacqueline stood in the doorway. She took one glance at Vera, who'd emerged from the carriage and then turned back to take Anne into her arms, and seemed to understand the situation without being told.

"Roland," Jacqueline said, "please roust the staff. Prepare the nursery. Have a bath brought up to the blue guest room in the meantime. And send a tray with soup and warm milk."

Roust the staff he did. No more than a quarter-hour later, Anne splashed happily in a copper tub that was far too large for her before a cheerful fire, a maid carefully monitoring the water depth and temperature.

"Did Stephen say what took him, then?" Jacqueline murmured over her tea.

They sat in the corner, close enough to observe the girl's bath, but far enough away that their conversation wouldn't be overheard.

"No, though I daresay he wouldn't have sent her here with me if there was any danger of contagion, if that's your concern."

"Stephen's too smart to make a mistake of that magnitude. I doubt he'd even let you handle her if that were a worry." Jacqueline tsked and shook her head once more. "The poor dear. First her parents, now Mr. Douglas."

Vera frowned. She could only see the top of Anne's head from this vantage point, but the girl's happy chattering and the sound of splashing belied her contentment.

"Do you think it's too much for her to overcome?"

"Not at all. Children are resilient, and she's at such an age where her pain may yet be overwritten. She'll need firmness, kindness, and constancy moving forward."

*But who would give it to her?* Vera wondered.

BY CHANCE, Vera happened to be coming down the stairs just as Stephen returned to the house. She took him in at a glance—the tired lines of his face, the mud upon his boots.

"How is she?" he asked, collapsing in a chair and yanking off one boot, then the other.

"She seems fine. I was about to ask the same of you."

Stephen shrugged. "Tired, mostly. And inexplicably starving."

"What happened?"

"There's no way for us to know. My best guess is he suffered an embolism during the night, or his heart simply stopped working. He appeared to go quickly, peacefully. There was no evidence that he even woke."

"That's good, then." She nodded.

It *was* good that Mr. Douglas hadn't suffered. It was a weight off her mind. So why were tears gathering on her lower lashes? Why did her hand come up to hide her wobbling chin?

"Ah, Vera. Don't cry." Stephen stood, and before Vera could quite reconcile what his intent was, he'd pulled her into his strong arms, her face cradled against the starched cotton of his shirt. "It's all right."

"Did we miss something?" She sniffed as she tried

desperately to control her hitched breathing. "Did we do something wrong?"

"Not at all." One large hand began a soothing trek up and down her spine. "Sometimes, there's nothing we can do. He was quite old; perhaps I should have listened when he said he was dying, but I didn't think it was more serious than a very stubborn cold."

"I just keep thinking that maybe if we'd gone yesterday…" Here, her voice warbled and she couldn't continue.

"It doesn't work like that, Vera. What took him—it would have happened, even if you had been sitting at his bedside."

That warm hand continued its slow path up and down her back. It was a soothing comfort, to be held in strong arms. Vera felt safe there. It didn't hurt that she couldn't help breathing in the scent of him. Soap, medical disinfectant, and a whiff of cedar—probably from the lining of his wardrobe.

They stood there in a comfortable silence. Vera couldn't remember the last time she'd shared a hug of this length with anyone. There was something uniquely restorative about it—the mutual solace of shared warmth, the gentle heaving of their breaths, the shared moment of grief for Mr. Douglas.

It was more effective than any tonic she'd sipped, and far more enjoyable. This was what friends did for each other, she supposed. They held each other, consoled each other, when terrible things happened.

Except, if Vera were being perfectly honest with herself, this simple hug had the danger of meaning too much to her. Her confusing feelings lurked just behind her grief, and as the moments slipped by, they threatened to whisper dangerous ideas into her ear.

"Thank you," she said, suddenly embarrassed.

She pushed back from the embrace and Stephen let her go. Vera dared not look into his eyes until she'd stepped back a careful distance.

"I'm sorry for—" Vera began, before she realized she didn't know how to finish the sentence.

*Sorry for crying on your shirt*? There was a patch of dampness on his chest.

*Sorry for feeling things you didn't mean the hug to evoke*? She could never admit to that.

"I'll have Mrs. Portence make you a tray," she finally said lamely.

Vera gave a tremulous smile and turned her back to head to the kitchens.

## CHAPTER 24- STEPHEN

Stephen wanted to call out to Vera as he watched her go, but he was struck momentarily dumb by the depth of his feelings. Had he thought he knew what love was before? Compared to the monsoon racing through him now, what he'd felt previously was a shallow puddle.

For a moment there, with her in his arms, he'd half imagined that she felt as he did. But no—she'd pulled away, an embarrassed flush on her features. Embarrassment for *him*, Stephen had no doubt. He never should have hugged her, but at the sight of her tears, he couldn't help himself.

Surely she knew now how he felt, what he'd been poorly concealing these past weeks. It could be that he'd ruined everything by pulling her into his arms. Stephen ran a hand through his dark hair and cursed beneath his breath.

Miss Beets trotted into the room and over to him. She

sat her furry bulk upon his foot, as if she knew what he was thinking and sought to distract him from it. He bent and rubbed one of her silken ears between his fingers. Down the hall, a flicker of motion caught his eye. Clarence the fox curled beneath the sideboard, staring at them.

"I live in a madhouse," he muttered.

"What was that?" his mother asked, coming down the stairs.

"Nothing."

"Are you quite well?" She stood before him and peered up at his face.

He nodded. "Is Anne all right?"

Her eyes flicked toward the second story. "Of course. She's been fed and bathed, and now Edna and Miriam are showing her the toys in the nursery."

"Apologies for throwing the house into an uproar."

"Nonsense. It's your house."

Stephen lifted a shoulder. Though technically true, this had always been his mother's and father's house. Title or no, he still deferred to his mother.

"The poor dear. I assume you mean to keep her?"

He frowned. He *had* been thinking along those lines, but how had his mother sussed that out, before he even realized he'd come to a decision? "What makes you say that?"

"Because you had Vera bring her here. Because both of you care deeply for the girl." She smiled. "I've been listening when you speak, you know. You've spoken of Anne nearly as much as you've spoken of all your other patients combined."

"I don't know if I'm the best guardian for a small child."

"Don't be ridiculous, Stephen. At her age, you'll be her father, not her guardian. Guardians are for children who've already *had* parents; this girl hasn't."

"That's a much taller order."

"I've no doubt you're up to the task, but certainly don't take it on if you're not going to commit to it. To her."

Stephen ran a hand through his dark hair. "I need to think about it."

"Of course you do. This is hardly a decision that should be made quickly. Only, don't wait *too* long. That poor little girl deserves to be settled after all she's gone through."

THAT NIGHT, after a hectic dinner that almost made the markets of Calcutta look tame and quiet, Anne sat tucked into Vera's side on the sofa in the library.

"Ah," Vera said patiently, for perhaps the thirtieth time. She angled the book just out of reach. "Remember, don't touch the pages. Only look."

The girl frowned but retracted her hand. Only then did Vera keep reading the children's book aloud. Benjamin had long given up listening to the story in favor of half snuggling, half playing with Miss Beets in the armchair closest to the fire. Now, he dangled a thread in front of the puppy's face. She half-heartedly snapped at it before collapsing into a sleepy puddle on the boy's lap.

"I'm taking her upstairs," Vera announced, swooping the blinking girl into her arms. "Say good night to everyone, Anne."

Anne simply yawned and stared blearily at them as Stephen and Benjamin offered their good nights.

After they left, Stephen turned to his brother. "Benjamin, I need to ask you something."

"About Anne?" He sounded resigned, his lips twisted to the side.

Stephen nodded. "About Anne. What would you think about her living with us?"

He frowned and plucked at his pajamas. "I guess that's fine."

"You don't sound very sincere."

"I just... Does this mean that I have to leave right away?"

"Leave?" Stephen frowned. "Where would you go?"

"To school. Reginald Stuart's parents sent him away to school when his sister was born."

"Reginald Stuart was ill-behaved at seven, and he must now be thirteen. Tell me—did time improve him at all, in my absence?"

"Last year he trampled all the washing into the mud when he didn't get a new horse for his birthday." The boy's eyes went wide with the shock of it.

Stephen smiled. "You see? I bet his parents were counting down the days until Eton would take him off their hands. Besides, you'll go to school when you're ready, and not a moment before. Aren't you looking forward to school, someday?"

He shrugged. "Not really. I won't know anyone there."

"What about Arthur? Certainly he'll go, when he's old enough. You're nearly the same age—perhaps you'll go together."

Benjamin's eyebrows rose. "Do you think so?"

"Yes, but that's still years off, yet. Tell me—what do you think of having Anne join our family?"

"She would be my sister?"

If Stephen adopted Anne, she'd actually be the boy's niece, but Stephen thought it best to keep things as simple as possible for the sake of this conversation.

"For all intents and purposes, yes. She would live here, be raised alongside you."

Benjamin thought for a moment. "I suppose that would be fine. I won't have to share too much with her, because she's a girl."

"Probably not. But you will have to watch over her sometimes, and teach her things, because she's younger than you."

"I can teach her how to ride a horse."

He nodded. "When she's old enough."

"And Mrs. Portence will bake her a special cake for her birthday, too."

Stephen frowned. He didn't even know the girl's birthday. Mr. Douglas hadn't known it, either. Just another thing he'd have to rectify.

"I'll tell you what, Benjamin. Since we don't know when Anne's birthday is, I'll let you choose it."

"Really?" His eyes were round with the magnitude of the responsibility.

"When do you think it should be?"

Benjamin stared into the fire, stroking Miss Beet's fur distractedly. The puppy had long since fallen asleep, her little jowls quivering with her dreams.

"How about in three days?" he finally said. "That's enough time for us to get her presents. We can look forward to it and plan a party, but it's not *too* long to wait."

"I think that's a great idea. What kind of cake do you think Anne will like?"

His brother gave a sly smile. "I think she'd like a vanilla sponge cake with chocolate frosting."

Stephen laughed. "Same as you? I suppose great minds think alike. Very well—you may tell Mrs. Portence in the morning."

THREE DAYS LATER, their household gathered for an afternoon party to celebrate Anne's birthday. There were presents—chiefly toys that the nursery lacked and an entire new wardrobe from the baroness—but the guest of honor was supremely uninterested in them, choosing instead to focus on the refreshments.

Benjamin had been correct when he chose the cake. Stephen thought that the girl couldn't have shown any more enthusiasm for her slice. Though she grasped a fork in one hand, she chiefly used her other to shove bites of cake into her chocolate-smeared mouth. Every time she did, she looked surprised at the experience—her eyebrows raised, she blinked. Stephen wondered if the girl ever had a proper cake before.

"You chose her nursery maid well," Vera murmured.

"Between Hortense and Miss Beets, Anne will be very safe, indeed."

"I'm not sure that the dog is any help at the moment, but perhaps she'll grow into the role." Vera smiled over at Miss Beets, who'd fallen asleep amongst some of the discarded wrapping paper.

"Undoubtedly."

Vera chuckled and shook her head.

He studied her face. "What is it?"

"Nothing. I'm simply surprised at how much can change in such a short amount of time. It wasn't that long ago that I was swinging a fire poker at your head."

"It's been months since that happened." He shifted and frowned. "Months is plenty of time to truly get to know someone."

"Indeed. But in that moment, I never would have thought I'd be delighted to see that man adopt a child. I wouldn't have trusted a stray dog to *that* man's care."

"Pardon me, but I am the same man," Stephen said in mock outrage.

"Oh, I know. I'm only speaking of who I *thought* you

were. Upon that point, you cannot take umbrage, for you were vastly mistaken about who *I* truly was, as well."

He shook his head. "Vera, there's a part of me that wishes you'd succeeded with the fire poker in that moment. For what I did next..."

"That is well behind us. So far, in fact, that I can laugh at it now."

"Truly?" His eyebrows raised.

Vera shot him a questioning glance. "Of course. It was a comedy of errors. Granted, at the time it felt like a very *dark* comedy. But that's in the past. Things have so markedly changed that I now consider you one of my dearest friends."

Stephen smiled, though his mouth threatened to twist. *Dearest friend*. Though he hadn't spoken the word, it still managed to leave a sour taste in his mouth.

He said, slowly, "You are mine, as well."

Vera's answering smile made him feel as if he'd been sipping warm amber whisky instead of tea and cream. Then Anne made some discordant cry, and Vera and Hortense instinctively converged to sort the girl's distress.

Stephen watched Vera go and thought about the words he'd spoken to her. He hadn't been lying. Vera was one of his dearest friends. The *very* dearest.

He also had meant the words another way. *You are mine, as well.*

Vera was his, in his heart, and he was most certainly hers. Now he just had to find a way to make it so in reality.

## CHAPTER 25 - VERA

Vera nibbled her lower lip and glanced at the clock. She had stayed behind to help with Anne, who had a stomach ache. Vera suspected that it might have something to do with the vast quantities of cake the girl had eaten the day before.

The little girl roused her sympathies to a degree that Vera was inclined to give her anything she wanted. This was an excellent object lesson that doing so wouldn't be beneficial for Anne; Vera would have to learn to tell her "no" and "that's enough."

Stephen had gone to visit Mr. Davis, who lived miles away. The man had a particularly stubborn lung condition that wasn't responding well to medicine. Still, Stephen had left in the early afternoon and it was now full dark.

"He should be back by now," Vera murmured for perhaps the third time.

Jacqueline said, "I'm sure he's fine. You forget that he traipsed all over India by himself. I daresay the back alleys of Calcutta are far more dangerous than the countryside of Devon."

"But the weather." Vera glanced at the rain-lashed windows.

"He grew up here; he's used to it. Besides, he has the carriage and his coat."

There was a frantic knocking at the front door. Vera stood—she recognized the cadence of that knock, though she had no idea who caused it. There was an emergency, one that required a doctor.

"Oh, Vera, no," Jacqueline chided. "Not in this weather."

Vera was already striding toward the hall. She wasn't a physician; she was no *Stephen*, but she could still do something to help. She'd learned quite a bit while under his tutelage these past months.

"Please," a man was saying when she reached the hallway. "She needs help."

"I'm sorry." Roland's tone was firm. "The doctor is out."

"Roland, what is it? Perhaps I can help."

Roland didn't dare contradict her, but his frown said enough.

A young man dripped water onto the flagstones of the entry. He gripped his sodden hat in his hands, unintentionally wringing the water out onto the floor.

"It's my wife, miss. She fell. Hit her head. My sister's with her, but please, come quick. She's not right."

A chill rolled down Vera's back; her stomach clenched. Head wounds were notoriously tricky. They could be nothing—no more than rest and a regimen of waking the patient—or they could be finicky and fatal. There wasn't anything Vera could do if it was the latter. Still, there was a patient's husband standing before her, asking for her help. She wasn't going to turn him away.

Vera turned to Jacqueline, who'd followed her out into the hallway.

The woman frowned at Vera's resolute expression and shook her head. "Very well, but take a footman with you."

"My lady, Lord Winthrop has the carriage," Roland protested.

"We have two, do we not?"

"Yes, my lady, but the curricle isn't sturdy enough to navigate the roads in this weather. They'll be thrown into a ditch."

Vera nodded brusquely, already pulling on the thick gloves and cloak she kept hanging in the entryway for occasions such as these. "That's fine, Roland. We'll take the cart."

"You'll be soaked through."

"It will make my bath all the more enjoyable when I return, then," she said lightly.

Vera was bluffing—she didn't relish the thought of being cold and drenched any more than the next person, but she sensed that if she showed an ounce of weakness, Jacqueline or Roland might forbid her from leaving at all.

The terror in this young man's eyes as he watched them debate transportation affected her greatly. He kept glancing toward the door as if he longed to run back home to his wife. What was Vera going to tell him—that he'd ridden all this way, only for her to be afraid of a bit of rain?

"Very well." The baroness nodded. "Have Mr. Frederick prepare the cart."

Vera picked up her basket and nodded at the man. "Lead the way."

Hours later, Vera stood and stretched, pressing a hand to the dull throbbing at her lower back. Mrs. Crawford was going to be fine, as far as she could tell. The woman had fallen on a freshly washed floor and hit her head on the corner of the kitchen table on her way down.

Head wounds bled like the dickens—no wonder the woman's husband had thought she was dying. It didn't help that she'd lain there stunned for a few moments before she rose—by the time she realized she was bleeding, a small puddle had formed.

"I fainted all over again, didn't I?" she'd said, sheepishly, holding a towel to her head. "Never liked the sight of blood. It makes me queasy."

"I was much the same before I took this position," Vera admitted with a smile. "I barely notice it now—it's like wiping a child's nose to me."

"Ugh, my Michael's nose might be worse than this scratch, that's for sure. At least in winter."

"It's amazing such small creatures can create such a great mess."

"Isn't that always the way, though?"

In the end, Mrs. Crawford needed only three small stitches. It was Vera's first time doing the procedure all on her own from start to finish—she was used to Stephen holding a lamp close and looming over her, humming his suggestions or approval as she went. Mr. Crawford had the dubious honor of holding the lamp—he looked the other way the entire time, gulping like he was about to be sick upon the floor.

Vera smiled and shook her head. It seemed that it was the way of things—normally strong men couldn't handle seeing their dear wives in any sort of distress. But Mrs. Crawford had swabbed the floor clean before they arrived with one hand while the other clamped the rag to her head.

"Are you sure you won't stay the night?" the woman offered again with a kind smile. "It's no trouble to rouse Michael. Or you can have our bed, and we'll sleep in the sitting room."

Calling it a sitting room was being generous—there was one small sofa and two wooden chairs near the front window. Still, Vera was touched by her words. Mr. and Mrs. Crawford had humble means but offered what they had, freely. It was a stark comparison to Vera's own mother and father.

"Thank you for the kind offer, but if I'm not home within the hour, the baroness will send a search party after me. I'd best be going. Besides, I think the rain's about to let up."

It was a lie and they both knew it. If anything, the storm had gained momentum. Much like an idiot who kept ordering rounds of ale at the pub, it was getting louder and more boisterous as the night went on. Still, Vera thought she saw a slight flicker of relief in the woman's eyes.

"And don't forget—neither you nor Mr. Crawford will be sleeping well tonight," she added. She turned to the husband. "You'd better not go to bed at all—watch the clock and wake her every hour on the hour. Ask her a few basic questions. If you cannot wake her, or if she loses her senses, come and get the doctor. I'm sure he'll be home by then."

Mr. Crawford nodded with wide eyes.

Vera smiled at his serious expression. "I don't expect any complications. Everything looks fine."

She had no doubt Mr. Crawford would fulfill her orders to the letter. It had been all she could do to make him go and change into dry clothes once they arrived at his house. Vera smiled wider and did her best not to show how wet and cold *she* was. The thought of a warm bath was all that had kept her going the entire evening. That and soup. Oh, how she hoped Mrs. Portence had saved some soup!

Even the footman had fared better than she had—he had a long, oilskin coat that he buttoned up to his chin. Not that she could resent the fellow for it—this was her first storm on the outside of a carriage, and he'd weathered many. She could hardly begrudge him better preparation.

The baroness had chosen him for this task on purpose—Mr. Frederick was fifty if he was a day, and though his figure was still large and imposing, he had grey around his temples and a wife and four children that he loved dearly. He was protection and as close to a chaperone as the baroness had managed, considering the conditions.

"Are you ready, Mr. Frederick?" She smiled brightly and tried not to show how little she looked forward to the miles-long journey back to Bertforth House.

Mr. Frederick nodded and led her outside, where he'd already hitched the horses. Vera was thankful they were exceedingly docile, as thunder rolled like a great bass drum across the countryside, punctuated by the sharp crack of lightning and the banshee howling of the wind.

The horses were drenched, the poor things. They stood, heads lowered against the gale. Vera couldn't help the sympathy that panged her heart. Mr. Frederick helped Vera up and took the spot next to her. She gathered her sodden woolen cloak around her and tried to ignore how cold she was.

Vera smiled to herself. How different things were now than when she'd started as Stephen's assistant! Just this very night, she'd neatly stitched a woman's head, all by herself. Now she was headed home in a terrible gale. She'd gained knowledge these past weeks—knowledge *and* courage.

Mr. Frederick gently slapped the wet reins against the wetter horses and pointed them toward home.

## CHAPTER 26- STEPHEN

"They should have been back by now." Stephen paced in front of the window.

He himself had only returned a quarter hour previously; he hadn't even removed his boots yet.

"That's funny—that's what she'd been saying about you." His mother paged through a book, looking utterly unconcerned.

Stephen frowned at her, then glanced at the clock. "What time did you say Mr. Crawford came, again?"

She sighed. "You heard me quite clearly the first two times. Are you certain *you* aren't the one with the head injury?"

"I would think you'd be more concerned. Your protectiveness of Vera seems to have markedly waned."

"It hasn't waned, my dear. It's been effectively transferred."

"What was that?"

Stephen had been checking the clock again—the

blasted thing was moving slower than the horse he'd once chanced a bet on. It was the one and only time he'd wagered on a race. Stupid thing, betting on animals—the loss had served him right.

His mother sighed as if quite put out. "I'm sure she'll be back any moment. Mr. Frederick's with her—that brute will keep her safe from harm."

"Tell me again—why is she unchaperoned?"

"I couldn't tell any of the maids to go out in this mess."

"Yet you could send *her* out?" Stephen's eyebrows were raised, as was his voice.

His mother paused, then slowly raised her eyes from the page. Stephen swallowed—he recognized that look.

Jacqueline's voice was deceptively light when she said, "I didn't *send* her. She went. And Mr. Frederick is extremely dependable. Vera's reputation is exceedingly safe. No one will be out in this mess, so there's no chance anyone will see her unchaperoned."

"Perhaps she should have come with me. Then she wouldn't have even been here to answer the blasted request."

"She was needed here, with Anne." His mother closed her book on her finger to hold her place. "This is a good lesson for you—that little girl needs a father *and* a mother."

"I don't want Vera to accept just because of *Anne*," he blurted.

His mother smiled as if she were the proverbial cat who got the saucer of cream. "I *knew* it."

"Yes, yes. You may enjoy your smug success later, perhaps. It's far too soon for it now."

"On the contrary. *You* were always the impediment to the issue. If you've decided to get out of your own way, I feel the situation can be charmingly resolved—and quickly. If you have the sense to propose to the lady, that is."

"This is hardly any of your concern."

"Is it not?" She raised her eyebrows. "Whose job will it be to help you raise that young girl if you don't secure Vera's hand in marriage?"

Stephen exhaled through his nose. He knew she had a point—if Vera turned him down, then his mother was the next most likely candidate to assist him.

She must have seen the truth of the matter upon his face, for she smiled again. "Exactly. So let me make this easier on you. I intended upon waiting to tell you this, but I feel now is the perfect time. I'm moving out."

"Excuse me?" Stephen couldn't have been more flabbergasted if she'd announced she was taking up a career on the stage.

"I'm relocating to the old groundskeeper's cottage by the end of the month. Rest assured that I'm taking my menagerie with me. This house will be yours, as is right."

"What about Benjamin?"

"I thought he'd stay here, with you. Of course he's always welcome to live with me as well, but some time together might be a good thing for you two. Plus, this is his home."

"This is *your* home."

"It's time you made it yours instead." She waved a

hand. "Oh, don't look so shocked. This is the natural order of things."

"Have I made you feel unwelcome? Because I've become accustomed to the animals."

It was a half-truth, and they both knew it. Stephen had only just become comfortable taking a bath without first feeling the need to search the corners of his bathing chamber for raccoons and whatnot.

"Not in the least. But it is high time that you start living your life. It's nearly impossible for a man to fully act as an adult if he's still living with his mother."

Stephen nodded. "As long as you're happy with the arrangement."

"Of course. It was my idea." Jacqueline flipped open her book. "When are you going to ask her?"

"I'm not sure—when the time is right, I suppose."

"Take it from me, Stephen. You don't want to waste any time apart from the one you love—time isn't guaranteed."

Stephen glanced at the clock on the mantel once more. "Enough of this. I'm going after her."

His mother hummed as she turned another page. "That's the spirit, dear."

## CHAPTER 27 - VERA

The bridge was washed out. Washed out! What was this, the seventeenth century? They'd had to go around. Mr. Frederick said he knew the road. However, as time went on, the road narrowed right along with Vera's confidence in his proclamation until finally, they were travelling at a snail's pace, her teeth clacking with the wheels over the ruts in what felt like little more than a rarely travelled footpath.

Vera had just turned to ask Mr. Frederick—for only the second time; she was quite proud of her own restraint—whether he truly knew where they were going. But a flash of light and a great *boom* directly overhead stole her breath and forced it out in a little scream. It sounded as if they were inside hell's bass drum itself.

Mr. Frederick yanked on the reins, trying to control the panicking horses; he didn't notice her small outburst. The beasts reared and screamed right along with Vera. The horses plunged to the side as if in agreement, right toward a smoking tree.

*It's been struck by lightning,* Vera thought stupidly.

She gripped the wooden seat with white knuckles and screamed again. Just as the horses pulled them off the dirt road into the gulley, part of the tree swung down like a great axe toward the cart with a groan.

The thickest part of the limb landed neatly between Vera and Mr. Frederick with a heavy *thunk*. Small branches scratched and slapped at Vera's face and struck her shoulder. They snatched her bonnet from her head and yanked the tied ribbons forcefully against her throat. Vera plucked the knots loose as she choked, then yanked the bonnet back from the grasping fingers of the branch.

"Miss Vera?" Mr. Frederick's panicked voice came from the other side of the fallen limb. It was the width of a medium tree, and he had to push the smaller branches apart to see her better. "Are you all right?"

Vera rolled her shoulder experimentally and worked her fingers to be sure before she answered, "Yes, are you?"

"Thank heavens." He gave a noisy exhale. "That was close."

*Close?* Vera wanted to say, but she bit her inappropriate sarcasm back with great effort. They'd nearly been struck by lightning! They were stuck in a gulley, their cart listing heavily to one side, and they'd been hit by a tree branch. "Close" seemed the wrong word for it.

"What about the horses?" she asked.

Mr. Frederick was already climbing down the side of

the cart to inspect them. Vera could barely see one of the horses—the branch had divided the animals as decisively as it had separated her and Mr. Frederick.

Her side of the cart was pressed against the hillside, so Vera extricated herself from the tangling branches and awkwardly climbed over the large branch and down the other side, yanking her skirts free of snags several times. When she jumped down from the cart, she landed in rushing water that soaked her to her ankles and wicked up her sodden skirts.

Vera scrabbled up the side of the gulley, back onto the road. She was grateful that Mr. Frederick had been too preoccupied with the horses to notice her ungainly trek.

"Horses are fine," Mr. Frederick finally said, charging up the side of the ditch. He'd made it look much easier than Vera had—he hadn't even needed to use his hands.

"Can we push it out?" Vera swiped her muddy fingers against her wet skirts and gestured at the cart.

"It's wedged too tightly, and one of the horses is trapped in by the branch." He put his hands on his hips and surveyed the scene again. "I think I should take the one horse and go back for help. I'll bring men and a saw, we can cut that branch, free the other horse, and get you home."

Vera blinked. *He was leaving her? Here? Alone?*

"I'm sorry, Miss Vera." He frowned. "That horse can't carry us both, but maybe if you rode it, and I led it..."

She shook her head. "No, that will take twice as long. I'll be fine. You know the way. Just leave me one of the lanterns, if you would. I don't fancy being alone in the dark."

"Of course." He plunged down the gulley once more and started unhooking the horse.

Vera swatted water from her face. The rain was relentless, coming in great blinding sheets, dancing back for a moment and pounding forth the next. She barely had time to comprehend that Mr. Frederick had freed the horse before he led it up the from the ditch. In the next instant, he swung easily up onto its back, holding one of the lanterns.

"Stay safe, Miss Vera. I'll be back shortly."

Vera nodded and gave a little wave. Then he was gone, the feeble light from his lantern swallowed by the gale in mere moments.

Vera shivered and looked around. *Alone.* She wasn't sure she'd ever been so alone in all her life. Not to mention, exceedingly uncomfortable and cold. Rain splattered the mud of the road, hissed against the water filling the ditch.

She stood in the center of the road for a moment until that felt far too exposed. She'd rather be back in the cart, even tilted as it was. She sloshed down into the gulley and clambered up the side of the cart, sitting in Mr. Frederick's place as she didn't fancy wrestling her way over the tree branch again. Several scratches stung along her legs; her stockings were torn to shreds.

At least she'd have something interesting to say the next time she got together with Candace. If only Vera's mother could see her now. The thought made her huff in amusement. Her mother would be horrified to know that her daughter was out in a rainstorm, muddied up to her knees, and soaked all the way through—and not out of concern for Vera. There was something satisfying about the thought, and Vera pulled that satisfaction around her like a warm blanket.

Her mother had inflicted the worst punishment the woman could imagine upon Vera, and despite the odds, she'd survived. One might even argue that she was doing more living now than she ever had before.

So yes, she would survive this too. What was it, anyway? Momentary discomfort? She was cold, but she knew a warm fire and a hot bath awaited her. And *soup*. And *tea*. And she was alone, for the moment, except not truly. She still had the horse for company—

At the thought, she glanced down at the animal. She gasped and stood to get a better look over the branch. The cart—wedged as it was—was acting as a sort of dam in the gully. The water which had once flowed freely was backing up against the impediment. At the start, the horse had only been standing in water. Now, the water was up to its flanks, and rising fast.

If she didn't take action, the horse would drown.

"Oh no," Vera gasped, even as she climbed down the side of the cart.

The water was deeper, tugging and pulling at her skirts. How had she not noticed it before? She struggled over to the branch. There was only enough room for her to duck beneath it, but she'd have to if she was going to unhook the horse from the cart. Vera gripped several branches and twisted and snapped them off to give herself more room. Then she said a silent prayer and ducked.

Vera submerged herself to her shoulders. The swirling cold water shocked the air from her lungs, stole every bit of warmth left in her chest. But she emerged on the other side and trailed her hand up the side of the horse. Its skin jerked and shimmied in response, its ears flat against his head.

"Easy. Easy," she said.

Vera tried to work the straps through the buckles, tugged off her gloves and tried again. All the while, she murmured words of comfort and consolation to an animal that she wasn't even sure could hear her above the rain, the water slapping against the side of the cart. She made her way around the animal, feeling low on its body, unbuckling every strap she could find, working her way around the front while praying that the animal wouldn't bite her.

Finally, the last of the tack came loose. The horse stamped in the water that was now up to Vera's waist. But the horse was still trapped. The steep bank of the hill closed it in on one side; the tree branch hemmed it in from the other.

"All right," she said. "I'm going to lift the branch. Then you should be able to get out. But you'll need to hurry—I don't know if I can hold it for long."

*Or even lift it at all,* she thought darkly as she climbed back up the side of the cart. Her dress now felt as if it weighed more than she did. She'd lost one boot to the sucking mud and she barked her toes against the step.

The end of the branch still lay on the high point of the

small hill. If she could use that point as a lever, if she lifted the branch high enough, the horse might be able to get out.

The animal certainly seemed eager. The water was rising. He stamped and flailed, water frothing around him. Every now and then, he gave a panicked whinny. His eyes were wide and rolling. She was glad he hadn't been so frightened when she was near him—she wasn't sure she'd have the courage to approach him as he was now.

"All right." Vera said the word to bolster herself more than the horse.

She leaned down and gripped the rough bark of the tree branch. She suddenly wished she had her gloves back, but those had been lost to the swirling water as soon as she tugged them from her fingers.

She hefted the branch, doing her best to ignore the scraping snag of the twigs as they clutched at her skirts on the way up, as they bit and bent against her skin. She grunted—the branch was at her chest now, but it still wasn't high enough for the horse. She braced the branch upon her chest and adjusted her grip. The rough bark tore at her skin; she gritted her teeth and hefted once more.

High, higher. Up above her head.

"Go," she grunted. "Go."

It was nearly a silent plea—she had no energy for much else. Worse, she couldn't see if the horse was able to or already had made its escape. She held the branch as high overhead as she was able until it wobbled, her arms nearly giving out. With her last dregs of strength, she pushed it away from her as it fell.

But the last of her strength wasn't enough—the branch landed with a thunk against her ankle. Vera cried out and doubled over, yanking her foot from beneath the weight in desperation. Thank goodness it had hit her booted foot, and not the bare one. Even so, the pain blinded her for a moment; she gripped her ankle and groaned.

Vera glanced to the side—the horse was free! It charged through the water and up the side of the ditch...

And cantered down the road into the darkness.

"You traitor!" she called to its retreating backside.

Not that she could be mad at the horse, not really. It was headed in the direction of home, and while she'd hoped they had come to an accord—one in which she'd release the horse and it would then take her with it when it left—Vera knew that it was wishful thinking. She'd never spoken a horsey language, and the animal was just acting prudently, according to its nature.

Still, that left Vera soaked to the bone, one boot lost to the quagmire of the gulley, the other ankle sprained at best. She was cold, frustrated, and quite wrung out by the fear she'd felt for the horse only minutes prior. It would have drowned if she hadn't taken action, so she couldn't be sorry for freeing it, even though the act had left her utterly marooned and alone. And in *pain*.

Vera hissed as she tested the weight against her ankle. She nearly buckled under the searing agony, but it held.

Funny how the presence of an animal felt like company. Without the horse, she was all too aware of her chilled state, of how dark it was, of how much her ankle hurt... But no—she shouldn't think like that.

"I'm thankful for my cloak. For the warm bath waiting for me. For the fact that someone knows where I am and will send help shortly, for the lantern to see by..."

As if on cue, the lantern snuffed out, leaving her in utter darkness.

# CHAPTER 28 - STEPHEN

At the crossroads, Stephen frowned. For a moment, he thought he saw... There it was again—a flash of light on the smaller path to his right. He reined in his horse and waited. Mr. Frederick and Vera had taken the long way around; that explained the delay.

Stephen frowned, wondering why they'd travelled so far out of their normal route. Mr. Frederick had been reared in this area of the countryside—he knew the small lanes just as well as Stephen did. Perhaps Stephen's trip had been an exercise in futility. Here he sat, damp and bedraggled, and they were only just late.

However, when the beam of light got closer, it was a lone horseman holding the lantern, not the cart Stephen had been expecting.

"Mr. Frederick?" Stephen called above the wind when the man drew nearer. "Where's Vera? What's happened?"

The man frowned. "Horses spooked and drove us

right into the gulley. The cart's stuck and we couldn't get the other horse loose. Miss Vera is safe enough—she's waiting in the cart. I'm going to get help to pull the branch off so we can get the other horse free."

"Branch? What branch?"

"From the lightning that hit the tree."

"You were nearly struck by *lightning*?"

Mr. Frederick frowned. "No, my lord. 'Twas the tree that was struck by lightning. Not us."

Stephen shook his head. "How far back is the cart?"

"A couple of miles, maybe less, maybe more. Somewheres between here and the fork, but you can't miss it on a road this small."

"Go on ahead to the house. Bring men back, and tell the household to prepare a hot meal and warm water for baths. Everyone out in this should have one once they're finished."

"Yes, my lord."

Stephen nodded and steered his horse down the dark lane. He could have asked for the lantern, but his eyes were well enough that he could make out the road, even in this gloom.

As he rode, he nursed an unfair anger toward Mr. Frederick. What was he thinking, leaving Vera all alone on the side of the road in a broken cart? There could be brigands!

Granted, it would have to be a particularly *desperate* brigand to be out in this weather, but still—desperate brigands were the worst kind of brigand. And sure, there weren't many who travelled small cart paths looking for prey—they usually stuck to the main thoroughfares that attracted wealthy carriages and offered clean getaways—but sometimes danger lurked in the last place you'd expect!

Of course, that horse couldn't have held the both of them—Mr. Frederick and Vera—but Mr. Frederick could have led the horse through the storm. Certainly that would have taken longer, but perhaps Mr. Frederick could have jogged alongside or something. There was simply no excuse.

It was perhaps a quarter hour later when a shape came barreling toward him out of the storm. It was the horse—the one that Mr. Frederick had claimed was stuck—wearing only its bridle. It stood there shivering and prancing in the middle of the road like a harbinger of doom. Stephen dismounted, his heart pounding. His boots squelched in the mud.

How had the horse gotten free if it were truly as stuck as Mr. Frederick thought? If Vera had managed to get it free by herself, why wasn't she *riding* the blasted thing?

Stephen gave a cursory inspection for injuries, took up the horse's lead, remounted, and rode faster through the night, chased by all his terrible imaginings.

Much later—hours or days, if one was to ask Stephen how long it felt, though in actuality probably only a quarter of an hour—Stephen's breath froze in his lungs.

The cart was tilted at a terrible angle, half-submerged in the small ravine. Vera was nowhere in sight.

"Vera?" he called, throwing himself down from the saddle. "*Vera?*"

Against the backdrop of the howling wind, he heard perhaps the sweetest sound ever.

"Here I am," she called.

A sodden, cloaked figure emerged from beneath the half-fallen tree.

"What are you doing? Get away from there; it's dangerous."

Though he couldn't hear it over the pelting rain and the raging wind, he swore he could see her sigh. "It's already fallen, Stephen. I thought the danger mostly passed."

Stephen leapt over the gulley—it was full now, more like a frothing river than a drainage ditch—his boots squelching in the water and mud on the other side. He held out a hand and she took it. She leaned awkwardly against him on the way back down the hill.

He frowned down at her. "What's the matter?"

"Why, nothing at all." She gritted her teeth as she stepped back down toward the water. "Just enjoying a lovely stroll."

"Stop, Vera. What's wrong?"

With the darkness, he couldn't see her face. He found he hated it.

"I sprained my ankle, helping that traitorous horse." Her voice lacked heat. She shortly added, "I'm glad you met the fellow, though. I was worried he might not find his way home."

Stephen couldn't help it, he pulled her into his arms and kissed the top of her sodden head. The relief thrumming through him, to his very bones—it could only mean one thing. He loved her. He was helplessly, madly in love with Miss Vera Ashbury. Of course he'd suspected as much, which was why his thoughts had turned toward marriage as of late. Still, this moment drove the emotion home soundly.

"Why are you hugging me?" Vera asked suspiciously. "Are you about to deliver bad news? Is there something wrong with the horse? I thought he looked all right—"

"Vera, shut up about the damn horse," he ground out.

She fell silent, and he was grateful for it. He could barely think over the howling of the wind, over the much louder howling of emotions raging within him.

Stephen could have lost her. The fear coursing through him wasn't just because of tonight, not just because of the stark terror he'd felt when that lone, riderless horse had loomed out of the darkness before him. No—he could have lost her in so many ways.

What if Vera had been accepted to a position before he'd even arrived home from India? They might have never met.

What if Vera hadn't possessed a great capacity to forgive? He could have lost her with his own arrogance, his own stupid, disbelieving cruelty.

And Stephen might lose her still—if Vera didn't feel as he did, if he couldn't convince her to love him back...

Not to mention the danger she'd faced tonight—she could have been gravely injured. Vera could have *died*. And here she was blathering on about the *horse*. As it was, she was soaked and shivering and had sprained her ankle...

And Stephen was holding her like a dolt in the middle of the storm, when he could be getting her to safety.

"Forgive me," he said, drawing back abruptly. "Let's get you home."

"That sounds wonderful. Can we please speak of fires and warm baths and hot tea all the way back?" Her lips stuttered on the consonants, belying just how chilled she was.

Stephen's mind nearly stumbled at the thought of Vera in a bath, but he recovered nicely—his thoughts flew at once to pneumonia, to pleurisy, to fevers. He cursed himself anew.

He swept her up into his arms; Vera gave a little cry of surprise. Stephen charged down the gulley. When he was ankle-deep in the water, he jumped and splashed into the shallows on the other side. His boots were of excellent make, but even oiled leather had its limitations—water seeped in at the seams and his wool socks began wicking the moisture upwards.

It didn't matter—he didn't care. Vera was far wetter and far colder than he was.

"Are you all right?" he asked.

"Fine," she squeaked, but he frowned down at her, unconvinced.

He set her atop his horse and swung up behind her, then set as fast a pace as was safe for home.

## CHAPTER 29 - VERA

*G*oodness' sakes, Vera, she chided. *Get ahold of yourself.*

But it perhaps wasn't her fault. Stephen had held her like she was unexpectedly precious. The dampness of her gown and cloak meant that the delicious heat of his body had transferred very easily to her. Vera told herself that it was only because she was so cold that she longed for him to hold her like that forever.

But then—as if the embrace hadn't been disorienting enough—Stephen had picked her up and carried her. It was just like all those romantic heroes in Candace's gothic novels. Except Vera didn't feel like a heroine so much as a bedraggled rat that had been wedged in a drainpipe. Her hair stuck to her neck like wet grass. Her one stockinged foot was muddy to her knee, and the other ankle felt like a painful grapefruit-sized lump.

Though she appreciated how quickly Stephen rode toward Bertforth House, she winced every other minute.

Her foot dangled awkwardly and bumped the side of the horse. Vera noticed that Stephen had dropped the lead of the other horse, the one she'd saved.

"Is he going to be all right?" Vera lifted her voice to be heard over the squelching hoofbeats and the rain that pelted and stung at her cheeks.

"Who?"

"The horse. You left him."

"You and that blasted horse. I don't care about the horse."

Vera frowned. "*I* do."

"He's keeping pace with us. He doesn't want to be alone in this storm any more than we do."

"He left me easily enough." Vera fidgeted and leaned, trying to turn her head and see around Stephen's bulk to check on the animal.

"Stop wiggling." The large hand that held her in the saddle spasmed on her stomach, and she froze.

Vera hadn't been aware that Stephen was holding her until that moment. Now, she didn't think she could feel anything else. The stinging rain, the cold of her limbs, even the throbbing in her ankle—it all dulled in comparison to that warm hand steadying her.

"The horse is there," he said, oblivious to her sudden inner turmoil. "Don't you trust me?"

"I do."

Vera realized the truth of the words as she said them. She *did* trust him. Despite the odds. Despite their terrible start. She trusted Stephen.

It was quite the feat on his part, considering that Vera's

trust of people had been at a low point after what her parents had done. In fact, how had Stephen managed to do it—to get Vera to trust him, after she'd sworn never to trust anyone again if she could help it?

It was probably how competent he was as a physician. Because he *was* a remarkable doctor—kind but firm, and he had a knack for knowing what was wrong with people, even if they explained it poorly.

Then there was the whole altruistic side of him. The part of Stephen that had prompted him to go to India was still alive and well. Vera hadn't been shocked when he took Anne in, not the same way others had been. Stephen possessed a brusque demeanor, but his insides were ordered in a warm and lovely way. Vera saw it in the way he cared for his mother, for Benjamin, and now for Anne, too.

Vera had once thought Stephen to be a brute of the highest order. He'd treated her abominably at the outset of their relationship, but he was the first to admit as much. He'd repeatedly shown her who he truly was—through his professional, courteous treatment as his assistant, with their long walks discussing everything, where he listened closely to her opinions and pondered them carefully before replying, even through his gentle handling of her this evening.

It was perhaps for the best, how they'd started, Vera mused. For if she hadn't hated him at the outset, she never would have had the courage to truly be herself around him.

Now, Vera felt something *new* blooming between

them. It was something she didn't dare name, something she didn't dare make direct eye contact with. She caught glances of it from the corner of her eye sometimes, and that was quite enough to make her shiver. Often she caught herself lying abed at night, staring up at the canopy, and not *not* thinking of what it might be.

But oh no! Suddenly, on this ride back to the house, with his great overcoat draped over her, with the heat of his chest pressed to her sodden back—*this* was the poorly chosen moment that her subconscious decided to drop the full weight of the realization that she'd been trying to ignore for weeks.

Vera was madly, irrevocably in love with Stephen.

She cursed her traitorous little heart. Why, the thing had been running ahead without Vera's knowledge or consent! Surely the rational side of her should have some say in the matter. But it was no use—when she checked in with the logical part of herself, she was dismayed to realize that it loved Stephen just as much as her idiot, fanciful heart did.

The *embarrassment* of it—to fall in love with someone who'd once treated her so terribly! Vera felt the realization of her feelings for Stephen as keenly as a physical blow. She even reared her head to silently beg the heavens for help—or, if proper sense was too much to ask for—a lightning bolt.

However, caught as she was in the maelstrom of her thoughts, Vera had forgotten that she was in the midst of a very *real* storm, and she wasn't alone.

"Vera?" Stephen asked, his words urgent and loud

against her ear. He spoke so closely that a gust of his breath warmed her cheek, and she shivered. "Are you quite all right?"

Vera had been lost to the throes of her own idiocy. She hadn't realized that when she'd thrown her head back in silent supplication, that she'd sagged her full weight back against him. Now she was all too aware.

Had Vera thought the heat coming off Stephen distracting? That was before she leaned fully against his muscular chest. The rain had thinned their garments, and she swore she could feel every ripple of movement, the taut control of his body as he steered the horse and supported her. His warm, capable hand was still pressed to her stomach.

Vera gave an inarticulate grunt of horrified realization —*she* had been the one to press them together. She struggled forward, trying to gain even a single, blessed inch of space once more. But that hand didn't let her go anywhere, not even away from his person.

"No. You must be exhausted. Sleep, Vera—I'll get us there safely." His words were low, resolute, and placed just along her jawline. Tears of embarrassment pricked at her eyes when she shivered at the feel of his proximity.

Stephen gathered his overcoat around her more fully and leaned into her, trying to shield her from the rain. Vera stifled a groan. He was making it worse, and by the briskness of his movements, she could tell that he had no idea the effect he was having upon her. At least there was that.

Vera suddenly wished for Hortense and her ironwood umbrella with a fierceness that nearly made her laugh.

WHEN THEY ARRIVED BACK at the house, Mr. Frederick was directing a group of men into a wagon. Stephen called out to them and dismounted, then helped Vera down from the horse. She stood awkwardly next to him—she would have stepped back, but she was obliged to accept his help.

Her ankle now throbbed with every beat of her heart. Previously, the pain had been dulled by her myriad other complaints—the dark, the cold, the wind, the loneliness and fear of it all. Now that warmth lay just across the very near threshold, she found she couldn't put much weight on the foot at all—not without pain searing through her leg, not without Vera gasping and gritting her teeth.

Stephen disbanded the search party and handed the wet horses off to the footmen, who were all very relieved they didn't have to go riding for an hour in the storm, after all. Then Stephen swung Vera easily into his arms and plowed up the front steps.

Jacqueline was suddenly there, her expression full of concern, and the housekeeper and Roland, who whipped the servants into a domestic froth. It was but minutes until Vera was ensconced in her bedroom and submerged in a hot bath under the careful ministrations of a solicitous maid.

Vera sighed and relaxed against the back of the tub.

Her hair and body had been washed. The chill had fought valiantly against the bathwater and the heavily brandied tea but had finally lost the battle in one final, violent shudder. Then Vera was finally warm through and through.

"Begging your pardon, miss," the maid said cautiously when Vera's eyes fluttered closed. "His lordship says you're not to sleep—not until he's had time to address that poor ankle of yours."

Vera sighed but dutifully opened her eyes. She knew Stephen was right, but just once, she wished he'd leave the competent doctoring behind. She was achingly, jaw-crack-yawning exhausted. Her ankle was bright red and very swollen. She'd hissed when Jacqueline had eased the boot off.

"Very well. Will you help me dress?"

"So soon? We have plenty more hot water, if you'd enjoy a longer soak." She gestured at the three large cans of water set to keep warm before the fire.

"Thank you, but I just want to sleep. Best to get this over with as soon as possible."

A half an hour later, Vera was propped up in bed against a veritable mountain of downy pillows. Her one leg jutted awkwardly from the bedclothes, the swollen foot propped on its own pillow, as if the offending ankle were a valuable antiquity being presented to royalty. She snickered at the thought, even as Jacqueline bustled in with a tray. Stephen came behind her with his doctor's case, knocking redundantly upon the doorframe.

"How are you, Vera?" He pulled a chair to her bedside and sat.

Vera couldn't help it—she laughed. "Don't you use that doctor tone with me. How many times have I heard you ask the same to a patient?"

Stephen smiled, looking a bit sheepish. "It's a classic physician's greeting. Why on earth would I deviate?"

*Because we're closer than that,* she wanted to say.

"Very well." Vera nodded. "You may proceed. But don't think I'm going to fall for any of your tricks."

"Tricks?" Jacqueline arched an eyebrow and placed the tray at her bedside. "Have I raised a sneaky son?"

"Two of them, actually, that I know of." Vera grinned. "But your eldest is possibly the worst. He's always dropping his doctor questions into casual conversation. The patients have told him everything before they even know they're being questioned."

"There's no need for subterfuge when it comes to you." Stephen grinned. "We live together. I already know your average diet and how many alcoholic beverages you regularly consume."

"After that tea your mother made me, my number is well higher than usual."

He grinned and swiped back his still-damp hair. Vera was glad he'd had the chance to bathe and warm himself, too. Stephen focused on her ankle then, sliding his fingers against the skin gently, probing and giving a thoughtful hum. Then he cradled the back of her foot and gently rotated the ankle, watching it first, then her face.

Vera sincerely hoped that any visible discomfort would be attributed to her injury, and not the riot of emotions that his bare fingers gently handling her ankle provoked.

"It's not broken, that I can tell. At least, the joint is whole. Cold compresses several times a day, and a lot of rest. You should be well enough within a couple of weeks."

"That's a relief. I have several balls to attend in the near future—I want to be sure I'll be able to waltz."

She'd meant it as a joke, but Stephen frowned. Vera's eyes slid to Jacqueline, who pursed her lips, raised her eyebrows, and busied herself with the tray.

Stephen cleared his throat. "Yes, well. I'm sure there'll be lots of dancing in your future, Vera."

He patted the bedding next to her foot awkwardly, gathered his case, and left.

Vera frowned after him, then turned to Jacqueline, whispering, "What was that about?"

"What was what?" She set the tray over Vera's lap. "Eat up. Cook swears by this soup—she weaseled the recipe from Canterbury's cook years ago and claims she's made it better with a bit of lemon."

Vera's appetite roared to life. Jacqueline kept her company through her supper, joking about Clarence and his reaction to the storm. Apparently, the rascal had buried himself at the back of Jacqueline's wardrobe and had to be bribed out with raw bacon.

Vera couldn't remember falling asleep—one moment she was listening to Jacqueline's animated murmurs about her pets, the next was comfortable darkness and silence.

## CHAPTER 30 - VERA

The following day, Stephen wouldn't hear of Vera leaving her bed. She had a sudden, new appreciation for how their patients felt when put on bedrest. It didn't help that her bedroom was too crowded for comfort. Edna sat near the fire, working on mending. Stephen had installed himself across the room at Vera's own writing desk as if to monitor whether she followed his directives.

It was only early afternoon and Vera already had to stifle the urge to scream. Not that she could navigate the stairs by herself anytime soon—her ankle was a lurid purple and red. Edna regularly changed out the cold compress that rested upon it. Otherwise, the maid draped a light linen towel over Vera's bare foot as if it were a cooling loaf of bread she was protecting from flies.

Vera huffed in indignation and checked the clock once more.

From the small writing desk across the room, Stephen arched an eyebrow in question.

She said, "I cannot believe you're *guarding* me so I don't get up."

"On the contrary. I'm simply here to entertain you while you rest."

Vera crossed her arms. "I hardly think you sitting in silence, scratching your pen on parchment across the room is *entertaining*."

"Very well," he said cheerfully and pushed his ledger aside. "You may help me with my correspondence."

Vera slumped against the mountain of pillows that held her in a seated position. "I'm not sure that would be any better than silence."

He ignored her grumblings and sliced open the first wax seal. "Ah, a letter from Dr. Halveston."

Stephen proceeded to read. Somewhere in the midst of the long letter, Vera forgot her irritation, instead entranced by the new medical procedure the man described. She was completely engrossed by the fourth page, where the man detailed one of his most recent cases at the hospital in London.

"But don't you think that individuals in clean houses are less likely to become ill than people in dirty houses?" Vera argued, an hour later.

"I don't think that you can isolate illness to cleanliness alone. Certainly in some cases such as infections from louse bites or pustulent wounds that are never properly cleaned, it's a large factor. However, I've seen the lords in the wealthiest houses brought low by fevers, the same as any coal stoker."

"Fine, but the rate of incidence is less. Isn't it?"

"True, but that might also be because close proximity can contribute to the spread of disease. People in grand houses have more room; therefore, they are less likely to become infected."

"You're playing the other side on purpose." Vera folded her arms.

"I'm pointing out other factors that may be just as important. That's the tricky thing with scientific endeavors—one must form a theory and then test it, all while keeping your mind open that your theory might be incorrect. You must believe what you're testing with all your heart, while remaining humble enough to remember that you might be wrong. Certainty is not the same as being right."

"Fair enough, but I still think that cleanliness plays a role in disease. If not in the initial catching of it, then certainly in how quickly the patients recover."

He nodded. "It very well might. It certainly cannot hurt things, though I would point out that Mrs. Edgar's house was spotless, and she remained ill for a full week."

"Because her husband was feeding her spicy foods while she had a stomach complaint!"

"There." He jabbed a finger into the air, grinning.

"You see? Even you admit that there are numerous factors in play when it comes to infection and healing."

She rolled her eyes, even as a smile feathered her lips. "I never said there weren't. I only posited that cleanliness is one of them."

"Cleanliness, diet, the general health of the individual before they became ill, age...they all affect how well a patient will recover."

"Exactly." She leaned forward, her eyes bright. "But we can only control some of those factors once the illness has set in. So shouldn't we focus on what we *can* control—with utter intensity—in order to give our patients the best chance?"

Vera flushed. She hoped Stephen wouldn't notice that she'd used collectives to describe them, as if she and Stephen were a unit, a pair.

*If only*, she thought before chasing the idea away.

"You make an excellent point." Stephen grinned. "It's nearly time for tea. I suppose my correspondence *was* entertaining enough. I'll go let Roland know we're ready for service."

"Enjoy your *walk*," she called to his back. "Enjoy your change of *scenery*."

His answering chuckle trailed down the hall.

The next day, Stephen allowed his patient to navigate the upstairs, as long as she elevated her wrapped ankle upon a pillow whenever she sat down. This was a far superior arrangement to being cloistered within her rooms. Vera spent the majority of the day in the upstairs library with Benjamin, Stephen, and Miss Beets.

Benjamin acted as her personal librarian, bringing her books he thought she might like—mostly books on warfare and diagrams of ships, but she thanked him all the same. Roland set a lovely tea service in the upstairs parlor, and afterward, Hortense brought Anne to the library for a visit.

"Hurt?" Anne said, patting Vera's leg. "Miss Vera hurt?"

"Yes, but I'll be better soon."

The little girl seemed to take her words at face value, and soon scrambled down to join Benjamin and Miss Beets before the grated fireplace.

"How is she?" Vera asked Hortense in a low tone. "She certainly looks well enough."

Anne did—it couldn't be overstated how large a difference cleanliness and proper clothes made. The little girl looked every inch the daughter of nobility in her starched white dress and velvet pelisse. Her hair had been combed, and though there wasn't enough to braid, Hortense had tied a bow in the ribbon around it.

Hortense murmured, "She's acclimating nicely. We're getting along very well. She's quickly learning how things are done here."

Vera nodded. "I'm sorry I'm not more available at the moment."

But perhaps it was for the best that Anne didn't get too attached or used to Vera's presence, for who knew how long she would be there? The thought sent a spasm through Vera's heart and an answering flinch across her features.

Hortense raised an eyebrow.

"My ankle." Vera nodded. "It's still quite painful."

"I'm so glad you didn't catch a fever out in that mess." Hortense shook her head. "I should have gone with you—if I had known…"

"Don't be silly. I'm fine, for one thing. And you have your own household to return to in the evenings."

Anne squawked; Hortense stood and crossed the room to investigate.

"How is your ankle feeling?" Stephen asked, taking the chair next to Vera's perch on the sofa.

"Just the same as it was when you asked me an hour ago," she teased.

"You must forgive me—it's impossible not to fall into the physician's role when a patient is in the room."

"I'm far more than a patient," she said lightly. "I'm your friend."

*Just a friend,* Vera reminded herself. *Just friends.*

Stephen levied a glance at her that carried an expression she couldn't quite read. It made her nervous, that look. She smiled reflexively so it wouldn't show.

"Indeed," he finally said. "Friends."

## CHAPTER 31- STEPHEN

Vera continued to recover at an admirable rate. The following week, she was well enough to gingerly make her way downstairs every day, one hand tucked safely into the crook of Stephen's arm, the other gripping the banister.

The week after that, Vera was able to make her way on her own. Stephen had mixed emotions on the subject. On one hand, he was thrilled that her ankle was healing so quickly. On the other, Stephen selfishly missed her hand clutching his elbow, missed bearing Vera's pleasant weight as he helped her down the stairs.

That particular day, the weather was cold but sunny. The temperatures had been hinting at snow, though it hadn't appeared yet. At the thought of snow, and based on his terrible memories of Vera wet, bedraggled, and stranded in the storm, Stephen had brought Vera into the front parlor and presented her with a gift.

"I look like an idiot." Her words came from somewhere within the great quantity of oilskin.

Stephen frowned. He was obliged to try to read her tone, for now that he really looked, he realized he couldn't quite make out Vera's face.

"But you'll be warm."

Vera turned toward him, but with the large collar of the coat pulled all the way up and the hat pulled all the way down, all he could make out were her eyes. They flashed with some emotion he couldn't identify.

"It's far too large, Stephen."

"They all look like that," he protested.

"That's not true. When you wear *your* coat, you still have use of your hands."

Vera held up her arms as if for his inspection, and he realized that the sleeves swallowed all but the very tips of her bare fingers. He frowned. What an oversight! He should have bought her gloves, as well.

Vera lumbered across the room, the oilskin whispering against itself as she walked. She paused in front of one of the tall mirrors that flanked the side table. Stephen assumed that she was examining her reflection based upon her proximity, but it was hard to tell for certain. He couldn't see her eyes from beneath the brim of the hat.

Stephen frowned. Perhaps the hat *was* a trifle overlarge, now that he truly studied it. The brim was far wider than his own hat, and a bit floppy, but he'd thought that would offer additional protection from the rain. And it could be said that the coat might need a *bit* of tailoring, but he'd wanted to make sure that it covered her thoroughly.

As he made his own perusal of the oilskin ensemble, he noticed she was shaking.

"Vera?" he sat forward. "Are you quite all right?"

"Quite." But her voice had a breathless quality about it —one that hinted at tears.

Stephen fairly leapt from the sofa. "No you're not. What is it? Is it your ankle?"

Inexplicably, she tilted her head back and laughed. "Stephen, *look* at me. It's the most ridiculous thing I've ever worn, and with a mother like mine, believe me when I tell you that's saying something. In fact, I never thought I'd look this terrible ever again."

He frowned. "Surely it isn't *that* bad."

She laughed again and waved her arms for emphasis. "Can you even tell it's me under all this?"

He twisted his lips to the side and refused to answer. "I wanted you to be warm."

She pushed the large brim of her hat back to look up at him. In the brief second before it flopped back down, he glimpsed her bright eyes full of mirth. But then they were gone, as was her face—swallowed anew by the great quantity of oilskin.

"Perhaps I might have gone a bit awry with the sizing."

"Oh, you think so?" She shook with a fresh round of giggles. "Stephen, it's *dreadful*. By far the worst thing I've ever worn, and all because you care so much. *Thank you*."

Vera abruptly flung herself at him, hugging him round the middle. Stephen frowned even as he returned the embrace—the coat really was unacceptably large—he could barely feel her at all through the miles of fabric. Still, he wouldn't turn down a hug from Vera, even if she was only giving it as a friend.

*You dolt,* Stephen thought. *No wonder she thinks you're just friends! You've given her only two presents. One of them regularly soils the rug, the other appears to be footman's garb.*

"Sorry," she said, pressing back from him abruptly.

"Not at all. I'm glad you appreciate the thought behind the gift, even if the execution left a bit to be desired."

"I will certainly stay warm and dry in this. Though I won't be able to see where we're going. Which is fine, as I've yet to learn how to drive the cart."

At least Vera sounded settled, as if she might stay. There had been times when he'd caught a certain softness in her eye as she looked at him. Still, Stephen couldn't be sure of her feelings, not until he asked her.

Not until he told her how he truly felt.

The letter in his inner coat pocket felt as if it weighed far more than it did. What if, when he gave it to her, she simply left? There was no bracing himself for such a possibility—it was simply a risk he had to take.

Stephen jammed his hands into his pockets to keep them from trembling. He gave a wide smile to hide his uncertainty.

"Well, the weather's clear enough. How about a walk to try out the coat?"

Vera brightened—until now, Stephen had been very stern about keeping her indoors. Suddenly he felt guilty.

The first time he'd suggested a walk, and he was going to use the time selfishly. After this walk, one way or another, their relationship would never be the same.

Vera beamed. "I'd love that, but I'm not wearing the hat. I won't be able to enjoy the sunshine."

## CHAPTER 32 - VERA

They slowly rambled down the hillside, Vera's hand tucked neatly into the crook of his elbow. She tried very hard to ignore that simple point of contact, the warmth radiating from it. She knew the corresponding glow in her heart was due to the emotions that she'd been trying—very unsuccessfully—to repress.

They walked largely in silence, but it wasn't uncomfortable on her end. She and Stephen were so often together they weren't beholden to the same constraints of politeness as they would have been if they weren't such good friends.

*Friends.* It was a word she'd been trying to reconcile herself to lately. And yet, it was too small a word to contain all her emotions. It was much like trying to shoehorn her ankle into her boot before the swelling had fully gone down.

"Vera," Stephen finally said when they stood at the

edge of the lower pasture. "There's something I need to tell you. Something I need to ask you."

Vera tensed. His tone held an element she couldn't read, something she didn't have a name for. That was rare when it came to him—she'd studied Stephen the same way she'd pored over the medical texts he'd lent her.

"Is anything the matter?"

She couldn't think of anything that might make him frown the way he was. At least, not anything between *them*. The last few weeks as her ankle had been healing had been among the happiest times she could recall.

Stephen had regaled her with past tales from his doctoring. He'd read her letters from his physician friends in London. Apparently, doctors were all the same—they loved to discuss new medical treatments and procedures, even in the tedious format of long letters. Vera loved that Stephen enjoyed sharing them with her, that he seemed to respect her ideas and opinions when speaking about them afterward.

If Stephen wasn't out seeing patients, he'd always been nearby. He'd taken to bringing his ledgers into the library. Sometimes, they'd sit in companionable silence, Stephen working at the desk, Vera reading.

Unfortunately, that time together hadn't muted Vera's feelings in the least. If anything, they'd only grown stronger. Her feelings were like one of those creeping vines that fought to enter the greenhouse. Vera plucked one thought or emotion, only to turn around and realize several new ones had taken its place.

"I've truly enjoyed our time working together," Stephen began, and winced.

Vera's face fell, her stomach dropped. Oh no—in the busyness of the past weeks, she'd forgotten their agreement. Rather, she'd forgotten that their time together was drawing to a close.

Vera rifled through her mind, trying to remember the date. They'd fulfilled their three months nearly a week ago —it was a day that she'd been looking forward to, at least in the beginning. How had it come and gone without her realizing?

Stephen held a folded parchment in his hand. He was going to do as she'd asked and send her away with a recommendation—just as she'd wanted at the outset. Terror and pain sank their claws into her heart.

Vera had no idea what expression was on her face; she couldn't have controlled it if she'd tried. All she could stupidly think was, *Not another letter telling me I'm not welcome in my family anymore.*

That was foolish—Stephen, Benjamin, Anne, and Jacqueline weren't her family. Just because her traitorous heart had claimed them didn't mean she had any *right* to them.

"Vera," he started again. "I know that we had an agreement. I want to offer you this before I say anything more. It's a recommendation—a glowing one."

Vera opened her mouth—to say what, she didn't know —but Stephen held up a hand. "Wait. I need to say this. You've been an excellent medical assistant. I've written to Dr. Halveston in London, and he's very interested in taking you on as an assistant there, in the hospital. They're using young women as nurses more, especially to help with ladies, who might not be comfortable with a gentleman physician."

Vera's eyes burned.

*Letters were funny things,* she thought, her eyes clamped on the folded parchment in his hand. *A splash of ink, a bit of pulp, could change your life forever.*

"But I hope you'll stay," he said.

"Wait. Pardon?" Vera glanced up at him, tears spilling over her eyelids and tracking down her cheeks.

Stephen's face was alive with...*something,* some emotion she could only hope she understood.

"But I don't want you to be my assistant anymore, Vera. I want you to be my wife."

She nearly staggered back. "What?"

"I don't want you to accept me because you feel that you don't have options," Stephen said quickly, the words tumbling out, one after another, as if he'd practiced them before and was in a hurry to have them done. "I promise that if you don't want me, you can still stay here. We can go on as we are. I'll *try*—" His voice broke on the word and he bit his lip. "I'll try not to make you uncomfortable with how I feel."

"With how you *feel*?"

*Good heavens,* she told herself. *Close your mouth.*

"I love you, Vera. So very much. I didn't know the definition of the word until you came along." Stephen's eyes were wide, the love in his face—for that's what it was, she realized now—radiated from every line in his smile. "It's funny—I've studied the body for years. Yet no one prepared me for how I feel when I see you walk into a room."

He held a hand to his chest. "No one's explained the possibility of the hold you have over my heart. The lightness I feel in it when you laugh. The way it flutters when you smile at me. The way it pounds when the candlelight softens your skin. And no one taught me how the mind can be completely split in two—how I can be utterly focused on what I'm doing, but that part of me still wonders where you are, and what you're doing at any given moment.

"And the hunger I feel here." Stephen pressed his hand to his stomach. "How I am still fully myself, just with a new obsession—that I long to know everything about you. When precisely you acquired each one of your lovely freckles. What you think about everything, all the time. How I find your interests just as fascinating as the ones I've always held for myself—not because they're inherently interesting to me, but because *you* are.

"I find I need to apologize again for how I treated you in the beginning. Yes, I do," he added as Vera shook her head, tears running unchecked down her cheeks. "For I only recently realized that I treated you so because you scared me. I found you beautiful upon first glance—breathtakingly so. And the last woman I'd looked at in such a way had hurt me deeply. I was foolishly trying to protect myself, and I did it at your expense."

"Stephen." She shook her head. "You don't have to—"

"Yes, I do. I adore you, Vera. And I know love is just a

word, but I promise I'll prove it to you every single day for the rest of my life, if you'll let me. I would be the luckiest, the happiest man in the world if you would stoop to being my wife. Will you?"

"Don't be daft," she choked out.

It was all Vera could manage to say for the time being. She was strangled by the depth of her emotion. Stephen thought *his* heart affected? Hers felt as if it would pound out of her chest and run through the pasture.

At some point during his recklessly romantic speech, Stephen had taken her hand. Now her palm was pressed to his chest, and her focus flitted between the warmth of it sandwiched as it was between his capable hand and his waistcoat, and Stephen's face—the hope and love she saw there.

Vera opened her mouth to give her reply.

"*Vera!*" a male voice bellowed from behind them.

They both turned. A man was half striding, half running down the green hillside behind them.

Vera pulled her hand from Stephen's in her shock. "*Bertrand?*"

"Who is this?" Stephen said, his voice low.

"My *brother*." Vera's tone expressed how improbable it was, though it *was* her brother, Bertrand—the younger of the two—hurrying down toward them.

As he got closer, Vera saw his face was red; a sheen of sweat graced his forehead.

"Vera, for heaven's sakes, *there* you are." He pulled her abruptly into a hug. "I've been looking for you everywhere."

"You *have*?"

Bertrand held her back by the shoulders. "Would have been here an hour earlier, except Canterbury and his duchess put me through the wringer answering their questions."

"They did?" Vera blinked.

"Not that I don't understand, once they finally explained it. Did you truly believe we'd written you off like that?" Bertrand yanked her back into a hug as if he couldn't help himself. "Dear heavens, Vera. You're my *sister*."

She squeaked some unintelligible response. Her eyes were leaking, this time in utter shock. Bertrand had been looking for her? He still acknowledged her as family? She couldn't help it—she began to sob into his chest.

"Aw, blast it, Vera." Bertrand patted her about the back awkwardly with his pudgy hand. "Don't cry. You know I can't handle that. It's awful. Jane's six now and she's already figured me out. I had to buy her a pony last month. A *pony*. Her mother's furious with me for being such a pushover about it, but Jane really does love taking her little cart into the park, so I think it's all worked out all right."

Vera just cried harder, clutching the front of his coat. She hadn't realized until now how much she needed to hear those words from someone. That she still was family. That she hadn't been thrown away, abandoned. Vera hadn't realized quite how deep that injury had gone—not until someone came along and salved it.

"You must be Baron Winthrop." Vera felt Bertrand offer his hand to Stephen, even while the other still held

Vera to his chest. "Very sorry to arrive unannounced, but it's a bit of an emergency."

She pushed back from her brother on a gasp. "What is it?"

"It's Mother. She's...she's dying, Vera."

IT ALL HAPPENED SO QUICKLY after that. Bertrand had already rousted the household, so Vera's trunks were being loaded as they made the drive. The baroness had instructed her own horses hitched to the front of Bertrand's carriage—a couple of her footmen would follow to bring them back the next time they changed horses.

Before Vera could quite reconcile what was happening, she hugged the members of the household in turn, uttered hasty goodbyes, flung one last, longing look at Stephen, and loaded into Bertrand's carriage.

"I hate to say it," Bertrand said a bit later, his mouth full of one of the sandwiches that Mrs. Portence had packed for their journey. "But Mother's gone mad as a hatter."

Vera tsked. Despite how her mother had treated her, she was still their mother, and politeness and respect had been ingrained early and often.

"No, Vera. Truly. She doesn't know who she is most the time. Other times, she knows us all. It's so strange.

Doctors say it happens sometimes, but they don't know why."

Something like hope lifted in her chest. "How long has this been going on?"

"In earnest? A few months. It came on quickly with her, doctor says."

A few months—not long enough to absolve her for the letter she'd sent Vera. Or was it?

"That's the hard thing—we don't know what was the illness and what was *her*. Because Mother has always been a bit off, hasn't she? That's why Father ignored it as long as he did, but then..." Bertrand bit his lip, shook his head.

"What? What happened?"

"Well." His belly shook with a laugh. "I'm sorry, Vera. It's not funny. I know that. Except that parts of it kind of *are*."

"Oh, dear. What?"

"Father and Mother went to dine with Lord and Lady Lewis. And..." He pressed his lips together, his eyes full of mirth.

"Laugh if you have to, Bertie, just tell me already."

"Mother made advances on the man. She *kissed* him."

"What?" Vera clasped her throat.

"Sat right on his lap during pre-dinner cocktails and planted one on him!" He slapped his knee, then glimpsed her horrified expression and tried to tame himself once more. "It's only funny to me because I've had time to sit with the information. Give it a week and you'll be laughing, too. Besides, that's nothing in comparison to what she gets up to now."

"What is that? Is she dangerous?"

"Only if you're a man. She pinched Harold's bottom last time I was there."

"She *didn't*." Vera leaned forward, eyes wide. "Their butler must be sixty!"

"Sixty-two, and I think he was secretly pleased. She'd already got all the footmen; I think it was starting to hurt his pride. Fellow walked taller for three days after that."

"Oh dear."

"But I swear to you, Vera," he said, sobering. "None of us knew what Mother had done. I only just found out, when Canterbury and his wife got to me."

"You say that as if they were cruel, and I know very well that they could never be so."

He raised his eyebrows. "Not *cruel*, per se. More menacing than anything. Have you seen their dog? Canterbury called it in and it growled at me!"

Vera waved his concerns off. "Arthur's been teaching Seamus to growl on cue. For cheese."

"I did wonder why it started drooling immediately afterward. Thought it wanted to eat me."

"Only if you're made of Stilton."

Bertrand ignored her. "Of course both of them are too genteel to come out and threaten me directly, but I think it was a narrow thing for a moment."

"Don't be ridiculous. Threaten you, indeed."

"It was very nearly the Spanish Inquisition over there." Betrand's eyes were wide. "At one point, I thought Canterbury was going to produce a rack and instruct me to heft myself upon it."

She shook her head, smiling. Bertrand had always been gregarious, bordering on ridiculous. It was one of the things she'd missed most about him.

"Those people care about you very much, Vera. But I was so confused as to why they were keeping me from you. Until it became abundantly clear that I had no idea what Mother had done. Surely you know *we* would never disown you. Don't you?"

There was hurt there, in Bertrand's gaze. And suddenly, Vera wondered why she *had* believed it of them so readily. Why hadn't she challenged it in her own mind? Why hadn't she even written a letter to ask? Certainly that said something about how she'd viewed herself at the time. Now, it felt properly idiotic.

Vera shook her head. "I'm sorry, Bertie. I don't know. Mother was…difficult. I know now that I should have doubted her more, but at the time it seemed real. I believed her."

His expression was serious. "Campton and I would never do that. And certainly Father had no clue of the truth—Mother had told him you were travelling with Lady Waldrey—er, the duchess—but he never even knew you ran off. He thought Mother gave you permission. She certainly kept up the charade—told him you sent letters, were having a lovely time. Of course, that was before the er… *pinching* started."

Vera shook her head, looked out the window. So the lie had just been her mother being herself.

Bertrand cleared his throat. "You look different. Better.

That dress suits you. Did someone, um...help you pick it out?"

Vera's mouth dropped open on a sudden suspicion. "Bertie—surely you know that I had no hand in those terrible dresses I used to wear. That was all Mother's doing."

He reared back. "What?"

"She didn't want me to marry! Not when she had you and Campton settled and making families. I was to stay home and take care of Father and Mother in their old age."

"That certainly explains a lot. I kept sending letters asking you to visit—told her I had a few gents all picked up for you to meet. Agatha was going to take you to the dress shop, get you sorted. Mother kept saying you were far too busy at home."

"Why didn't you tell *me*?"

He shifted in his seat. "Well, I didn't want to embarrass you—make you think you couldn't find your own chap."

"But I *couldn't*." She slapped the seat next to her in emphasis, half laughing. "Not with Mother dressing me in cast-off upholstery and chasing away every man who looked at me."

Bertrand considered that for several moments, then grinned. "Look on the bright side—it could have been worse. Now she scares them off for a whole other reason." He brought his thumb and forefinger together in a pinching motion.

## CHAPTER 33 - VERA

London was much the same as it ever was. Only now, Vera wrinkled her nose at the waste in the gutters, at the ripeness of the alleys they passed. She would never take fresh air for granted again. In the distance, the bells of St. Paul's Cathedral chimed noon; birds erupted from the trees in the nearby park. The carriage pulled up to the familiar brick rowhouse. Bertrand stepped out first and offered a hand for her to follow.

They rushed up the stone steps and were met by a grim-faced Campton.

"She's worse—much worse," Campton said, even as he hugged her. "Vera, so glad you came."

"Of course."

"The doctor says it could be anytime now. You both should go see her."

Bertrand wrinkled his nose. "Is she still pinching? Should I keep my back to the wall?"

"We're well past that, I think. She hasn't left her bed these last four days."

"Oh." Bertrand frowned. "Let's go up."

Lady Callista Ashbury reclined against pillows in her bed. The thick draperies were thrown back to let in light, and as they arrived, a maid hustled across the room. Instinctively, Vera inhaled deeply through her nose. It was an underrated form of diagnosis, the nose. But she smelled no infection, no sourness or sickly sweetness on the air.

In fact, the room smelled of fresh linens and the sprig of eucalyptus placed on the fire. The staff was doing an excellent job of caring for her mother—it wasn't easy keeping someone who was bedridden clean at all times.

"Begging your pardon," the maid said in a low voice, bobbing a curtsy. "She's sleeping at the moment. The doctor was just here, said she needs her rest."

"We'll watch over her for a while." Vera nodded to the door. "We'll call if we need anything."

A look of gratitude passed over the young woman's face. She bobbed another curtsy and headed for the door.

"Was that wise?" Bertrand said. "Sending her away? What if something happens?"

"What would a maid be capable of that we are not?"

He shrugged and took one of the chairs facing the bedside. "Lots of things. Fetching tea. Changing linens. Stoking the fire."

Vera smiled. "There's a bell pull over there, if need arises. But Mother's color looks relatively good. She's breathing evenly. I don't think she'll shake off this mortal coil in the next thirty minutes."

Bertrand frowned. "You seem different."

"I *am* different. I lived so long frightened of what Mother would do if I didn't follow her every whim. Then the one time I rebelled, the worst *did* happen, and I survived."

*More than that,* she thought, thinking of Stephen. *For the first time, I lived.*

Stephen was never far from her thoughts. Certainly not here, in a sick room so similar to the many others where she'd spent countless hours with him. Vera kept turning her head, half expecting to see him sitting in the corner or washing his hands in the basin.

He'd be impressed with how orderly everything was, how much sunlight streamed in. So many people thought death should be a closed-shades affair, as if the act of dying was some secret, shameful thing.

"I wish I had known," Bertrand said lowly, pulling her from her thoughts. One hand was balled in a fist atop his thigh. "I wish I would have known what she was doing to you. I would have taken you from here. I would have stopped her."

Vera laid a hand over his. "It all worked out precisely how it was supposed to. Mother would be dismayed, but in the end, I managed to accomplish what she always dreaded."

"Yes, I've already told you your dresses look fetching."

Vera smiled at the teasing note in his voice.

Bertrand cleared his throat. "It's that Winthrop fellow, isn't it?"

"Yes."

He frowned in something that resembled a glower. It was a shocking expression for one as good-natured as Bertie. "Now look here, Vera. I know that you might not think you have many options, but if you don't like the fellow, you don't have to marry him. He hasn't been at all improper, has he? I know you were assisting him, but we don't have to tell anyone. I daresay many a thing has occurred in Devon and other countryside locales and not a whisper of it ever reaches London—"

Vera patted his hand. "It's not that way at all, Bertie. Though I thank you for your protective and practical instincts. I love him and he loves me."

"Oh, well—"

Bertrand sounded as if he might choke if he ventured further. Vera hid a smile while he cleared his throat again and recovered.

"Has he proposed, then?"

"Truly, you have the worst timing in the history of mankind. If you'd waited five more minutes, the deed would have been done."

"How much time does a fellow need?" Bertrand said, umbrage clear in his voice. "You've been there for *months*!"

"Yes, but we didn't like each other the first bit."

"Why? Is he a cad? Vera, I wasn't lying. I have a list of gentlemen who'd be delighted to have you. Several of them are quite rich—"

"He's not a cad, and he proposed that very moment."

Bertrand frowned down at her hand. "I don't see a trinket. Gentlemen ought to offer a trinket to seal the deal. Everyone knows that."

"He asked, and I didn't have a chance to answer, because someone began bellowing my name from the top of the hill."

"I didn't *bellow*." He patted his stomach. "Bellowing is something portly fellows do. I'm still quite trim."

"Not if you keep eating all the biscuits."

"I told you—I thought there were more. I thought they were divided into two parcels."

"There were at least a dozen biscuits in the hamper, Bertie, and I didn't get one."

"Travelling makes me peckish. 'Tisn't my fault. I'd already taken a grand tour of the countryside that morning, trying to find you. First the marquess—who was in high dudgeons when I rang the bell. How was I to know his wife was napping? How was I to know her condition? Such things are private for a reason."

Vera bit back a smile.

"The fellow fed me straight to Canterbury. I had no idea what I was in for, otherwise I would have demanded biscuits from the marquess before I left. Then Canterbury and his wife. Mercy, those fellows are being led around by the nose by their ladies. So *tetchy*."

Vera rolled her eyes. "Tell me, brother, what did you get for your wife last Christmas?"

Bertrand frowned. "Now *that's* different."

"What was it again? A new ballroom, I believe?"

"It only made sense. Ambrose Place didn't have one, and Agatha loves to dance. Besides, we had the room and the funds, and really it's none of your business what I get my wife for Christmas, anyway." He punctuated the end of his good-natured rant with a poke to her side.

"Vera, darling. Is that you?" her mother murmured.

They stood and Vera took her wrinkled hand, leaning close. "Yes, Mother. I've come to see you."

"You look beautiful, my girl. Just lovely. Hair just like mine, you know. Before it went grey."

"Thank you, Mother."

The words were uncharacteristic of Lady Ashbury. No doubt they were brought on by whatever illness was claiming her, mind first. Still, Vera was affected all the same. She'd always wanted to hear such words from her mother; it hardly mattered what had brought them forth.

Her mother patted her hand listlessly. "My darling girl. I love you so much. I wish you to be with me, always."

A tear snaked down Vera's face. "I'm here. I'll stay with you."

She smiled and closed her eyes. "I'm just going to take a little nap."

"I'll be here when you wake, Mother."

Vera was there every time her mother woke, for the next four days. And when Lady Ashbury finally slipped into the deepest sleep of all, her three children were gathered at her bedside, and her husband held her hand.

## CHAPTER 34 - STEPHEN

Stephen slouched on the leather sofa in the parlor. His elbow was cocked, his head resting on his hand. At his feet, Miss Beets chewed happily on a massive, smoked bone he'd procured from the local butcher.

One of the only good things about his mother's penchant for collecting strange animals was that many rooms on the first floor lacked rugs. Even still, some poor servant was going to have to mop up the small puddle of drool collecting from Beets's current delight. A tidy dog, she was not.

Funny—Canterbury hadn't warned him about the great quantities of drool that mastiffs produced. And the *consistency* of it. Someone really ought to perform a study of the stuff. Surely there was some use for a viscous material that, when wet, could hardly be wiped away. And it dried to the consistency of cement.

*Don't be daft,* Vera had said.

She'd said it fondly, hadn't she? At the outset, Stephen was sure of it. Her eyes had been warm and full of *something* that made him press on. Her expression had kindled hope within his chest. If only her brother hadn't interrupted at that *precise* moment.

But as days of her absence passed, Stephen's confidence wavered. His memory reformed, turning her fondness into contempt.

"Don't be daft" was hardly a comforting response to that all-important question.

"Yes" was the gold standard, but Stephen would have gladly accepted a "certainly" or a "sure," or even a "maybe" or an "I must consider it further."

But she'd left him with "don't be daft."

Stephen sighed. His mother stiffened across the room where she was sorting books, but didn't turn. The tomes on animal husbandry and care were going with her. He'd asked her to make a list—he didn't like the idea of depleting Bertforth House's library; he was going to send for replacements from London.

"Well, I asked her," Stephen finally said.

His mother turned, several books in hand, her eyes bright. "Oh Stephen, how wonderful. Congratulations."

"You may keep your congratulations on ice. She didn't have time to answer before her brother whisked her back to London. The entire experience was ghastly—I bared my heart and received no response at all."

Stephen wasn't positive, but he could have sworn his mother's lips trembled in something that looked suspiciously like laughter. He narrowed his eyes. She gave a noncommittal hum and turned back to the bookcase before he could confirm her expression.

Outside in the hallway, there was a sudden eruption of childish conversation and giggling. Benjamin and Anne had entered through the front door, trailed closely by Hortense. The maid was just beginning to show her condition, but Stephen had always thought it unnecessary that women were cloistered away when the effects of marriage began to show.

*Ridiculous.* Certainly they were to be treated with additional care, but women didn't cease to *function* when with child. He could think of none better to watch the children than Hortense—she wielded her firm tone and that fearsome ironwood umbrella with equal amounts of precision.

"Well?" Stephen finally prompted once the happy gaggle had retreated up the stairs.

"It sounds like a trying experience, darling. Hopefully, the next time, it will go better."

"The next time?" For a head-swimming moment, Stephen thought his mother meant the next *woman*. He sat straight, his heart suddenly playing the part of a bass drum in a discordant symphony. "There will be no next time, Mother. It's her or nothing."

"I'm so glad to hear it. You two are a perfect match."

"You meant the next time I *propose*."

"Indeed." Jacqueline added several books to the pile and bent to make neat markings upon her parchment.

Stephen thought about her words. It *had* occurred to him that there would have to be another conversation, but if he were being honest, he'd thought that his initial question and declaration of love would stand until he received an answer. He'd asked; Vera was required to answer... Wasn't she?

Except that things had changed. Her circumstances had been dramatically altered from one moment to the next. He'd proposed to the woman he loved—a penniless lady without household or family. Now, Vera had been restored—and rightly so. But the way Stephen had handled the initial proposal was not at all the way he'd have handled things if he'd known Vera *hadn't* been disowned by her family.

There was a proper procedure, and in the haze of his affection—and because he believed her cast off from her family—Stephen had disregarded all of it.

He jerked to his feet. Miss Beets gave him a curious side-eye but kept munching her bone. Her back turned, his mother gave a cough that sounded suspiciously like a hastily covered laugh.

"Mother, will you please stay on at the house awhile longer and look after things? I must go."

"Good heavens, *finally*." Jacqueline shook her head. "I swear, if you weren't such a fine doctor, I might suspect you were a bit of an idiot."

Stephen ignored her and strode out the door.

## CHAPTER 35 - VERA

*Don't be daft*, she'd said.

Vera had planned on following the words with "of course I'd be thrilled to accept an offer of marriage from the man I love," but there hadn't been time. Bertrand always did have the worst timing. Not that she truly regretted it—if she hadn't left right then, she might have missed saying a final goodbye to her mother.

Though possibly *five* minutes more wouldn't have been amiss.

Vera's heart longed to return to Devon, to return to *Stephen*, but she'd had no idea how busy dying was for those who remained. There was the funeral, of course—a stately affair in which her mother was laid to rest in the family vault.

During the procession, Vera could barely look at the wagon that carried the casket, even decorated as it was with swaths of black fabric. Despite the rituals that surrounded the event, Vera knew that her mother was gone. After all, funerals were for the living, far more than they were for the dead.

But mourning only seemed to begin with the funeral, and Vera possessed just two dresses appropriate for the occasion. One was black taffeta, the other skirted the line of propriety in a grey bombazine. Which was why, early one morning, she arrived at the door of Madame Aubert's.

She'd requested a special appointment, so Vera was surprised when—just as she lifted her hand to take the brass knob—Dahlia Warrington opened the door from the inside and went to step out. Face to face, they both blinked.

Dahlia recovered more quickly, as Vera couldn't help but feel a deep shame over her behavior when they'd last met—that terrible afternoon at Candace's tea party.

"Vera." Dahlia took her gently by the shoulders and deposited a breath of a kiss on each of her cheeks. When she retreated, she left behind a pleasant scent of jasmine and lilac. "I'm so sorry for your loss. How are you?"

"As well as can be expected." Vera paused for a moment, then nibbled her bottom lip. "I'm so sorry—" Vera began, right as Dahlia said, "You must—"

There was an awkward, half-smiling wince on both their parts.

Vera took advantage of the silence and plowed forward. "You must forgive me for my behavior when we last met. I've regretted it ever since it happened; I only didn't know what to say to make it right. Which is no excuse, of course. I should have written to you."

Dahlia shook her head emphatically before Vera had

even finished, setting her lovely ribbons fluttering. "Absolutely not. The fault lay entirely with me. I should have considered how it would feel, having a near-stranger interject themselves into your private affairs. I can only assure you that any conversation that took place which mentioned your name wasn't at all at your expense. If you will accept my apology, let us consider the matter fully settled."

"Of course." Vera smiled—she felt much better with that resolved.

"Are you here to see Madame Aubert?" Dahlia wrinkled her nose. "How silly of me. Of course you are. Would you like some company while you browse the mourning fabrics, or would you like to be left alone?"

The question was asked openly, with no insinuation of offense were Vera to refuse. Dahlia's lovely eyes were wide with the earnestness of her inquiry. Vera found suddenly that she wouldn't mind the company at all.

"If you have the time to spare, I'd love your help."

It was the truth—though Vera had imagined it many times, she'd never been to Madame Aubert's alone. The thought of facing all those fabric options without a friend to run them by was overwhelming.

Dahlia beamed. "I always have time for you. And for clothing," she added with a wink.

Vera laughed and followed her into the polished hallway. The maid who usually occupied the chair by the front door was nowhere to be seen, but Dahlia led them through to the fabric room, where the gas lamps were already lit.

"I assume you're here for mourning clothes? Or is it

another gown that you need to shop for?" She asked the question with a tilted head, but added no sly smile that hinted of gossip.

Vera found herself regretting their last meeting all the more—she thought she could like Dahlia, very much.

"Mourning clothes. This is the only one that's truly appropriate, and it's one Mother chose." Vera drew a hand down her person as if to better display the awkward cut of the gown.

Thankfully, since the dress was stark black, it wasn't nearly as offensive as some she'd donned in the past. Vera had felt a strange sort of nostalgia at the bulk of the shoulders, the excess of clumsy pleats at the waist that made her look much larger than she was.

"Indeed." Dahlia took her in at a glance. "Any fabric preferences?"

"Well, this might be a strange request, but do you know of any fabric that might hide stains well?"

"Stains?" Dahlia tilted her blonde head and blinked her clear blue eyes. "What sort of stains are you expecting?"

"Er— *blood* stains?" she whispered.

"Oh, that's right. You're assisting the baron; I'd nearly forgotten. Do you intend on returning to Devon, then? You'll be wanting wool or cotton. Very clever of you, to find another use for these dresses, past the mourning period. I'd recommend a dark charcoal instead of a flat black—no one will know you've ordered them out of anything other than practicality."

Dahlia crossed to one of the walls filled top to bottom

with bolts of fabric. She deftly pulled four options, humming to herself before choosing another two. She lay them upon the large table in the center of the room, one by one. Two lampstands were clamped at the ends of the table, offering excellent light.

"Now, this is a lovely stripe. It's very muted, but I think it would look stunning in a walking dress with a trim jacket." She gestured to the next. "This one would lend itself to a more formal setting—accepting visitors over the next few weeks, perhaps. And this one...well, if I were you, I'd have Madame create a slim skirt with just the *hint* of a train, and ask for two tops—one, a stark jacket with a nipped waist that would go over a black shirt with a tuft of lace at the throat; the other, the top for a dinner gown, off the shoulder, to show off your lovely collarbones, and decorated with cloth roses of the same fabric."

It was only through good manners that Vera's mouth didn't drop open. "Dahlia, you're a genius."

"Yes, but don't tell anyone."

Though there was a twinkle in her eye and good humor around her lips, Vera somehow got the impression that the young lady was quite serious in her request.

"Of course. I'll give all credit to Madame Aubert, if you wish."

"Thank you."

Vera considered the fabrics and nibbled her lip. "Do you not think it shocking, to reuse a mourning dress as a dinner gown?"

"It's only shocking if you tell people. Otherwise, no one will ever know."

Vera slid her fingers across the fabric. Something about Dahlia's words spoke of one with experience keeping secrets. Secrets that were far deeper than turning a mourning gown into a dinner gown. But Vera couldn't muster the courage to ask about it—what would she even say?

Before she could capitalize on the strange moment, Dahlia moved on. "Of course, you'll need more than just those." Dahlia pointed at a subtly patterned twill at the end. "This would make a lovely walking or travelling dress. It also could be paired with a matching shirt for the time being, but after mourning, a crisp white lawn would do very nicely."

"Forgive me, Dahlia, but is everything all right?" Vera finally managed to ask.

The lady turned to her with a puzzled expression. "Yes, why?"

"Oh, it's nothing. Pardon me." Vera held fingers to her temple. "I have much on my mind."

"Of course you do." Dahlia's smile was suddenly strained. "I was very young when my mother and father passed, but it's still painful sometimes. It grows easier, which somehow hurts in its own way, too."

Vera nodded. It was different for her. Vera's relationship with her mother had been so fraught, so difficult. Even at the funeral, she hadn't mourned her mother as she was, not really. Rather, she'd mourned the relationship she *wished* she'd had with her mother—the one that would never be.

There was something about her grief that felt fraudulent—Vera had to swallow back guilt when people consoled her. Some of them had very real tears in their eyes. They'd imposed their grief over her own—they imagined what she felt based upon what *they'd* felt, when their own loved one died.

Still, Vera felt compelled to nod and accept the condolences. Even her brothers didn't quite understand—they'd had a different mother, a loving mother. Vera was nothing but bewildered when her brothers passed about their pleasant, shared memories of Mother. It was the same as hearing people describe a dinner party she'd never been invited to—no matter how great the detail used, Vera still couldn't quite picture it.

Then there was the faint, flickering anger that Vera did her best to squelch down and smother. When the preacher described Callista as a loving mother, Vera nearly stood up and corrected him. The last week of her mother's life was the most pleasant their relationship had ever been. Vera didn't know what to feel about that—that only madness had made her mother say she loved her.

"Are *you* all right, Vera?" Dahlia asked softly.

Vera realized she'd been staring at the spotted fabric, petting it over and over like a treasured lapdog while she ruminated on thoughts of her mother. "I'm sorry. I got lost for a moment there."

"No apology needed."

At the compassion in Dahlia's gaze, Vera felt her tears welling up for the first time since her mother had passed. She stepped back as if she could put more distance between herself and the emotion.

"Oh, dear. I'm sorry." Dahlia produced a handkerchief and handed it over.

Vera took it gratefully; she'd left hers at home. And didn't that just say everything? How deep could her mourning be, if she'd forgotten that basic necessity?

"I fear I'm not up to this, after all."

Dahlia nodded, then bit her lip. "If—if it would be helpful, I'm happy to relay an order to Madame Aubert on your behalf. I take it the measurements that she last used are still correct?"

Vera nodded and dabbed her eyes, choked by her own confusion. Of all the times for grief to surge within her, why did it have to be now?

Perhaps it was because what Dahlia had done for her here was exactly what Vera wished her mother would have done, when she was alive. Weren't mothers supposed to help their daughters choose fabrics and think of which ensembles would suit them best? But not *her* mother. Her mother had done the exact opposite. On *purpose*.

"I would really appreciate you placing the order, if that's not too much trouble."

"Not any trouble at all, Vera. Truly. I'll take care of everything."

"Thank you, Dahlia."

Though she'd taken the carriage to Madame Aubert's, Vera sent it home and walked. The footman only protested once—Madame Aubert's shop was in an excellent part of town, mere blocks from her father's house. Vera hadn't even brought a maid on the errand.

In truth, Vera had acclimated to the freedom of the

countryside. She enjoyed her solitude, her long walks about the grounds. Her ankle felt much better now, and how she longed for fresh air and greenery!

Mist still clung to the ground and hovered undisturbed in the mouths of the alleys. Vera didn't want to return directly to the squared-off rooms of the brick townhome, filled with sour memories and her mother's collected trinkets. So instead of turning right toward home, she went left, toward the park.

*A half an hour,* she told herself.

No one would miss her for that length of time. It was still early—the house wouldn't even be open for visitors for an hour or more. There would be plenty of time for Vera to pinch some color into her cheeks and decide whether she wanted to risk frowns in the grey bombazine.

The park was lovely, even at this time of year. There was something crisp and clean about air surrounded by greenery. It was a pale comparison to Devon, but Vera would take what she could get.

She missed Stephen with a breathless intensity whenever she was alone. When she'd left, she'd naively thought she'd be back within a fortnight, a month at most. Vera hadn't thought to be tethered here by her family's grief and expectations.

Vera wished now that she'd flung her arms immediately around Stephen's neck when he'd proposed. She wished she'd interrupted him with an eager "yes" when he'd declared himself. But she'd been choked by the depth of her emotion and the beauty of his words. She'd thought she'd have more than a single moment to make her reply.

She thought she'd have more time with him. She'd thought she'd have *all* of it, actually.

Vera plunked down upon a bench that overlooked a small pond. A wreath of mist clung to the shoreline and lazily drifted overtop the still water. At the far side, a swan lifted its head to inspect the intruder, then tucked its bill beneath its wing once more.

Now who knew how long it would be until she saw Stephen again? Perhaps she *should* write him a letter. She'd started one, several times, but she selfishly wanted her answer to be given face to face. Vera wanted to see him *hear* it, the first time she confessed her love.

Vera plucked at the stiff taffeta of her skirts and frowned. Surely he would wait for her. Surely he wouldn't take her lack of a response as a denial...right? But in that moment, Vera suddenly wasn't sure. It must be a difficult thing, to declare oneself and ask for a lady's hand. Far worse to ask and then have the lady say nothing at all.

Across the pond, the swan lifted its head once more. Vera turned to see what had captured its attention. A gentleman approached through the mist. Some nobleman taking his daily constitutional around the park, no doubt. At this distance, Vera could almost imagine it was Stephen walking toward her. The man had similar height, dark hair, a similar gait.

Several moments later, Vera stood with a slight gasp. It wasn't her wishful thinking—it *was* him. The improbability of it staggered her for a moment. What on earth was Stephen doing in London?

When he got closer, he called, "Vera."

Vera had the sense to close her gaping mouth, but that was all she could manage.

And then Stephen was there, and real, and pulling her into a hug. Vera dug her fingers into the fine charcoal wool of his coat and sagged against him.

"I'm so sorry about your mother," Stephen said.

"What are you doing here?" Vera's bewildered words were muffled against his chest.

Her head was tucked quite neatly beneath his chin. She could smell the combination that was uniquely him—soap, cedar, and just a hint of medical disinfectant. To Vera, it was the headiest cologne in the world.

"I'm here for you, naturally."

One hand soothed Vera's back in slow strokes, leaving a wash of pleasant warmth behind every pass. The beating of his heart was a steady thrum beneath her ear. He was strong, sure, and she felt safe in his capable arms.

After long moments where Stephen simply held her, he finally set her back far enough to peer down at her face. "How are you, Vera?"

"Much better, now that you're here. I feel terrible about how we parted. I hope you know I thought of you every day since I've been gone."

*More like every hour*, she thought, though it felt reckless to admit such a thing.

"And I you." His warm smile crinkled the corners of his intelligent eyes.

"Now that we're together again, I must answer your question—"

"No." Stephen held up a hand.

Vera's heart lurched. What did he mean, *"no"*?

"I don't want you to answer the question, not when it was so inappropriate in light of the circumstances."

"Circumstances?" she echoed faintly.

The only thing keeping her tethered was the fact that Stephen still held her waist. Vera's fingers clutched deeper into his coat, as if he might thrust her from him at any moment.

"Of course. It's not how things are done. Though I confess I never *meant* to cut your father out of the rightful proceedings, but both of us were working with faulty information. It was easily rectified."

"It was?"

Once again, his words had turned Vera into a deranged echo. She clamped her mouth closed and decided not to utter another word until she caught the full meaning of what he was saying. It was one thing to be stupid—it was another thing to let on by speaking every moronic thought in her head.

Stephen's smile deepened, as if he could read her thoughts. As if he considered her dull repetitions adorable instead of idiotic.

"Of course. I just came from speaking to your father."

*You did?* Vera thought, but kept the promise she'd made to herself and sealed her lips.

"He's agreed to let me ask you a very important question."

Here, Vera was obliged to let go of his coat, as Stephen dropped to one knee. She thought it was safe to do so—he could hardly make a run for it from that position, and she'd kick him hard in the knee if he tried.

"Vera Callista Ashbury, I love you. Deeply—"

"*Vera!*" someone hollered from behind them. It was her brother Bertrand, emerging from the trees. "*Where are you?* Ah, there you are!"

Stephen gritted his teeth and muttered, "Dear heavens, I'll shoot that man. Physician's ethics or not—I swear I will."

"Bertie Ashbury," she yelled, pointing at the far tree line. "If you don't leave right *now*, I'll let Canterbury set his dog on you."

Bertie jerked to a stop, turned round, and went with all due haste.

"He doesn't like dogs?" Stephen tilted his head.

"Arthur's been teaching Seamus to growl. For cheese."

Stephen opened his mouth, shut it, and shook his head. "Please put me out of this miserable suspense. Will you marry me or not?"

"Yes." Vera beamed down at him. "Nothing would make me happier. I love you, Stephen."

Stephen grinned and stood, then pulled her into his arms. His lips found hers. And though she'd studied the textbooks that he'd given her, she suddenly found them lacking, too. For she'd never before read that a person could fly while their feet were firmly upon the ground.

Yet she *was* flying. The mint and tobacco of his breath told her he'd been nervous—he only indulged in a cigar when he was anxious about something. She reveled in the warmth of his skin, the tender movements of his lips against hers, as if he wished to learn her.

Vera dazedly wondered if she'd ever tire of this. No wonder they cautioned young ladies against kissing a man, even one that you loved! Now that they'd started, how would they ever stop? It was a wonder there weren't scandalous displays of this kind all over London!

"*Vera!*" Bertrand sounded like he was choking on the impropriety of it all.

They broke apart.

Vera whirled, her hands clenched into fists, murder snapping in her eyes. "We're *betrothed*, Bertie! If you interrupt us again, I shall cheerfully strangle you myself!"

Bertrand went, hopefully for the last time. When she turned back to Stephen, he was laughing.

Vera shook her head. "I'm not certain I *am* glad to be back in the family fold."

But they both knew she was lying—it was trying sometimes, to have people care about you, but it was far better than the alternative.

Stephen grinned. "I hope you don't find it too presumptuous of me, but I've already made plans to call on Dr. Halveston this afternoon."

"Are you unwell?"

"I'm in perfect health, I assure you. But I don't have any patients in London, and Dr. Halveston has more than he can see. I thought to ask if he'd send them my direction, start building a practice."

Vera frowned and stepped back. "Here? In London?"

"I thought that, being so recently reunited with your

family, perhaps you wouldn't be keen on putting such a great distance between you so soon."

"I'm very keen on returning to Devon, though it has nothing to do with putting distance between my family and me."

"Truly?" Stephen grinned. "You wish to make our home in the countryside?"

"I do. You don't need to establish a practice here; you already have one in Devon. My family may come and visit as often as they like."

"You do realize that you are getting a package deal, accepting me? Not that I'll let you out of it now that you've said yes, but Benjamin will live with us until he's ready for Eton, and Anne will be with us indefinitely."

"You know I love Anne. In fact, perhaps I'm accepting you just to act as her mother," she teased.

Stephen smiled in that tender way he reserved only for her. "I'm not proud; I'll still have you no matter why you've agreed. I'll just have to work very hard to make you love me over time."

"I already do, you know. Love you."

"I love you, Vera. Immensely. Oh!" He set her back once more and rummaged in his coat pocket. "I almost forgot. This is for you. Though I suppose I've bungled it by not offering it to you while on my knees. Shall I do it again?"

"No. I believe you already have some goose droppings on your knee from the last time."

He grimaced, angling his leg to inspect the damage.

"I've always heard romance can be a messy business, but I never imagined they meant *this*."

Vera cleared her throat, her eyes on the small velvet box he held in his hand. Stephen laughed and opened it, letting the morning light play over the large, light-blue stone set in a simple gold band.

"Do you like it?"

"It's stunning. I adore it."

"It reminded me of you." He slipped the ring on her finger.

Vera held it up to the light, enjoying the pleasing weight, the fact that Stephen had chosen it just for her. "I do love blue."

"Not just because of that, though I'm glad to hear it. It reminded me of you because it's a diamond, but it's rare. No one will know it's a diamond to look at it. I thought that was much like you—infinitely precious, and none of those idiots could see it, and I'm so *grateful* for it."

Vera's chin wobbled; she blinked back the tears that threatened to blur her vision of the stunning stone.

"Thank you, Stephen," she finally managed to whisper.

"But we'll have to get you a simple, smooth band to wear, too. That stone is far too large to wear during medical procedures—it will catch on the bandages and get in the way of your stitching."

Vera laughed.

## CHAPTER 36 - VERA

One month later, Miss Vera Ashbury and Lord Winthrop stood before a small grouping of family and friends in the parlor of Devon Manor. The bride wore a beaded, light grey silk dress, one that Dahlia had slipped in amongst the orders for her mourning period.

*It was as if she'd known*, Vera thought.

Undoubtedly, it would have been a scandal for her to marry Stephen so soon at all—custom dictated that Vera be in full mourning for her mother for at least three months. However, Vera decided that she'd given enough of her life up for her mother and wasn't going to continue to do so after the woman was gone.

Her veil was the most romantic delicate lace, and it swathed her from head to toe. When Vera appeared in the doorway, clutching a bouquet of pale pink cabbage roses, the groom nearly staggered beneath the weight of her beauty. Neither of them could tear their eyes from the other during their vows, even when Anne began to fuss and was removed by a tutting Hortense.

The Marquess of Salisbury had insisted upon hosting the celebration, as his wife had insisted upon attending the event. She was to give birth to their first child any day, and Percy's worry had grown right along with his wife.

"He's hired a footman to stand at every staircase to assist me up or down," Adelaide said later, at the wedding luncheon. "It's completely unnecessary—I'm well able to use the handrail."

Vera secretly doubted it—the woman could barely sit close enough to the table to reach her plate.

Just then, a discordant clanging erupted from the sideboard.

"That blasted clock," Percy said, shoving back from the table. "I've reset it a hundred times and it still clangs at odd hours. If it hadn't been a gift from you, Candace, I'd chuck the thing."

Vera rolled her lips inward and raised her eyebrows when she glimpsed the terrible clock. It was a stack of porcelain lemons, limes, and oranges in a basket. The thing was positively ghastly, and Vera knew full well that Candace had never intended upon purchasing it in the first place. Then again, that was an entirely different story.

Across the table, Candace caught Vera's eye and gave her the barest of winks. It threatened to topple her straight into laughter, and she forced herself to look elsewhere before she succumbed.

"How's the new house, Jacqueline?" Adelaide asked. "Are you feeling settled yet?"

"I must confess it does feel a bit lonely."

It was only because she happened to be looking at him at the moment that Vera saw Hamish go very still.

"Even with your animals?" Candace said.

"Indeed. Perhaps I will add to my collection."

"What are you thinking?"

"Something larger this time," the dowager baroness said lightly.

"We haven't yet divested ourselves of all Seamus's offspring," the Duke of Canterbury said. "Would a puppy be welcome?"

Jacqueline wrinkled her nose. "I'd prefer something already house-trained."

Hamish's expression now contained stark hope.

"Children are out, then," Percy grumbled from down the table. "Do you know that a newborn needs a fresh nappy upwards of twelve times a day?"

Adelaide shook her head, one hand on her belly. "No one wants to hear about it, my love. Especially not at the dining table."

"It's not as if you'll do the job yourself," Candace said.

Percy frowned. "I could. If I so chose. If I *wanted*."

"But no one *does* want to."

"I bet Canterbury did it."

"He'd never be so crude to speak of it, if he had," Candace said.

"And certainly *not* at the dining table, Percy," Adelaide added, more firmly this time.

"Very well. It was a shocking number, is all. I don't even think dogs need to relieve themselves *that* often—"

"Percy!" Adelaide snapped.

Percy clamped his mouth closed and mulishly stabbed at his slice of cake.

Candace smiled. "I think it hilarious that my brother repeatedly attempts to keep us away for fear we'll upset his wife, when it seems that he does the job better than any of us could."

Percy glowered at her.

"It's our husbandly duty, my dear," James said. "To vex and provoke our wives."

"I hardly think that should be a *goal*."

"It lends a lovely fire to your eyes."

Candace turned to him, scowling. "Are you saying I'm prettier when I'm *angry*?"

"You see? You've proven my point, dearest."

Candace pursed her lips and returned to her dessert.

Vera gave a small smile as Stephen finished his first piece and motioned for another. How the man stayed trim with a sweet tooth like his, she'd never know. If she ate as Stephen did, she'd look...well, she'd look like Bertrand in a wig.

"Do you regret that your family isn't here today?" Stephen murmured as the table struck up a debate about betting on the Salisburys' new arrival.

"I swear you read my mind sometimes." Vera smiled. "But no. I wouldn't change anything. My brothers and father met you while we were in London, and that's more than I thought to have. I'm perfectly happy."

"I'm sure they'll visit soon."

She nodded. "Father says he plans on coming in the spring."

"I love you very much, Vera. I'm thrilled you didn't kill me with that fire poker when we first met."

Vera nearly choked on her bite of cake; she coughed. "I thought we'd moved past that nicely."

"I'd say this is a very unexpected resolution to our beginning, yes."

"A very *delightful* resolution."

"And yet," he said, picking up her lace-gloved hand and depositing a warm kiss upon her palm, "this is just the beginning."

"Twelve times a day, Stephen!" Percy bellowed from the end of the table.

"*Percy!*"

# CHAPTER 37- STEPHEN, ONE YEAR LATER

Stephen ducked under the awning and flapped his coat, sending a hundred glittering droplets to the flagstones below. He paused to knock the mud from his boots before opening the front door. Things weren't the same without Vera by his side on nights like these. It was much harder to leave the house without her, and he longed to return as quickly as possible.

He sat on the wooden chair by the door and pulled his boots off, stacking them near the small stove to steam. He draped his coat over the rack, ruffled the excess of water from his hair, and set off down the hall in his socks. Perhaps some might have found it shocking, his lack of shoes, but it was one of his favorite things, sneaking up on his family. It was his tiny reward after a night such as this, where things hadn't gone the way he hoped.

Stephen found them in the front parlor. Benjamin and Anne were freshly washed, ready for bed. Anne had insisted she have a dressing gown to match Benjamin's, so she wore a quilted robe of scarlet belted over her nightdress. She was slumped against Vera's side, barely keeping her eyes open. Benjamin was focused on the pages of the book Vera read from, looking at the pictures.

As for his wife—Stephen suspected she knew he lingered in the doorway, watching, judging by the small smile on her lips. Or perhaps she always smiled like that. His eyes softened at the hand at her waist. It was a new habit, a protective gesture that he'd seen a thousand times before from other women.

Vera was just starting to show. She hadn't told him about this one until she was nearly three months along. He didn't blame her; they'd lost their first early. The pain of it had taken him by surprise. He'd always thought of it as a woman's loss. Now he knew better.

It wasn't until she'd thrown up while assisting him with some stitches that she'd finally said the words out loud. Words that made it real, made them both feel vulnerable once more. He didn't tell her that he'd known from nearly the beginning, when she ordered Mrs. Portence not to serve any fish.

This time it was going well, it seemed. And though they both missed her working alongside him, it was more important that she be rested and not exposed to all manner of ills or infection.

Vera glanced up at him, smiling. It seemed his time as an observer had come to a close.

"Papa!" Anne cried, her chubby cheeks bunching with her smile.

She held her hands up to him eagerly and he took her

upon his lap with a melodramatic groan. "You're getting too big for this, Anne."

"No, I'm not."

She wasn't, not by a long shot, but it delighted her to argue the fact every time. And perhaps it was a reminder to him, that it would one day be true. Stephen intended to soak in the years before she wore petticoats and beaux came knocking at the door.

Vera raised her eyebrows in silent question. Stephen shook his head; her smile slipped.

"Are you going to listen to the story?" Anne asked.

"That sounds perfect. Benjamin, will you read us the next page?"

He nodded and began. Stephen listened intently at first. Benjamin's reading was much improved these past months. The tutor he shared with Canterbury's son must be doing something to earn his wages, then. The fire flickered and popped. He glanced over, making sure no errant ember had made it through the tight lattice of the screen. But all was as it should be; all was well.

Soon, Stephen slumped against the sofa cushions, his head tilted back, his eyes closed. With the warm weight of Anne against him and his feet upon the padded ottoman, he began to drowse. Later, Vera rousted him by gently squeezing his shoulder.

"Are the children in bed?" he asked, cracking a yawn.

"I certainly hope so, as that's where I put them."

Stephen sat up and blinked. "I'm sorry I nodded off."

"He didn't make it, then?" Vera asked, her voice canted low.

"His lungs were too full; the fever never broke."

"I'm sorry, my love. Was Hamish a help, at least?"

He nodded. "Offered the man a carrot to make him feel better, though."

"He did not." Vera shook her head, a reluctant smile upon her face.

It was a running joke. The first time he'd helped Stephen, Hamish had made a comment that he was good with horses, and that humans should be easier to help.

It was a fair point—humans could describe their ailments and horses couldn't, but Stephen had never forgotten how Hamish had as much suggested that his experience with farm animals was equivalent to a medical education.

Stephen stretched his arms over his head. "How are you feeling this evening?"

"A bit tired, but pretty well. Anne tried to sneak a tart that wasn't fully cooled yet, so that was a delight." Vera snuggled into his side and folded her legs up next to her onto the sofa. "She shrieked like a banshee when she bit into it."

"Is she all right?"

She nodded. "Not even a blister. Mrs. Portence made her shaved ices all afternoon. I think she felt bad, though it was completely Anne's fault."

"Not with sugar, I hope."

"Just plain ice. Anne didn't seem to notice. Tomorrow will be interesting—I'll see if I can wean her off the habit."

They sat like that for a moment, her against his side.

"I've been thinking," he said. "About taking on a real apprentice."

"Oh?"

"Horse jokes aside, Hamish is wonderful, but he's only helping for now because I need someone. Dr. Halveston says he has several promising students. One has a lung condition that makes him better suited for country life, and he's asked if I would take him on."

"That's high praise from Dr. Halveston, that he'd ask you to do that."

"I thought the man could live in the cottage near the gatehouse for the time being. Once he's fully trained, he can take lodgings wherever he likes, or he can stay there, for all I care. The house is sound and no one's living there; if it stays vacant it will just fall into disrepair."

Vera gave a hum, but he couldn't tell if it was agreement, and he couldn't see her face with it pressed against his chest.

"I wanted to talk to you about it first." He picked up an ash-brown curl and slid it between his fingers, watching the light play off the strands. "Would that be all right?"

"I think it's a lovely idea. You'll be an excellent teacher. And heaven knows I'll have my hands too full to help you."

"Are you sad about it?"

"Yes and no. It's strange—I have fond memories of that chapter and it's bittersweet to see it come to a close. Yet I'm filled with excitement and hope for the next."

"I'm happy to hear that." Stephen tightened his arm around her. "I want you to be happy."

"I am," she said. "Truly."

# EPILOGUE - DAHLIA

I f fish and visitors stink in only three days, then what was to be said of a lady starting her fourth Season? For she must surely be as stale as the stinking fish, and hardly better received.

Dahlia Eloise Warrington was very unhappy, but she had little to complain about, and she knew it.

Three years ago, the wealthy Marquess Salisbury had darkened the doorway of her sisters' little cottage and changed their lives forever. Seemingly overnight, they'd gone from abject poverty to wealth and comfort. Dahlia was old enough to remember the change. She would never take it for granted.

Wealth was the difference between overwatered, plain porridge eaten before a smoking fire, and sterling silver racks of buttered toast enjoyed with strawberry jam before a roaring flame. It was the difference between shivering in a coat that had been worn thin far before it was handed down, versus a fine worsted wool that was tailored to perfection.

Dahlia remembered, and she vowed she'd never return to poverty.

Poverty wasn't romantic, like the way it was written in some books. It wasn't sweeping pastoral views and wistful sighs. It was fear and panic—the sound of a mighty wolf outside a door too thin to keep it out.

Dahlia remembered.

Now she found herself in a strange season of life. Her two elder sisters were happily married—love matches, both—and her two younger sisters lived with the eldest, splitting time between the marquess's London townhome, the Duke of Devonshire's London estate, and various country houses.

Dahlia was aware that their upbringing was unique—very few young ladies had experienced so much protection and luxury. Sometimes she worried that her younger sisters would forget how cold an attic garrett was in winter. Sometimes she was frightened that they would make foolhardy choices that would put them back in that garrett once more.

But not Dahlia. She was never going back.

Even if that meant remaining unmarried. Even if that meant marrying for security instead of love.

Of course she *wanted* to marry for love. Anyone who said differently was a liar, or perhaps they loved themselves too well to want to involve anyone else in the process.

Dahlia had gone into her first Season as wide-eyed and hopeful as any young lady. And she was a rare beauty—

golden hair, large blue eyes surrounded by a thick fringe of dark eyelashes. Her cheekbones were high, her nose finely formed, her teeth white and straight.

Apparently her figure had a positive effect on the male set, too. Dahlia thought her best asset were her clavicles—very fine, those clavicles, and she endeavored to show them off whenever possible. But she suspected it wasn't *just* her clavicles that had the men very nearly throwing themselves at her feet.

A Frenchman had once wept while they were waltzing when she'd turned down his offer of marriage. Not that she could be blamed for it—she could barely understand the fellow and had thought he was joking. It was their first dance, for heaven's sake—they'd only just been introduced.

With her two eldest sisters off the marriage mart within the first months, Dahlia had emerged as the premier young lady to court.

And court they had. Dahlia had never met so many young men; never received so many smiles, or *presents*. She'd taken up one of her blank sketchbooks and made a list of all the gentlemen—a grid, actually, with spaces for her to fill in with pertinent information.

Attractiveness. Kindness. Intelligence. Title.

And wealth.

She distinctly remembered the day she'd crossed the first man off her list. It was only three weeks into that first Season, and a disturbing rumor reached her ears about one Lord Simon. Up until that point, the young lord had been the forerunner of the pack. Young, handsome, charming, witty, and kind. A title that was well-esteemed. A good family, with parents who'd still make voluntary eye contact with one another.

Yes, Lord Simon had her eye.

But then she found out that he favored the gambling dens. And whisky. A heady combination, to be sure, and one that had gotten the young lord into trouble. He'd lost his favorite horse in a card game. He'd *loved* that horse. She was a beautiful grey spotted mare, lovely and gentle. Lord Simon had extolled her features in the park only several days earlier, while he and Dahlia rode together.

He'd loved that horse, but it hadn't stopped him from gambling her away. There was no possible way Dahlia would trust such a man with her future, with her security.

Dahlia had admired the mare, so right after she scratched Lord Simon's name out in her book, she jotted a quick note to the owner of the gambling hall, found out who'd won the horse, and made an offer.

Lord Simon's eyes grew round the next week when she rode Lady Grey through the park and refused to acknowledge him.

Dahlia remembered the cold, the hunger, the fear. She wouldn't forget now, not when she was finally in a position to stay warm and comfortable and secure.

Not even for all of Lord Simon's winning smiles.

One by one, the others had been crossed off, as well. The misers would never approve of her ghastly expensive wardrobe habit—they were out. The young ones had too short of a track record for her to judge. She wouldn't marry *just* for money, either. Lord Fettiwig had offered, and he was wealthy, but she didn't fancy spending the next four years spooning soft foods into an aged, spluttering mouth.

The French were out; so were the Italians. She didn't understand foreign banking systems—their economies might collapse, and then where would she be?

Back in the garrett. And she knew that every attic garrett was the same, more or less. Cold, drafty, and full of beady-eyed rats.

In her first Season, she scratched out a dozen names. She went through ten options her second Season. Eleven in Season number three. Now it was her fourth, and she wondered whether she'd bother to make a grid at all.

By this time, more rumors were swirling—rumors about *her*.

She was frigid, some men claimed. A gold digger—though that was easily disproved, as she'd turned down several wealthy men. One denied suitor had gone so far as to claim that she was touched in the head and should be relegated to Bedlam.

*That* particular rumor stung a bit, though Dahlia supposed she couldn't blame the man for his ire. She'd told him that she'd rather be trampled to death by horses than be his wife. But what else was she to do? She'd already answered him quite firmly three times, and in plain language, too.

Dahlia had always been grateful for the interest the Duke and Duchess of Devonshire had shown to her family, but she possibly had never been *more* grateful than when the duke took four of his largest footmen to

Lord Pastial's house and quelled that rumor at the source.

She was staring down the barrel of her fourth Season, and the whirl of balls and theater attendances and dinners would have grown tiresome at best, if it weren't for one thing.

The Clothing.

The only thing that Dahlia truly loved was clothes. There was nothing like the subtle shimmer of silk, the zing of light across satin, the warmth and sheen of a fine wool, the structure of a rich brocade. She adored shopping for new gowns, adored poring through the fashion plates for ideas.

Dahlia may not have trusted the French economy, but their designs were another thing altogether.

Most of all, she loved sketching her own ideas.

She'd been doing it for nigh on four years, the sketching. Before Percy came into their lives, Dahlia would just daydream about dresses. Now, with the welcome addition of paper and fine charcoal pencils, she could record them.

Lately, she'd taken up a new hobby—a dangerous hobby. It was simple—she'd sit somewhere where she could view other ladies of the peerage without being disturbed. Then, one by one, she'd sketch the dress they had on, and just next to it, she'd design a new one. Perhaps she'd move the sleeve length or the neckline to better flatter the wearer. Or she'd make notations on the color. *Peach makes her look sallow and wan. Aubergine or navy would be much better*, she'd scrawl.

Dahlia had found her passion, but she was obliged to

keep it private. None of the ladies she drew would be pleased to know that she'd found fault in their ensembles, especially now that Dahlia was garnering a reputation for being a snob toward the gentlemen the rest of the ladies were clamoring to marry.

Once—only *once*—had she deviated from the strictness of her secret.

It had been the middle of her first Season, years ago.

Miss Angelina Carter was so kind, so lovely, but Dahlia couldn't help but wonder if she, her mother, and her lady's maid had all been struck by the same version of colorblindness. It was something that Lady Ashbury would have admired for her own daughter—but only to keep the suitors away.

Miss Carter was wealthy, kind, and witty, but her *gowns*. They were hideous. Breathtakingly so, in a way that can only be accomplished when one possessed not a single ounce of taste and frequented a modiste who didn't care *what* one wore, as long as the notes were paid.

Dahlia had been hiding from Lord Pastiel behind a potted fern in the Marquess Ellis's ballroom when she'd heard the exchange.

"Too bad about that one," one gentleman murmured to another, nodding at the serenely ignorant Miss Carter, who was being swept about in a waltz by some fellow or other.

"Why's that?"

"Lord Harrison wants to marry her, but his mother won't have it. And you know if his mother says no, his father won't stand up to her."

"What's the matter with her?"

"Her style is *dreadful*."

"Who cares? She's pretty enough."

"Harrison's mother is afraid she'll insist on redecorating the family seat."

There was a round of chortling, and the conversation moved on.

Dahlia had seethed. Of all the things to preclude a lovely young woman from marriage—her terrible clothing choices?

Dahlia spent the next day cloistered in her bedroom in a furious flurry of deep thought and scribbling. When she'd finished, she'd written an anonymous letter.

*Dear Miss Carter,*

*You don't know me, and therefore have little reason to trust me, but I hope you will, anyway. It has come to my attention that Lord Harrison wishes to marry you, but your wardrobe is keeping him from it.*

*Excuse me for saying so, madam, but your taste is terrible. Please accept these renderings in the spirit they are meant—as a gift to help ensure your future happiness.*

*Bring them to Madame Aubert, and—if in doubt—accept all of her suggestions moving forward. There's no point in pretending to be good at things we aren't—not when there are experts so readily available to help.*

*Most Sincerely,*

*A Secret Friend*

*PS. Though it is not my place—none of this is—may I suggest that a young man who's unwilling to stand up to his mother before the marriage starts is far less likely to do so after you're wed? Surely there is one better for you than the aforementioned lord.*

DAHLIA HADN'T THOUGHT that Miss Carter would take her suggestions, not really. So she'd stifled a surprised cry of delight in the park a fortnight later when she saw Miss Carter walking in a day dress of her own creation. It was just as Dahlia had imagined—the palest pink to offset her luminous skin, the trim waist, the bodice decorated with thin bands of trimming.

Miss Carter hadn't stopped there—she'd ordered all of Dahlia's designs. Two months later, she wore the emerald-green ball gown when she held the Marquess Ellis's elbow as he announced their betrothal. Last Dahlia had heard, they were still equally delighted with their marriage, and the marchioness had been a faithful client of Madame Aubert's ever since.

Dahlia's secret pastime had been born. And though she never shared a single sketch with anyone ever again, nearly every lady in the *ton*—from the elderly Dowager Duchess Kentbury to the youngest Miss to have a Season—had received a complete, imaginary wardrobe. The drawings were locked away in a trunk in her bedroom.

Along with her personal hopes for the future.

For she'd yet to meet a man who fulfilled all her requirements.

She was beginning to think he didn't exist.

THE END.

BUT EVERY END is a beginning of sorts.

Dive right into Dahlia's story in *Miss Warrington's Portfolio for Designing a Betrothal*!

# ACKNOWLEDGMENTS

First thanks goes to Jesus, for saving my soul. Reader, I don't know where you stand with Jesus—whether you know Him, whether you've drifted away from Him, or whether you've outright rejected Him.

But I do know that Jesus can handle whatever you want or need to say to Him, and He's listening. He will never reject you—He is waiting for you. So wherever you are, you can talk to Him.

Second thanks goes to my supportive husband, Adam. I'm not lying when I say I could not do this without you. Thank you for all of your support. Thanks for telling me I can do this.

Thanks also to my fabulous beta-reading/editing team: Kari Hodgen, Babs Veneman, Heidi Hollander, Jana Miller, Jamie Weatherfield, and Jenny James. You guys are amazing! This book would be riddled with errors if it weren't for you!

**Thanks also to you, Reader. I so appreciate you taking the time to read this book. I hope you loved it! If you did, would you please take a moment to review? Reviews are the difference between success and failure for indie authors. Your review helps other**

readers find me, and enables me to keep writing books!

## ABOUT THE AUTHOR

Hi! I'm Jill M Beene. I write Fantasy, Historical Romance, and Action Adventure with humor, banter, and heart. I'm addicted to good coffee, can't get enough of snuggling my mastiff Rupert, and I'm madly in love with my handsome husband, Adam. Shoot me an email at JillMBeene@gmail.com. You can also follow me on Instagram at @jillmbeene, and on Facebook.

I really hope you enjoyed the book you just finished—there's more where that came from! Join my mailing list to be the first to know!

> Check out my books and sign up for my list at:
> JillMBeene.com

ALSO BY JILL M BEENE

### Regency Romance-

Mr. Pickwick's Guide to Marriageable Young Ladies

Lord Salisbury's Ledgers on How to Woo a Wife

Lady Waldrey's Gardening Almanac for Cultivating Scandal

Miss Ashbury and the Anatomy of Mending a Heart

Miss Warrington's Portfolio for Designing a Betrothal

### Young Adult Fantasy-

### The Weapons of Leiria Collection:

A Sharpened Axe

A Bone Dagger

A Drawn Bow

### The Battle for Leiria Trilogy:

A Poison Vial

An Edged Sword

A Heavy Hammer

## The Elayna Miller Series-

Kill Girl

Fury Girl

Legacy Girl

Hyde and Seek- An Elayna Miller Novella

Made in United States
Troutdale, OR
12/10/2025